THE SHOWDOWN

With regret he realized that White Horse, in coming forward alone, was getting a good look at everything—their strengths and weaknesses. *I made a mistake in not going to him,* Gary thought.

White Horse saw the downed buffalo calf and said: "The buffalo is mine. I take now."

"No," Gary said. "The buffalo belongs to the man who killed it. Even among your own people, this is so."

"Buffalo mine," White Horse said again. "When Indian take horse of white man, he must give back or pay. It is the rule of the chief at the fort. My buffalo. You take. You pay me."

Gary was losing his argument, and it galled him and worried him, because this was his second mistake and a most serious one. He said: "If you want meat, take what you need. That is payment enough."

White Horse struck his chest with the flat of his hand. "You have many bullets. We have few. Give us bullets, and we let you go in peace."

"No bullets," Gary said. "If you had enough bullets, there wouldn't be any peace."

"It is a white man's way to have all the bullets," White Horse said. "The Indian must fight with a stick against bullets. Give me bullets, and we go now."

This was, Gary was sure, the showdown, and what he did next would determine whether they lived or died. . . .

Other *Leisure* books by Will Cook:

THE DEVIL'S ROUNDUP
ELIZABETH, BY NAME
SABRINA KANE

WILL COOK

UNTIL DAY BREAKS

LEISURE BOOKS NEW YORK CITY

A LEISURE BOOK®

June 2004

Published by special arrangement with Golden West Literary
Agency.

Dorchester Publishing Co., Inc.
200 Madison Avenue
New York, NY 10016

Visit us on the web at www.dorchesterpub.com.

UNTIL DAY BREAKS

Resting here until day breaks and shadows fall
and darkness disappears.
From the gravestone of Quanah Parker

Chapter One

After he had made the speech, the whole thing seemed a little ridiculous to him — the twenty-dollar-a-plate dinner and the overwhelming ovation afterward. A man would think that he had said something important. From the moment he'd received the wire, he'd been nervous about the whole thing. He couldn't see any justification in bringing him from his command in Texas, clear to Washington, just to make a speech.

He stood by the cloak room, waiting for an orderly to bring his hat and cape, and he thought: *It must have been those damn' papers I wrote for that journal.* The newspapers had picked them up and had made a big thing of them. He could understand the senator's attitude, for any sincere plan for peace meant a drastic cut in troops, a savings to the taxpayer, and more votes at the polls.

Some of the high brass didn't like his speech, he knew. He had seen General Burley's immense frown, and a bell of warning sounded in the back of his mind. Better not make any more speeches, not with eleven more years to go before retirement.

Colonel Tracy Cameron was a tall man, grown gray in the service. He was in his late forties, as thin as a whip, yet possessing a surprising strength and vitality. Although his skin was dark, it seemed very thin, like old leather dried too long. And every bone in his face was a hard ridge, like the bracings of a tent, serving to draw his flesh drum-tight from cheekbone to jaw hinge. He had a long nose with a slight crook in it, only noticeable when viewed full face. His lips were like a healed

7

scar, thin and flat against his even teeth. Gray had invaded his hair at the temples, and he combed it back so that it made two contrasting streaks past his ears. His forehead was a broad, flat plane with eyebrows as dark as two thunderclouds, gathering on a still day. When he became irritated, the flesh bunched together into irregular lines, and every officer on the post below the rank of major searched his soul for past sins and wondered which of them had finally caught up with him.

The orderly came with his cape, and Cameron stepped over to put it on. He had a noticeable limp, which naturally brought to an observer's mind some unspoken moment of bravery on the battlefield. At one time in his life, Tracy Cameron set straight anyone who spoke of it, but in later years he'd learned to keep quiet, for the truth was quite without glamour. He had been kicked by a quartermaster's mule.

During his thirty years of service, combat had somehow circumvented him, and the closest he had come to it was in the fall of 1863, when a shell exploded a hundred yards down the road from staff headquarters, wrecked an Army escort wagon, and killed two mules. He was keenly aware of his one-sided career, but somehow had been unable to change in any way the events of his life. From the first he had been assigned to staff as an aide-de-camp; then after the Civil War he served five years in Europe as a military liaison officer and observer to the German army.

"Your carriage will be around in a moment, Colonel."

The orderly's voice aroused him, and he nodded. "Thank you, Corporal." He walked outside to stand in the shelter of the porch. A light, spring rain was falling, making the street bright beneath the electric street lights.

He had been a bitter man in those days, thinking about the trouble on the western frontier, thinking about his piddling duty in Europe. He had been certain then that promotion would pass him by, but it didn't. He found himself advancing with unaccountable regularity, as though he had had some unknown champion in Washington. And then he'd been mixed up in that damned border affair over there, too. He'd come close to ruining his career there — of that he had always been certain. Officially he had had no business acting as a go-between for warring governments, or sitting in as mediator to the peace terms. But he'd carried it off, and a little later he'd been recalled and given his captaincy.

A carriage rounded the corner and came toward the curb, lacquered sides bright with rain, glowing in the light of the side lamps. A sergeant smothered in rain gear drove, and he hopped down to open the door for Tracy Cameron.

"A good night to catch the pip, eh, sir?"

"If you like the pip," Cameron said, and got into the coach.

He took off his hat, laid it on the velvet seat, and leaned back so that he could see out the window. The driver held to a sedate but steady pace, and Cameron admired the smooth street, and the street lamps, and once in a while he would rub his hand over the velvet upholstering and think how good this was, how different from the accommodations to which he was accustomed at Fort Elliot, thirty-six miles to the nearest railhead, and almost fifty to the stage line.

Every man can stand a little spoiling once in a while, he decided, and leaned back to enjoy the ride to his hotel. It really didn't matter why he'd been brought to Washington. It was a good vacation for himself and his wife. He hadn't been away from the frontier for nearly six years. And lately he hadn't been feeling too well.

Cameron had always wanted to serve on the frontier, but for a time he thought he never would make it. After his tour in

9

Europe he'd been in staff — nearly two years of that — and then they sent him West, not to subdue Indians, but to investigate peace possibilities. He didn't like to think of those things. It was an era of failure for him, an era that carried over to this very moment. He had established a peace with the Kiowas, only to have it broken in eleven months, and warfare more ferocious than before sprang up over a thousand square miles.

His dealings with the Cheyennes had also ended equally badly: a year of quiet, then thrusting raids and war parties. He began to live with a sense of failure, and constantly searched his soul for the flaw that permitted it.

The driver stopped before his hotel, and Cameron got out while the doorman touched his hat. "Good night, Sergeant," Cameron said, and went on inside before he got wet.

A clerk hurried forward with his key, his heels tapping on the marble floor. Cameron walked up the broad stairway to the third floor, pausing once to catch his breath. This short-windedness bothered him, more now than it had in the past. *I'll have to see a doctor,* he thought, and knew that he wouldn't.

He unlocked the door to his suite, saw that the light was still on, and knew that his wife had waited up for him. She always did that, and he felt warmed by it. It was a devotion he felt that he did not deserve.

He took off his hat and cape and hung them up, and she came from the bedroom, dressed in a robe.

"Two minutes to twelve," she said. "I thought you'd be later."

"I didn't want the coach to turn into a pumpkin," he said.

She was younger than he, a little plump now, but still shapely, still an attractive woman. He put his arms around her and kissed her, then she made him sit down. "How did the speech go?"

"Good," he said. "I think they liked it. General Burley didn't, though. He still thinks a cavalry charge will cure the world's ills." He bent over to take off his shoes.

"You didn't drink too much? You've got to remember your liver, Tracy."

"I had a few," he said. "I took my olive oil like a good boy." He reached out and patted her. He turned his head as a low whistle came out of the speaking tube on the wall. He got up and crossed to it, and put it to his ear.

His wife said: "Blow in it. That way the person on the other end. . . ."

"I forgot." He puffed his cheeks and blew, then put it to his ear again. The instrument was strange to him, and he never knew when to listen through it or speak through it, so his wife took it and conducted the conversation.

When she hung up, she said: "Senator Chaffee will be up in fifteen minutes. I ought to get dressed."

Tracy Cameron laughed and said: "Nonsense, dear. Only a fool would call at midnight and expect the hostess to be in an evening dress." He took a cigar from his pocket and lit it. "Well, since we're taking the eleven o'clock train tomorrow, I suppose it's all right. Only these senators never have anything important to say."

She came over to sit on the arm of his chair. "Tracy, it's been a wonderful ten days. I mean, the city is a nice change, with the streets and walks and shops. Will we ever have such things at Fort Elliot?"

"They have street lights in Dallas," he said. "I saw them there nearly four years ago." He put his arm around her. "You've had a hard life, old girl, but you've worn damned well. Next year the boys will be through school, and we'll have them with us for a while. I promise you that."

"For the summer, anyway," she said. "Perhaps you'll get a

11

change of command. I'd like to go to California. To San Francisco."

"I'll test my political influence," Tracy Cameron promised, and they both laughed.

She went into the bedroom to change into a dress. He had known she would, for she was a proper woman, aware of her rôle as his wife, and occasionally it amused him, how seriously she took everything.

He could not imagine what Senator Chaffee wanted. As far as Cameron was concerned, they'd talked themselves out at the dinner, before and after his speech. He liked Chaffee, in spite of the man's pomposity, but then he supposed that the man had been in the public eye so long that he just couldn't do anything else but gesture and parade a little. This was a part of life, of a man's *costume*, and Cameron understood it, for the Army was that way, full of parades and protocol and saber-shaking to keep the people interested. When it was over, the work began, the dull routine that never made the newspapers or the dispatches to headquarters, because they had routines of their own and didn't want to be bothered with yours.

Senator Chaffee was punctual. He rang, and Cameron went to open the door. Chaffee shook Cameron's hand and said: "I trust you'll pardon this late intrusion, Colonel, but I just had to see you again before you went back to Texas."

"I'm glad you could take the time, Senator. Our train leaves at eleven tomorrow."

"Yes, I know, that's why I called." He gave Cameron his hat and coat and cane. "I have a committee meeting in the morning at nine. This was really our only chance to get together."

Edith Cameron came from the bedroom, and Chaffee gave her his brightest smile and bent over her hand a moment before his lips brushed it. "So nice to see you again. My wife and niece send their regards. They enjoyed the tea so much."

"Thank you, Senator. I've sent down for some coffee."

"Good," Chaffee said. "*Wugh,* that Scotch! I swear, if Billings had proposed one more toast, I was going to get up and leave." He took the chair Cameron offered, and one of the colonel's cigars. "Again, I must say that I found your speech most stimulating, Colonel. And, of course, I've read your articles. Your viewpoint is most refreshing."

"Perhaps, but it lacks popularity," Cameron said. "I'm not doing my career any good by hammering at it all the time. Still, only a fool will pursue logic which concludes that only a dead Indian is a good one. That kind of thinking doesn't stop when the Indians are dead, Senator. It goes on, and one day may be turned against Swedish Lutherans or someone else." He shook his head. "The Army places too great an importance on a man's ability to fight, rather than negotiate. We're running out of enemies, Senator. There's no one else to fight. So we have to change from an army of reprisal to an army of policy, where a politically-oriented officer is more valuable than one with a sterling war record. The army function has slowly changed, and the value lies not in the ability to wage war, but to keep peace."

"The Indian trouble isn't over, Colonel," Chaffee pointed out. He sat in the chair like a man ready to get up and fight. He seemed to find it difficult to relax. He was a big man, thick through the chest, and his voice was a rumbling bass of untapped power. His mustache was dark and thick, and his brown eyes were quick-darting, restless, as though he could never see enough of what went on around him.

"Politically," Chaffee said, "we're very aware of the fact that Western expansion has not yet taken place. I suggest that as soon as the land is made safe, the population will triple west of the Mississippi. We've got to be prepared for that, Colonel. We've got to have men there who will know how to handle it." He reached over and tapped Tracy Cameron on the knee. "The whole political picture is changing, Colonel, and, when it changes, the Army is going to have to change, too. Colonel, I'm chairman of a very important committee. We create Indian policy, and we're trying to do it right. The only hot spot left is Texas . . . and the Comanches."

Tracy Cameron shrugged. "Senator, we've kept them from gathering. I'd say we were doing a pretty good job, considering there hasn't been a shot exchanged between the Army and the Indians for nearly three years. In my opinion, the fighting is over. I predict that there will never be another major engagement between the United States Army and the Indians. But, unfortunately, men who rank me don't feel that way. And I hate to say it, but it's my studied opinion that they're waiting for the day when they can launch a new campaign against the Comanches."

"I agree, sir, but it just can't happen," Chaffee said. "Colonel, my committee can take a general and squeeze him into line, if we have to. Sherman is an excellent commander. I think he'd take a peaceful negotiation over another armed uprising by the Comanches. Give me sixty days, Colonel, and I believe I can put you in a position of power in Texas. Your remarks tonight made a tremendous impression on my colleagues, and an informal poll of votes seems overwhelmingly in your favor, as a logical choice. Would you accept?"

"I'm not sure what I'd be accepting, Senator."

Chaffee leaned forward to tap his cigar ash into a dish. "Next year is election. We want to go to the polls with a record that will stand like stone. For thirty years now there's been one bloody Indian affair after another, one peace treaty broken while another was being made. We want to be done

14

with that, Colonel. We want a peace so firm, so just, that no man in his right mind will ever doubt that it is a final one."

Tracy Cameron frowned. "It's rather a noble thought, Senator, but it loses some of its luster when you consider the motives behind it."

Chaffee took no offense. "No motive for wanting peace could be wholly bad, Colonel." He leaned back and looked steadily at Tracy Cameron. "You've never commanded a unit in battle, never lead a charge, or organized a retreat. By some thrust of fate, you've always been the clean-up man, the one who went in after the glory was gone and brushed up the mess that heroes left behind. That makes you a most peculiar man, Colonel Cameron. Sort of like the red-headed stepchild no one wanted, but who saved his money through the years and came in the clutch to pay off the mortgage. You have a talent for peace, Cameron, and very little capacity for war, and we need that, desperately. Yes, I'd say that you were not only one of a kind right now, but also a first of his kind, a soldier whose purpose is not to fight."

"It's rather amusing, the way you put it, Senator."

Chaffee smiled. "But true. Cameron, I believe I'd trust you as far as you wanted to go in this matter. There's a brigadier in it, if it matters to you."

"It doesn't," Cameron said. Then he laughed. "Senator, I'm afraid I haven't fooled you. I'm a dedicated man with an obscure and unpopular cause." He suddenly thrust out his hand. "I'd be glad to accept the responsibility."

Chaffee slapped Cameron's palm, then gripped the hand firmly. He turned to Mrs. Cameron. "Madam, I think your husband is a great man."

Tracy Cameron puffed briefly the bitter stub of his cigar, then crushed it out in a dish. "You're reckoning without General Sherman, Senator, and he is still Departmental Commander. And knowing the general, sir, he has plans of his own concerning the Texas Indians."

"I'm sure he has," Chaffee said. "Cameron, I'm not going to try to tell you that we're going to get our unopposed way in this matter. There are factions in Texas politics who want the Army to wipe the Comanches off the map, and there is some solid military thinking behind this. George Custer isn't the only glory-hunting officer in the Army. I know of half a dozen of staff rank who'd like nothing better than to sink their teeth into another good, offensive campaign, and drag it out for another year. That's just something you'll have to handle in your own way. Naturally, my committee will do everything it can to keep authority in your hands. We've got to try, Cameron, even if we fail."

"A few months back," Tracy Cameron said, "I was at Fort Griffith, talking to Ranald Mackenzie. He'd just come from a staff meeting at Fort Union, and was quoting General Miles. The gist of it is a late campaign. Mackenzie's for it, and he's got enough of a record as a fighting man to draw about him the best cavalry companies on the frontier." He glanced at Chaffee. "Miles isn't going to be an easy man to dissuade. If there was ever a heroic Indian fighter, it's Nelson Miles. Why, the moment he assumes command of a campaign, the public naturally assumes it will be soon reading of stirring battles. And every junior officer with him will be thinking of getting mentioned in a dispatch, coming that much closer to a raise in rank." He shook his head and drank his cold coffee. "Any man who departs from Miles's conception of how Indians are handled will be fighting on two fronts, the Indians and the men in his own service. Peace, Senator, is what everyone says he wants, but it is still a radical concept. There are times when I think it is an alien concept."

"People won't trust it because it's always too good to be

true," Chaffee said. "But it has to become a reality, Colonel. Look at Wyoming and the Dakotas once the Indian trouble was put down there. They're expanding at an unprecedented rate. Eyes are turned to Texas now. The country is rich, big, wide open. And with the windmill, a dry farmer can sink a well and turn the desert green. Only he can't do it with the Comanche threat lurking over the next hill. People won't do it. Cameron, we've used up our hearty pioneer stock. They don't want to die for the land any more." He slapped the arms of his chair and stood up. "Well, it's late, and I must be going. You'll hear from me shortly, Cameron. I'd say within ten days, or shortly after you return to Fort Elliot."

Cameron's wife fetched the senator's hat and coat, and, as Chaffee slipped into it, he asked: "What's Fort Elliot like?"

"Hot and dusty and lonely out there on the plains."

"Sounds miserable," Chaffee said. He shook hands. "Have a good trip. One of these days I'd like to come out and have a look at your country."

Cameron frowned. "You haven't seen Texas, Senator?"

Chaffee laughed. "I haven't been west of Iowa. Good night, sir . . . Missus Cameron. Don't bother, I'll let myself out."

After the door closed, Edith Cameron said: "I thought he was a senator from Texas. He's a strange man, Tracy."

"Because he can feel for someone he's never seen?" Cameron thrust both hands into his pockets and stood that way for a moment. "He's a visionary, Edith. He could look at a desert of waste and see farms there, and cattle grazing in the pastures, and grain growing in the fields. There are men like that, old girl. They can't see a plain without visualizing a railroad across it, or a telegraph line, or a bridge across the rivers."

"And you, Tracy . . . do you look at Fort Elliot and see it not there any more?"

17

He smiled at her. "I see it decaying, Edith, because the need for it will be gone. In fifteen years, there won't be a Fort Elliot or a Fort Griffith, because there won't be any Indians hostile enough to look after. The function of the frontier Army is to operate so well that it will remove the need for its existence. We must, in a sense of the word, work ourselves out of a job. For many years now troops have been stationed where they were needed. That will change. We'll see the day when troops will be stationed where it's convenient to train them, nothing more."

"Did you say that tonight?" she asked.

"Yes."

"I'll bet General Burley frowned. You know, it's his dream to make Fort Union, New Mexico, the jumping-off place for the next Indian campaign."

"He rather scowled," Tracy Cameron admitted. "But time and tide will take care of Saber Sam Burley. Soon, Edith, a man will have to point his ship in the right direction, or find the tide too strong to sail against."

"He has two stars," she pointed out. "Now, if you were a brigadier. . . ."

"But I'm not," Cameron said, "and I don't think Senator Chaffee has that much pull, good intentions notwithstanding." He turned out the light and went into the bedroom, unbuttoning his dress blouse. "But it's nice to think about . . . retiring as a general. You know, when I began my career, I was willing to settle for a major's rank. I used to dream of going back to Vermont to be a country squire and let everyone call me Major, like some misplaced southern gentleman." Then he laughed. "It would be quite a surprise to the men at Fort Elliot, wouldn't it? I mean, the post has never rated a brigadier general for a commander. It might do a bit for morale."

She studied him for a moment, then came over and put her arms around him. "You want it, don't you, Tracy?"

"Yes," he said. "I'd like to feel that it doesn't matter, but it does. I believe I have it coming, and I know I'd work hard at it. Still, I'm not totally happy with the thought, Edith. One part of my mind rejects it and tells me that I should give everything for love of duty, and hang the reward. Another part tells me that I need the money and the prestige, that I want it just to have it." He sighed and freed himself from her embrace. "I've never been fond of any officer who used rank as a ladder, but now I find myself doing it. He offered me a brigadier, Edith. My God, I'm a man of flesh . . . how could I be expected to resist it?"

"Don't," she said. "It would be foolish." She turned her back to him. "Unbutton me. I had enough trouble getting into this alone. I'm not going to get out of it the same way."

"Well, I haven't got it yet," he said, working on the row of fastenings down her back. "So there's no use sewing on the stars. But it's something to think about, Edith. It's pretty big to any man, and it makes him think . . . make an appraisal of himself." He reached down and slapped her on the rump. "You'll have to put on a little weight, old girl. I've never heard of a general's wife as good-looking as you."

Chapter Two

A bit wearily, Tracy Cameron stepped down from the railway coach, then handed his wife to the station platform. Hardly had the cinders crunched beneath his feet when a young officer trotted up, clicked his heels sharply, and nearly tore the beak off his kepi with a salute.

"Colonel Cameron, sir. I have a detail to take care of your luggage, and an ambulance for you and your wife."

"Thank you," Cameron said. "Who the devil are you?"

"Lieutenant James Mayhew Gary, sir. Your new A.D.C."

"An aide?" Cameron frowned. "Where did you come from?"

"Fort Union, sir. Two days ago. I was ordered here by command of General Sherman, sir."

"Well," Cameron said, smiling, "I'm not going to argue with General Sherman. All right, Mister Gary, carry on. I'm going to step over to the telegraph office. Be ready to leave in fifteen minutes." He gave his wife a pat on the arm. "Excuse me, my dear."

He walked over to the side of the waiting room and asked the telegrapher to check and see if there were any wires. While the man went through the stack of papers, Cameron half turned and observed Lieutenant Gary. The man was efficient, handling a dozen small details at one time, yet Cameron reserved his firm judgment. He needed an aide-de-camp like he needed another toe on each foot, yet he was willing to give Gary every chance. He was a handsome young man, tall and muscular, pretty much of a show piece with his parade-ground manners. Yet it took more than swagger to make an officer. It took time, a lot of routine, and a little hate for the Army to mold a man into a strong leader.

"Nothing, Colonel," the telegrapher said. "I sent a batch out with the rider yesterday. Likely they'll be on your desk when you get there."

"Thank you just the same," Cameron said, and went over to the ambulance. Lieutenant Gary was there, and, when Cameron approached, Gary brought his heels together, cracking them like two blocks of wood. Cameron said: "Where did you learn that, Mister Gary?"

"A Prussian drill master in military school, sir. Two years of it before the Academy, sir."

Cameron felt like telling him to confine that to once a day — in the morning — but he held it back and got into the rig. A sergeant drove, and Gary sat primly on the other seat, while an armed escort and a buckboard brought up the rear. They had a long ride ahead of them, Cameron knew, and he didn't intend to endure it in silence.

"So you came from Fort Union. How long were you stationed there, Mister Gary?"

"Eleven months, sir."

"Tactical?"

"No, sir. Administrative." There was a touch of regret in his voice, and perhaps even reluctance to admit that he had not been on a single patrol.

Cameron understood the feeling well, and it generated a touch of sympathy within him. He smiled and said: "Well, we'll see if we can't find a patrol now and then for you . . . something to get you off the post."

Gary's smile was like a suddenly lit lamp. "Why, thank you, sir. I must say that this assignment failed to arouse a proper enthusiasm, sir. That is, it came rather suddenly,

21

if you know what I mean."

"Things are liable to happen suddenly from now on," Cameron said.

"A new campaign, sir?"

Cameron studied Gary's eagerness. "Why do you suggest that?"

"Well, the way I was transferred, sir. A telegram ordering me to report immediately. Most unusual, wouldn't you say, sir?"

"We're entering an unusual era, Mister Gary. A very unusual era."

They talked of many things as the day wore on. Gary was from a middle-class family, a hard worker who took the chances given him and made the best of them. He had manners and poise, and a good opinion of himself, which was all right, if a man didn't carry it too far.

That night they camped on the prairie, and Gary attended to each small detail, seeing that the tent was pitched and a proper cook fire made. Cameron observed him carefully, for he knew that Gary was new to the country, and he wanted to see how he adapted to it. They were in that part of Texas that is full of monotonous flats, where the day's sun is liquid fire, and the darkness of night is an ink blanket, and even the stars seem farther away, unbelievably remote.

The Mexicans called it the *Llano Estacado*, the Staked Plains, and the Indians considered it a place of bad medicine. Certainly it was no place for any man who could not endure the empty miles, the biggest skies he had ever seen, and the lonesomeness of land completely unchanging. Still this was only the northern fringe of it. The really bad part stretched far to the south.

At dawn they broke camp and pushed on, and by early morning they entered slightly rolling land. Shortly after noon they raised Fort Elliot. Gary sent the sergeant on ahead, and a guard detail was assembled by headquarters, while the officer of the day trotted across the sun-hardened parade ground.

Cameron dismounted by the headquarters building, and told Gary: "Take Missus Cameron to Quarters A, and see that the servants are on duty." He answered Gary's salute and turned to the shade of the porch.

The O.D. said: "Glad to have you back, sir."

"It's good to be home, Bingham. Come on in and bring me up to date." He entered the outer office, moved past the orderlies at attention, and went to his office. A thick heat filled the room, and Cameron flung open the windows, knowing well that it wouldn't do any good until evening; a breeze always sprang up then. He sat down in his chair and sighed and looked at the paper work waiting for him, but he felt good, as if he belonged here and nowhere else.

The patrol reports were on his desk, he was sure, still he didn't feel like digging through them. "Sit down, Bingham." He waved the lieutenant into a chair. "What's the activity around this part of Texas?"

"Well, generally quiet, sir. The Indians aren't doing any gathering or dancing, but that's because we're out there all the time, looking down their necks. Two weeks ago, an Indian took a shot at Captain Jennings's patrol. Winged Trooper Busik in the arm, but it wasn't serious."

"Did Jennings return the fire?"

Bingham shook his head. "No, sir. They pursued the Indian, took away his rifle, and turned him loose. Jennings has a good head on him, sir. He isn't easily rattled."

Cameron felt a deep warmth within him. It was a feeling all commanders get when they know that orders are deeply ingrained in the minds of the men, so securely set that they become a will of their own. "It's damned easy to start an inci-

23

dent," he said. "Well, there's one Indian who can't complain about being mistreated." He pushed himself erect. "I'm going to my quarters for an hour, Bingham. I'd like to see all company commanders at four. That'll give me time to bathe and shave and smoke a cigar and go over the patrol reports."

"I'll have them here, sir," Bingham said, and went about his duties.

Cameron walked across the parade, feeling the heat through the soles of his boots. He entered his quarters, spoke to the orderly, and then went down the hall to the bedroom. Edith was changing into a cooler gingham dress.

"How does home feel?" Cameron asked.

"Good," she said. "I dreaded the thought of coming back, but the nearer we got to Tascosa, the better I began to feel." She wiped sweat from her face. "My, it's hot. But good."

"I'd like to invite six officers for supper. Mind?"

"I think company would be nice this evening," she said.

Their quarters were the largest on the post, and perhaps the furniture was a grade above that of captain. Still none of it was first-class, and most of it had been handed down from one commanding officer to another, or shipped to the post for Cameron's use. He had seven rooms, including a large study and a dining room, and there wasn't a junior officer on the post who didn't think it was grand, with the papered walls and rugs on the floor. But Tracy Cameron knew it was second-rate and didn't like it. Not that he wanted fine things for himself. It was of his wife that he thought. She deserved better than Quarters A, Fort Elliot, Texas.

If he were stationed at the Presidio in San Francisco, they'd have a house, or live in an apartment off the post, and it would be something fine. Probably not too large, for his salary only went so far with two sons in college, but it would be good, something they could call their own.

24

"I'm going to write a request to departmental headquarters," Cameron said, "and have this place done over. The outside needs painting, and the inside is showing wear." He gave her a kiss on the cheek. "One of these days, old girl, I'm going to figure out some way to buy you a new set of china, and get it here without half the pieces getting broken."

"Tracy," she said, "there isn't a wife on the post who doesn't understand a chipped dish." She gave him a playful shove. "Your bath is waiting. I'll put out a glass of whiskey and a cigar for you. You know, when you're tired, you always complain about this house, and about my chipped dishes. Tracy, you are an easy man to understand, and a very nice man to be in love with."

The bath did make him feel much better, and he shaved carefully, except for his upper lip. He decided that a mustache would give him a touch of distinction, and they were coming back in style. He examined the hair follicles closely and concluded that his mustache would be dark, with very little gray in it.

He arrived at his office a good half hour before the scheduled meeting time, and, after closing the door, he went over the patrol reports in detail. There had been no slackening of activity in his absence. In fact, he detected an even more strict adherence to duty, as though every man were determined not to offer an area of criticism upon his return.

Since assuming this command, Cameron had considered a dozen possible avenues of military activity. But what he boiled it all down to was a campaign of watchful alertness, keeping troops always on the move, keeping the Indians always under the eye. He had met with resistance, for these men were soldiers, men who had fought before and wanted to fight again, and Cameron was conducting a no-fight policy. He swung them to him in time, for with his way there were

25

no empty saddles, no burials in the field, no worry about re-placements, or getting the hell licked out of you, as Custer did.

It had taken time, but they were behind him now. They trusted him and believed in him, and they liked his way, and he believed the Indians liked it. They could hunt the buffa-loes and have their dances, and the soldiers weren't always entering their camps or stirring them up. And when an Indian broke the rules, he was handled as Captain Jennings had han-dled it, reprimanding the Indian by disarming him and sending him back to his people. That was more of a disgrace than putting the culprit in the stockade.

In Cameron's methods there was no sense of turning the other cheek, no question of cowardice, for it took courage to do the right thing, and it took courage to maintain peace when another man's thoughts were on war. Every man rose to the challenge, and in Cameron's mind these four hundred and ninety-two men were the cream of the crop, the finest troops he had ever soldiered with.

He knew his company commanders would be prompt, and Lieutenant Jim Gary came in first, carrying folding camp chairs. He set these up, placed a few saucers about for ash trays, then asked: "Would the colonel like a bottle and glasses?"

"I hardly think anyone is ill, Mister Gary, so there's no need to drink to anyone's health."

"Yes, sir." Gary opened the door and ushered in the offi-cers who had been waiting in the outer office. When they were all seated, he turned to leave, but Cameron waved him back.

Cameron left his desk and shook hands with each man in turn, then said: "Gentlemen, I'm happy to say that you look the same. I've been going through your reports of patrol activity. Are there any personal opinions you'd like to air . . . unofficially?"

Captain Leeds, a dark, barrel-bodied man, spoke. "Colonel, this is, of course, just an opinion, and nothing more. But there seems to be a good deal of Indian movement in the area. I hesitate to call it a gathering, sir, but it's most peculiar. Indians move when they're hunting or raiding, but in the last three weeks I've seen two of Kicking Bird's bunch in two localities some distance apart. I'd like to ask, sir, if we couldn't round up Kicking Bird and send him back to the reservation."

"I think not," Cameron said. "If we sent him back now, he'd break out again. No, we'll leave him alone, let him do what he wants, and, if it fails, he may get it out of his system." He paused to consider Leeds's remarks. "Of course, Captain, your observation may be pure coincidence."

"Yes, sir, I thought of that, until I compared it with Captain Jennings's report and Lieutenant Sawyer's, sir."

Cameron glanced at these two officers. Jennings was a graying, raw-boned man with large hands and feet. "We've made the same observation, sir. In fact, we were fired upon by a lone Kiowa. We captured him, disarmed him, and sent him home, but it seemed to me that he was quite fearful of us, as though we'd find out something. Sir, I think all this movement is a banding together of all the Kiowas and Cheyennes that have jumped the reservations and are now living in the Staked Plains country. I believe Quanah Parker of the Comanches is calling them into one force, sir."

"I share that opinion," Lieutenant Sawyer said. He was a rather young man with a new pair of silver bars, but he was Texas-born, and his opinions were always worth consideration. "It's been three years since any of us took a shot at an Indian, sir. I think they like the way things are going, but they can't believe it'll last. Parker is the big man among the Comanches, and he mistrusts us. He may want to hit one of our patrols, or some outpost of buffalo hunters like Adobe Walls, and test his strength. We'd have to fight then, sir, and it would all go to hell . . . all this patient work."

Tracy Cameron lit a cigar, and they took this as permission to light their own. Within minutes, the office was dense with smoke, and non-smokers like Lieutenant Gary coughed and moved closer to the open window.

"Gentlemen," Cameron said, "when I was in Washington, I was heartened to note that our efforts here have not gone unnoticed. I wish I could say more. I wish I knew more to say, but I urge you to hold on a little longer, to maintain this attitude of peace even against mounting threat. The future of the Comanches and ourselves and the people here in north Texas may well hang or fall on how we conduct ourselves in the next few months." He looked from one to another. "It would be unkind of me to insult you with an order not to fire when fired upon. I intend to leave these individual problems entirely to your own judgments, but I want it clearly understood that we are after peace and not war. Captain Jennings, I'm going to mention you in a personal dispatch to General Sherman for your handling of that affair with the Indian. Believe me, gentlemen, these problems can be resolved without shooting. I pray that they will be, or peace will be many years in coming. We've got to let old wounds heal. We've got to stop hitting back every time we're hit. It is our charged duty to set the example of peace, and, believe me, it no longer matters a damn who started the trouble."

"Hear, hear," Jennings said, and they all nodded their approval to this.

There was no more discussion of their problems, just a casual free-for-all conversation about Cameron's Washington visit, and he entertained them by recounting all the social events and the plush accommodations of his hotel suite.

Before they left his office, he invited them to dinner, brushed aside their excuses, then shooed them out. Lieutenant Gary remained, and he tidied up, emptying the saucers and putting away the folding stools. Then he cleaned off Cameron's desk and filed everything while the colonel looked out the window at the parade ground. Cameron could see nothing that had changed particularly since he had assumed the command. The grounds were kept a little cleaner, and there had been some repair work done, but the real changes had all been more subtle, all in the attitudes of his men from the newest trooper to the oldest officer.

He turned and found Jim Gary waiting. "Sit down," Cameron said. "So you want to be a fighting man."

"I want to be a good man, Colonel. If fighting is a part of it, I'll fight."

"What do you think of the officers on this post?"

"They have my deepest respect, sir, with one or two exceptions, and they were not present tonight." He folded his hands and looked at Tracy Cameron.

"Mister Gary, do you mean to tell me you have formed this opinion in a few days?"

"Yes, sir. I can form an opinion in two minutes, but it probably wouldn't be any good."

Tracy Cameron laughed, then turned to the door. "I think that will be all for today, Mister Gary. I arrive at my office shortly after six every morning, breakfast at seven-thirty, and get down to serious business at eight. Generally I eat lunch here, and supper at six. I trust you can adjust your habits to that."

Jim Gary risked a smile. "Sir, at twenty-two most of my

habits are bad and have to be broken anyway."

During the next three weeks, Tracy Cameron reacquainted himself with every minute detail of his command. He didn't want anything going on that he didn't know about. Personally, he led three patrols, and on two of these Lieutenant Gary went along, conducting himself with the same level-headed efficiency that seemed to mark everything he did. Cameron was beginning to understand Gary, to appreciate his agile mind, and to be annoyed at times by his eagerness to perform well.

He was, Cameron decided, more than a handsome showpiece, and he revised his earlier estimate. Gary's deportment was a model for every officer on the post, and at the rifle butts he made top score, three weeks' running. At mounted and dismounted saber, he had no peer. How he was with his fists, Cameron didn't know, but he was willing to bet that Gary could stand toe-to-toe with another man and not do any backing up.

Fort Elliot patrols lasted five days, and they didn't go eight or nine miles out on the prairie and bivouac, either. These were riding patrols — looking patrols — ranging south to the Salt Fork of the Red River, then east to the Washita, and as far north as Wolf Creek, which came close not to being in Texas at all. To the west they reached Adobe Walls, the nest for buffalo hunters. All the land in between they crossed and criss-crossed, and rode circles around it and triangles through it until half the jack rabbits were recognized on sight.

It was, Cameron knew, the only way to know a country, to live in it, work it, and then your observations became important and could be properly evaluated. Quite possibly there were more patrols going and coming out of Fort Elliot than out of any other two posts in Texas, but that was the way

Cameron ran his share of the Army, and he was getting no complaints.

Patrol, report, evaluate, plan — that was the cycle for him, and he spent long hours in his office because of it. Each week a rider went to Tascosa for mail and telegrams, and these always meant more work, for departmental headquarters always loaded him down with advice. Everyone, it seemed, was an authority on another man's business.

He received a letter from Senator Chaffee and read it several times, trying to decide what was good news and what was bad. Chaffee had kept his word. He had convinced his committee that Tracy Cameron was the man to conduct the peace settlement with the Plains Indians. General Sherman had been advised and would communicate in the near future to map out a complete strategy. Chaffee was eager to get the whole thing under way, because he had made a few promises that the negotiations would be a success, and that it would be completed by the end of summer.

This was one of the things that disturbed Cameron. That, and the fact that he was still taking orders from Sherman, who strongly favored General Burley and Nelson A. Miles to run the whole affair.

"I'm going to have trouble there," Cameron said aloud.

He started to open this latest batch of telegrams. There was a wire from the commander at Fort Bascomb. He'd been having a devil of a time, losing men to desertions because of the silver strikes near the fort. He wanted the temporary transfer of two companies to swell his table of organization until he could bring back the deserters. Cameron threw the wire in the wastebasket.

There were other requests, and he ignored them. Then he opened one of the envelopes and stared at it, reading it three times before putting it down. With hands that trembled

31

slightly, he put a match to a cigar and sat there like a man thinking of far-off places.

It was official, all right. As official as any order could be, and he got up and opened the connecting door. "Corporal, will you find Mister Gary for me?"

He went back and sat down, and a feeling of elation was beginning to grow now. It was like a warming fire on a cold night. A few minutes later he looked out his window and saw Gary hurrying across the parade ground, and Cameron thought: *That boy can sure hurry.*

Gary came into the office. "Yes, sir?"

Cameron hesitated, and then spoke calmly. "Mister Gary, will you have a notice posted with the officer of the day that I've been promoted to the rank of brigadier general. I believe one notice at the guardhouse, one in each mess, and one in the sutler's store will be sufficient."

"Well, I'll be damned," Gary said.

Cameron felt like laughing, but he knew he didn't dare. "What was that, Mister Gary?"

Instantly the young man sobered. "I was only expressing my surprise, sir, and my pleasure." He saluted, then did an about-face to the door. But instead of stepping out, he let the stiffness of attention run out of him and turned back. "Wait until I write my sisters about this. An aide to a general!"

He dashed out in a most unmilitary manner, and then Cameron's tension broke, and he began to laugh. Both orderlies heard him and looked in to see what was so funny.

Chapter Three

Adjusting the lamp on his desk so that he could see better, General Tracy Cameron fumbled with a silver-braided star and needle and a dress tunic that was unmanageably held on his knees and wondered why the blazes he'd forgotten to affix his rank on his dress tunic in the first place. He wouldn't be doing this himself except that his wife was entertaining, and the commanding general was barely eight miles down the road, and approaching fast.

Having been captain of the Academy saber team for two years running, it irritated him to have such an insignificant thing as a needle turn clumsy in his hands. Already he had pricked his fingers twice, and each bright drop of blood was a point on the rising graph of his temper.

Then Lieutenant Jim Gary came into the office and slammed the door, and General Cameron stuck his finger again. He flung the garment on his desk, turned to his apple-cheeked aide, and tried to keep the bite out of his voice.

"What is it this time, Mister Gary?"

"Signal from the heliograph detachment at Crooked River, sir. The general's party passed there three minutes ago."

"He'll be at Sudro's in an hour. Mister Gary, is every man turned to his duty?"

"Yes, sir. Lieutenant Adams has a detail cleaning the stable. Mister Beamish is in charge of the barracks, cleaning from end to end. And C Company is policing the grounds." A touch of a smile changed slightly the contour of his lips. "And

33

I've left a standing order with every company commander on the post that each enlisted man will bathe before evening mess."

"Very thorough, Mister Gary," Cameron said. "In my entire career as a general, which is nine days, three hours, and approximately ten minutes, I have never seen such efficiency."

"Thank you, sir," Gary said, holding back his smile. "If the general will pardon me, I believe you've sewn the star on crooked."

"Oh, blast it!" Cameron said irritably. "I'll use it as a conversation piece." He reached for the humidor on his desk, lifted out a cigar, then licked it to make the loose tobacco wrapper lay flat. Considerable changes had taken place in the last few days, and he wasn't used to them yet. Six escort wagons had arrived, loaded to the bangboards with furniture and trappings, enough to fill his quarters and replace his office equipment. He passed on the old to a grateful supply officer. There was, he suspected, more of a gap between the rank of colonel and general than he had once thought. They even supplied him with a lot of knickknacks, such as a bootjack for his office and the cigar humidor and other clutter for his desk. He still felt a bit clumsy around it all.

Cameron put a match to his cigar and puffed it robustly until a cloud of rank smoke hovered around his head. Then he said: "Mister Gary, as soon as the detail is finished with the cleaning, bring them here and dung this place out. I want all the spittoons emptied, the windows washed, the floor scrubbed, and the damned stove polished."

"The stove, sir?"

"Everything is to shine, Mister Gary." He waved his hand idly. "Get along and keep me informed of the general's progress." He gnawed his cigar. "I suppose I'll have to call a com-

34

pany out for a reviewing body. And inform the bugler that if he blows 'The General' in the Infantry key of G, I'll have him in the stockade for the rest of his enlistment."

"Yes, sir," Gary said, and saluted. He rushed out of the building in an even greater hurry now.

Cameron turned back to the problem of the star he had sewn on his tunic. Gary was right — the damned thing was on crookedly. He studied the problem and wondered whether or not he should do it over, and decided to let it go. The general would likely see it and comment on it. William T. Sherman had an eye for small details, but would no doubt blame it on Cameron's tailor.

Early in his career, Tracy Cameron had learned not to try to outguess a commanding officer, yet he could not avoid some speculation on Sherman's sudden visit. Senator Chaffee evidently had more power than Cameron had realized, for the man was really giving the wheels a spin.

What kind of mood Sherman would be in was anyone's guess. If he was submitting to pressure, he'd be in a peckish frame of mind, and the whole thing would turn out unpleasantly. But Sherman was somewhat of a peacemaker himself. He'd conducted negotiations with the Plains Indians before, although unsuccessfully. But then, who had been successful?

Cameron shed his dusty blouse and slipped into the dress tunic. He listened a moment to the sound of the orderlies, cleaning up the other room. No doubt Sherman would appreciate the elbow grease that always preceded such a visit, and quite likely he would retain the impression that Fort Elliot was commanded efficiently.

To Tracy Cameron it really didn't matter if he got that impression or not. Sherman wasn't traveling this far to inspect the post, although he'd go through the motions of looking it over. That was Army, and a man just couldn't get away from it.

He passed through the outer orderly room and stopped on the porch. The sun was well down now, and, when he looked toward Quarters A, he saw that the lamps in the downstairs half were brightly turned up. Edith was giving a party, not because she enjoyed the social whirl, but because it got all the officers' wives out of their quarters so they could be cleaned. Sherman would make his rounds, and any captain considering a future promotion would have his home ready to receive him.

Tracy Cameron used the side entrance so as not to disturb the gathering in the parlor, but his wife heard him come in and left her friends to join him in the study. He embraced her briefly, and asked: "Good party?"

"We don't have anything new to talk about, so we're practicing being civil," she said. "How long is the general going to stay, Tracy?"

Cameron's thin shoulders rose and fell. "Generals are like flies. They move around a lot. Well, we'll be a good host. Still, I'd give a bit to know what kind of a mood he's going to be in. If Chaffee has forced an issue with him, he's going to be a perfect bear." He laughed briefly. "It's kind of like having some fool point a gun at you, while you stand there figuring out if it's loaded or not."

"It could be a social call, Tracy."

He smiled, for she was the eternal optimist, and it amused him, this naïve attitude she had about the Army. During his career he had met many wives of officers who were so intensely interested in their husband's work that they knew every phase of his activity; some became so well-versed that they could offer sound advice regarding military tactics. But not his Edith. She was a woman first, last, and always, a wife, not a field commander. Although he was irked at times by this lack of interest, he was more often thankful, for he could quit the day and go home to the comfort of a woman, not an associate in petticoats.

"I came over to tell you that I'll probably be at headquarters until late," he said. "Don't wait up for me."

Disappointment came to her round, smooth face, but her voice remained soft and pleasantly domestic, as though she were accustomed to this and long ago had learned there was nothing she could do about it. "Wouldn't you and General Sherman like some coffee before going to bed? Really, Tracy, I don't mind waiting up."

"You're a good old girl, Edith," he said, then turned his head as someone knocked lightly on the side door. She opened it, and Lieutenant Gary stepped inside, sweeping off his kepi and bowing politely.

"Sorry to intrude, sir. I realize you just got home, and I. . . ."

"Get to the point, Mister Gary."

"Heliograph from Sudro's, sir, just before sundown. The general's left his detachment and is riding the rest of the way alone." He plucked a stem-winder from inside his blouse. "I'd say he'll arrive within the hour, sir." He replaced the watch and stood at attention.

Tracy Cameron frowned, then spoke to his wife. "As quickly as you can, shoo these hens back to their own roosts. Mister Gary, you remain here and escort them. I'm sure none of them will turn down an opportunity to take the arm of the handsomest officer on the post."

"Really, sir, I have pressing matters. . . ."

Cameron's eyebrow lifted. "Argument, Mister Gary?"

"Oh, no, sir! I have ambitions to become a first lieutenant, sir." He offered his arm to Edith Cameron. "Shall we join the others, madam? And as the general says, shoo the hens . . . ?"

"That was only a figure of speech," Cameron said firmly. He picked up his hat and turned to the door, pausing when his wife spoke.

"Try and come back before the general arrives, dear. One of your stars is on crooked."

"Yes," Cameron said, automatically raising his hand. "To be sure. Report to me as soon as possible, Mister Gary." He stepped out and walked across the parade, his long stride making short work of it.

It was just like Sherman to forge on ahead of his detail. The man probably thought he was making another march to the sea. Blast men and their ridiculous poses! Cameron knew the whole routine, for he'd seen it before, some general storming onto the post and flinging off with that — "God, what a ride!" — attitude. Then they'd brush aside the officer of the day and stalk around, finding fault, taking down names, and making every officer in sight feel that his promotion chances were gone for at least five years.

Cameron had never conducted himself in that manner, and he had difficulty understanding men who did. Perhaps, he thought, it was because he had no tactical experience, no glorious battles behind him. He had never been a public hero, and for that matter not even a private one. The best, he was sure, that could be said of him by any officer who had served under him was that he had been efficient, firm, and easy to get along with. From day to day he tried to remain the same and in this way to end the eternal guessing game of what he would do next. Consistency, he believed, was the keynote. All the world understood and admired a consistent man.

The orderlies were finishing their clean-up, and Cameron had to admit that it was an improvement. He looked out the freshly washed windows and could not remember the view of the guardhouse and the main gate being so clear.

When he entered his office, he noticed that the spittoons had been emptied, cleaned, and polished to a luster, and the pot-bellied stove glistened with a new coat of lamp-black. Even the glass chimney of his desk lamp was shedding a greater brightness than before. He found that the duty roster and the horse books and all the company commanders' records had been properly filed, and so unaccustomed was he to this order that he had to search a bit to find what he wanted.

Going over it all in his mind for possible flaws, he could not honestly find anything that the general might get into a lather over. As a rule, Fort Elliot was in a constant state of semi-disorder, and the men spent more time on patrol than they did drilling, and he supposed it had been ten weeks since he'd held an inspection of any kind. But then, he hadn't figured it was necessary. He trusted his officers to do their duty, and they did it and would not grow too lax with the business of keeping their houses in order.

It irritated him to order them to hump it now, just to polish for General Sherman. Generals were like visiting grandfathers. You had to go around and hang up all the pictures they liked, and get their favorite chair down from the attic, and warn all the kids to be nice because Grandpa was getting on, and it would be a shame, if Aunt Clara and Uncle Herb got it all, since you'd already done so much. You dreaded their arrival, walked on eggs during their stay, then cried at the train when they left, as though you were sorry to see them go.

Lieutenant Jim Gary completed his duties at Quarters A, and reported to Cameron's office. The stable clean-up was completed. The officer of the guard wanted to know whether he should have tattoo blown promptly or not, and did the general want sentries posted to watch for Sherman's arrival?

Cameron thought about it and told Gary to have tattoo blown and to forget about the sentries. Since Sherman entertained the notion that his actual time of arrival would be a surprise, let him go on thinking so. Cameron was positive that the heliograph detachments had sent their messages undetected and that Sherman had no knowledge that Cameron was kept continually informed. Cameron was proud of this, for the use of the heliograph was his own idea and had been operating now for two years. He had always felt the lack of field communication was a serious threat to any plan, and he had solved it neatly. At strategic points on the prairie, pits had been dug, below-ground shelters built, and heliograph detachments set up with a four-man, armed escort. Actually he was putting in practice some of the things he had learned in Europe — how to disguise positions so well that they were undetectable except at a few yards' distance.

At fifty yards, his heliograph outposts looked like buffalo wallows, and every patrol carried a surveyor's transom and polaris to plot positions accurately from one outpost to another. This was necessary, because the heliographs were shuttered and shielded, and, unless a man was within a few degrees of the exact aimed point, he would not see the flash. The operators were a clannish bunch and took great pride in their work, and in two years now Cameron had rarely been surprised at any Indian movement, because word was always sent on to him, so he could act wisely and not waste a patrol's strength in idle ramming around the prairie.

Two-way communication, he had achieved it, and he wasn't going to write a paper on it or tell General Sherman about it, either. Why should he? He was having success, and they were wondering how he did it or were putting it down to a superior ability to command. He wasn't going to spoil the illusion and reveal himself as only an officer of modest capabilities.

He glanced at Gary and realized that the young man had been standing there, waiting. "As long as Sherman's on the post, I want you at his elbow constantly," Cameron said. "If the general reaches in his pocket, I expect you to divine whether it's a cigar he's after, or his watch. If it's a cigar, have a match burning before he gets the cigar to his mouth. If it's a watch, supply him with the correct time before he can ask. See that the general has a drink in his hand, but never pour too much for, if anyone saw it, they'd think he was a heavy drinker. If he asks a question, answer briefly but say that I'm more qualified than you to answer. Remember, you get your promotion from me, but I get mine from him. At all times you must create the impression that you are sincere, alert, devoted to his pleasure, sober, and intelligent. Mister Gary, a general of Sherman's importance must be courted with as much ardor as a woman you hope to marry, and perhaps the whole thing will prove more frustrating, because with a general you never know if you've succeeded or not."

"It all sounds like a silly game, sir."

Tracy Cameron laughed softly. "Playing politics is an important part of being a soldier, Mister Gary. The higher you go in rank, the more you'll see it." He looked at Gary, still at attention. "Will you please sit down? God damn it, not on the edge of the chair! Relax a little. Here, have a cigar. Oh, go on, take it." He raked a match alight, and, after Gary got the smoke going, Cameron lit his own.

"In the months to come, I'll need Sherman . . . need him badly. I can't say what's in the man's mind. He may be coming here to scald me alive. If that's the case, I've got to swing him to my side. But if he's behind me now, even a little bit, I've got to firm my position with him. Do you follow me, Mister Gary?"

"Yes, sir. We woo him, either way."

"Don't make that sound like a dirty word," Cameron cautioned. "Every junior officer on the post butters up to his superior. It's part of the routine . . . like shaving. But there's more to it than seeking promotion. Every commander needs more men, more equipment, more horses, more co-operation from general headquarters, and more understanding from the civilian population. You just don't get those things by asking for them, Mister Gary. You get them by partying with generals and politicians, and dancing with their wives. And if you have any spare time left over, you soldier a little, try to do your job. When I was in Europe, I discovered that more battles were won in the drawing room than in the field, and that a drawing-room officer was as valuable as the charger at the head of his command. For without the drawing-room officer, there would never be enough men or money to fight with."

A step sounded in the orderly room, and the officer of the guard knocked before opening Cameron's door.

"Sorry to bother you, sir, but I believe the general's approaching. Not more than twenty minutes away."

"How do you know that?"

"The scout has been keeping his ear to the ground, sir, and he swears he hears a horse running." He looked blankly at Cameron. "Shall I just let him come onto the post, or have the bugler blow flourishes?"

"Hell, blow 'The General' as ordered. Let him think he's waking up half the post. It'll be good for his morale." He waved the man away. "Mister Gary, when Sherman arrives, meet him, then bring him to my office."

"Yes, sir. But wouldn't it be more fitting, if you . . . ?"

"No," Cameron said quickly. "They're a suspicious lot,

and, if I acted eager, he'd think I had something to hide. It will be bad enough, just my being in the office at nine o'clock. Quite naturally he'll think I'm either behind in my work or trying to straighten out a mess I've gotten into."

"Very complicated, the thinking of generals," Gary said.

He went out to take a station on the headquarters porch, where he would be able to dash immediately to Sherman's horse the minute he came through the gate.

Cameron remained in his office and toyed with the idea of strewing some papers around on his desk, so he would appear overworked. He decided not to, for that would be going too far. In his mind's eye he could see Edith scooting about, ordering the servants to a flurry of tidying, probably gathering up every whole cookie left over from the party, because Sherman had a sweet tooth and would think it most thoughtful of her to have remembered it.

She was, Cameron thought, a very wonderful woman, and he made up his mind to tell her that more often. He didn't spend enough time with her, he knew, and regretted it, but his duty called him at odd hours, and she never blamed him for being so thorough. She only tried to make dearer those moments they had together. That must be devilish hard work for her, he thought, for at times he could feel her straining to pull together the ends that always seemed to drop unattended. Perhaps it would be different when the boys were through school. They might be together for a while, then. He could take a year's leave, and they could all go back to Europe and just wander around, seeing the sights. It was nice to think about, but he wondered if it would really come to pass — so few things one planned ever came out that way.

The thunder of approaching hoofs startled him, then the sentry called out, and General Sherman stormed onto the post as the bugler blew his trilling call. Jim Gary made his dash off the porch and took the reins just as Sherman plowed to a stop.

With both office doors open, Cameron could hear Sherman's laugh, and the creak of saddle leather as he dismounted. In a moment he was coming in, stripping off his beaded gauntlets, and flinging them into a handy chair. He was a man whose every movement was a mild storm of activity. He embraced Tracy Cameron, and rank clouds of dust rose from his flailing arms as he whacked Cameron on the back. Then Sherman unbuckled his riding cape and sort of dropped it, as though he knew Gary's hands would be reaching out for it. Then he sat down, and Gary barely had time to slide a chair under him to meet the general's descending rump.

"Catching up on a little late work?" Sherman asked mildly.

"Waiting for you, General," Cameron said.

"Eh?" Sherman laughed. "Don't try to fool an old fox, General." His hands dropped to his pocket, and Gary cleared his throat.

"It's a quarter after nine, sir."

Sherman seemed surprised, but he covered it quickly. "Thank you. Come now, Tracy, I surprised you . . . admit it."

Cameron hesitated a moment, wondering whether he should go along with the general's wishes, or set him back a little. The temptation was too strong to resist. "Mister Gary, when did General Sherman pass Crooked River?"

"Nearly three hours ago, sir."

"And when did General Sherman leave his detachment?"

"At Sudro's, sir."

Sherman frowned, then slapped the arm of his chair. "How the devil did you know that? My God, it's impossible for you to know it." He squinted at Cameron. "What kind of

44

tricks do you play out here, Tracy?"

"None, sir. Just a sound application of military principle."

"Hah, that's a likely story." He dipped his fingers into a pocket for a cigar, and started when Gary snapped a match on his thumbnail. Sherman puffed a moment, then said: "You've got an alert boy here, Tracy. But all the bright ones are being sent to the frontier. You ought to have the one I have in department." He rolled his eyes to heaven, and laughed. "Is that soap I smell in here?" He twisted in the chair and looked around, letting his glance swing back to Tracy Cameron. "You made a hit in Washington. Burley sent me a long and very detailed report."

"He didn't say it was a hit," Cameron commented.

Sherman smiled. "Quite the opposite, and from that I gathered that you made a favorable impression." He waved his cigar at Cameron's shoulder stars. "I was surprised, when the order came through, but pleased just the same. I always said it was possible to become a general without doing any more than count laundry." He saw the change in Tracy Cameron's face and hurried to add: "You know how I meant that, Tracy. We've worked together before, and it's been a good team."

He puffed on his cigar, then laughed. "Hell, if Senator Chaffee hadn't selected you, I would have. I can recall your earlier efforts to bring peace. A good, thorough job, Tracy."

He was lying. Cameron knew his efforts had been a bust from the start. The Army had demanded too much, and the Indians had promised too much.

"Not too thorough," Tracy Cameron said. "If it had been, I wouldn't be keeping patrols busy watching the Comanches. And Kicking Bird wouldn't be preaching war. He'd be clear of the Staked Plains and back on the reservation."

"You're nit-picking," Sherman said quickly.

"I'm quoting the facts," Cameron said. "You know them, and I know them. Washington knows them, too."

"It all boils down to peace or war," Sherman said. "And believe me, Tracy, I have capable men who can wage war."

"General Burley and General Miles. And, of course, we shouldn't forget Mackenzie. He'd love to march south and wipe them out."

All that had just boiled out, and now Cameron waited for Sherman to take offense, to slap him back in line, but Sherman didn't. He rolled the cigar from one corner of his mouth to the other and looked at Cameron. "I'm too old a fox not to know the baying of hounds, Tracy. Chaffee didn't ask my opinion. He gave me his and came straight to the point. Congress has been doing some adding, and they've come up with some mathematics, some dollars-and-cents arithmetic . . . it's simply cheaper to put down a weapon than to pick one up. Chaffee made it clear that the last time I tried to negotiate a peace, I relied on Custer, and the damned hothead only wanted a fight."

Gary poured two whiskies and handed one to General Sherman, the other to Cameron. "Thank you," Sherman said. "Now, that's what I call an aide. As I was saying, Tracy, this thing is getting big, very big. I don't mind it being dumped in my lap, so to speak, because I've been ordered to dump it in yours. But you talked with Chaffee and knew it was coming. The only thing is . . . I didn't want it now, and you did."

"The issue needs settling," Cameron said. "You know that, General."

"Of course, of course, but I haven't written papers and made speeches about it. Well, the wheels are turning, General Cameron. You may damned well get ground up in them, but they're turning anyway." He saluted Cameron with his drink, then tossed it off. "It may interest you to know that Chaffee is bringing a party to Fort Elliot to look over the situation. Some Congressmen whose backing is highly desirable right now. I expect you'll provide the proper entertainment for them, let them hear the things that have to be heard, and see what is best for them to see. You're experienced in this sort of thing, so I'll leave the details to you."

There were, Cameron knew, no two ways about this. Sherman was giving him an order, worded to sound like a request. Well, he'd accept it, as though it were a sought-after thing, and maybe that would bother Sherman a little. "General, you don't have to give it another thought. I rather look forward to these affairs. But I'll rely on you to keep Burley and Miles and a few others out of it."

"They're hard men to hold down," Sherman said. "They have views quite opposite from yours, Tracy. And then, too, there're the facts to consider. Not too rosy facts, either." He ticked them off on his fingers. "We have White Bear in prison, and many of the Kiowas and Cheyennes on the reservation, but not Quanah Parker. He's a god to the Kwahadi Comanches, and he's been calling together all Kiowas and Cheyennes that are still free on the Staked Plains. Parker's said it before, and he's said it again. He'll never go on the reservation or take his people there."

Sherman puffed on his cigar and found it dead, and Gary quickly offered a light. "Thank you. Tracy, the buffalo hunters are moving south, and you know as well as I that the Army can't stop them. But the Comanches could, if they set their mind to it." He spread his hands in a clear gesture of inquiry. "What would Chaffee say, if he knew all this, saw this? He'd say there wasn't a dog's chance of carrying off a true peace. And you couldn't blame him, Tracy. Not one damned bit."

"No, I couldn't," Cameron said. "But I'd want to try, before he made that decision."

"Well, you've bought that chance," Sherman said. "The price may be pretty dear, though. You fail, put Chaffee on the spot, and you'll be retired damned fast."

"General, don't we all have to take a few chances?"

Sherman laughed. "You amaze me, Tracy. Nothing seems to frighten you. I like to see that in a man, a will so strong that it pushes fear aside."

"Who says it does?" Cameron quipped. "Well, I got what I always wanted. It'll take a little more time to see who's right."

"I want you to be right," Sherman said, then reached across the desk and slapped Cameron on the arm. "Show me a bed. I've had a fast ride." He stood up and chuckled. "My escort ought to be straggling in soon . . . say, in an hour or so. Can't get good men any more."

"My wife's looking forward to seeing you again, General," Tracy Cameron said. "Shall we go to my quarters?"

"It'll be a pleasure." He glanced at Gary. "You come along too, son. By God, I like the way you light a man's cigar." He took Cameron's arm, and they went out, still talking. "Half the aides you get these days either burn your nose with a match, or make you stretch your neck out of joint reaching for it."

Gary, trailing them, closed the doors behind them, paused an instant, and, puffing his cheeks, blew out a silent breath. Then he followed them across the dark parade ground.

Chapter Four

C Company took the full load of a standing parade-ground inspection for General Sherman, and he found many things to comment on unfavorably. Then the entourage made the rounds of the officers' mess and the barracks, and the general spoke to the "boys" to keep up their morale. After that, Sherman looked in at the guardhouse, the stables, the quartermaster, and hay sheds, paused briefly for lunch, then began a run of guest appearances at each officer's home.

Lieutenant Gary never left Sherman's elbow. He kept re-lighting the general's cigar, which had a habit of going out, and seeing that he had a little something to drink at each place, and that he sampled the cake or cookies or whatever the major's wife or the captain's wife had to offer. And so they'd have something to remember, the little children were trotted out, pushed forward to show off their carefully rehearsed manners, while the proud father stood there and swore up and down that his little Edgar was going to be cavalry, or he'd disown him.

As they went along, Jim Gary began to detect the air of rehearsed informality about each performance. He saw the ritual each went through, with the carefully told jokes, the laughter prompt and hearty, and the visit at each of the quarters never prolonged beyond the demands of protocol. It was a duty to receive the general, and an obligation on Sherman's part to meet all of them. So from the major's quarters right on down the line to Lieutenant Beamish's small rooms, Sherman went with a grim determination not to neglect anyone. Gary lost count of the drinks he managed to down, and he noticed that Cameron's eyes were taking on a shine, and there was a barely detectable thickness of the tongue when he spoke.

Gary felt sorry for young Beamish and his wife. They were relatively new arrivals to Fort Elliot, and even while calling on other wives Susan Beamish had been ill at ease and inept, for she was seventeen and not Army at all. Harry Beamish was younger than Jim Gary, and he had found the Academy a hard pull, graduating nearer the bottom of his class than the top. Then on his way to his first assignment he'd stopped off at an Iowa farm, married his childhood sweetheart, and plopped her down in the worst quarters in Fort Elliot, which was, without argument, the hottest, dustiest post in north Texas.

Beamish met them at the door and ushered them in. He wore his dress uniform, and it was a little tight for him, since Susan's cooking was mainly starch, and Beamish had a natural tendency toward plumpness. As Sherman and Cameron stepped inside, Jim Gary caught Beamish's eye and winked, and Beamish smiled a little weakly, like a man who is going to have his leg amputated and has just been told it won't hurt a bit.

Their quarters were small — two rooms and a cramped kitchen. Susan had on a pink party dress, and her dark hair was swept high into a tightly coiled bun. She curtsied rather clumsily and turned to the pitiful tray of snacks she had prepared.

In a burst of pure pity, Jim Gary abandoned his proper place behind his rank and took the wine bottle from her hand. "Permit me," he said softly.

Her warm, brown eyes touched his, brimming with gratitude. "Thank you, Jim." Perspiration made her nose shine and formed small globules on her full upper lip.

He poured for General Sherman and for Tracy Cameron.

Sherman was saying: "Mister Beamer, many a man would take a reduction in rank to be an officer in this command. Consider yourself fortunate."

He'd gotten the name wrong, and Gary wondered whether he should correct him or not. Sherman said: "What is your duty, Mister Beamer?"

Harry Beamish looked quite stricken, and Jim Gary spoke quietly. "Mister Beamish is our procurement officer, sir. He is also the post morale officer."

A frown formed on Sherman's forehead. Then he smiled and wiped it away. "A responsibility, to be sure." He looked at Tracy Cameron. "This position of post morale officer is something new. Your own invention, Tracy?"

"Yes, General." His glance touched Gary briefly.

"It sounds interesting. Send me a paper on it. I'll give it some study, and, if I like it, I'll cut an order for it for other commanders. You know I hate pioneering, Tracy. I've always said that to have a good Army, there must be some slight change continually. The problem, of course, is to keep the changes slight. Policy is the backbone, you know, and a soldier is an instrument of war, pure and simple. If he wasn't, he'd have been issued a broom instead of a carbine."

"This is excellent wine, Mister Beamish," Cameron said. He set the glass down, although it was not yet empty. "But I'm afraid we must be going."

Sherman didn't like to have someone brush him aside like this, but he wasn't going to take up the matter at that moment, and Gary felt some relief. He could see a nasty row coming on.

Sherman was shaking Beamish's hand and pausing over Susan's. Her face flushed, and her eyes were bright, and

51

Sherman laughed, for it pleased him to be able to bring color to a pretty girl's cheeks.

As they walked toward headquarters, Jim Gary thought of the evening ahead. The bachelor officers were sponsoring a dinner in the general's honor, and afterward there was to be a cotillion in the big hall next to the sutler's. This would surely last until the small hours of the morning.

General Sherman wanted to go to his room in Quarters A and clean up a bit, and Tracy Cameron said that he had some work to take care of. Gary figured they were both making excuses. Sherman walked toward Quarters A, his step a bit unsteady, and then Cameron said — "Come along, Mister Gary." — and turned toward headquarters. As soon as they stepped inside, Cameron said: "Close the door." He turned and looked at his young aide. "Will you explain to me, Mister Gary, just what the hell was the idea in telling Sherman that Mister Beamish was our procurement officer?"

"Well, he does buy hay and grain for the horses, sir."

"All right, I see that we're going to tread technical ground there. Explain, if you can, his duties as post morale officer, whatever that might be." He sat down behind this desk and waited patiently until he was certain Gary had nothing to say. "Can it be that Mister Beamish attaches some stigma to his duties? Fort Elliot is a large post, Mister Gary, with thirty-five officers and nearly four hundred troopers. Someone has to be in charge of the honeypots and the laundry." He wiped a hand across his face. "Now I've got to write a damned paper for the general, only you're going to write it, and . . . let me tell you . . . it had better be excellent."

"Yes, sir."

"That will be all, Mister Gary. You're excused for an hour and a half."

"Yes, sir," Gary said stiffly and walked out, trying to keep his heels from telegraphing his anger.

The sunlight was fading as he walked over to his quarters. It cast a long shadow before him, and each ripple in the parade-ground dust became a dark depression. He did not understand Cameron's insensitive attitude, for only a blind man would have missed Beamish's complete misery there in his quarters. Beamish was unsure of himself to begin with, and the company of two generals was almost too much for him.

Gary wondered if Beamish had ever written home and told them what he did in the Army. Of course, there was no disgrace to being in charge of the stockade prisoners, but Beamish couldn't see that. All he saw was that each day the prisoners had to empty the post's slops and do the laundry, and it was a humiliation to him, a stain on his mind that wouldn't come out.

Walking along the duckboards in front to the officers' picket quarters, Gary saw Harry Beamish, coming toward him, and wished there was some way of avoiding the meeting. Beamish came on, a round-bellied man with a rolling gait hardly becoming to a cavalryman.

"I've been sort of watching you, Jim. Susan wants you to come to supper."

"I really shouldn't bother you," Gary said.

"She wants you to," Beamish said. "How about it, Jim?" He took Gary by the arm, and his hand trembled a little, and Gary turned away from his own door. Beamish smiled and spoke, as they walked along together. "You helped me out of an awkward spot this afternoon. Thanks. I hope General Cameron didn't say anything to you about it."

"We're the best of friends," Gary said, and he held up two fingers tightly pressed together. He didn't want to confide in Beamish, who wouldn't honor a confidence anyway, so he thought this would satisfy the man. It didn't take much to do that.

Susan Beamish met them at the door and, unexpectedly, gave Gary a quick, wet kiss. "You're a gentleman, Jim Gary," she said. "Isn't he, Harry?"

"The best," Harry Beamish said. He led the way into the cramped kitchen. There was just enough room for Gary to squeeze in between the table and the wall, when he sat down.

While Susan put the food on the table, Harry Beamish said: "I wish we could offer you better, Jim. Meat and potatoes and stewed tomatoes are hardly what I'd call. . . ."

"It looks good to me," Gary said quickly, shutting him off. He didn't want to hear Beamish talk like that, always apologizing because the food wasn't better, or because his uniform was regulation issue and not tailored, or that he had no personal horse, as all the other officers had.

Susan sat down, crowding in beside Gary. He thought that she sat unnecessarily close, her leg often touching his, and he wished he could move a bit, but the corner blocked him effectively.

"What's the general here for?" Susan asked.

"Oh, a look around, I guess," Gary said. He knew so vague an answer wouldn't satisfy her, so he looked at Beamish and smiled to take the edge off his next words. "You know better than to pump me. An aide has no ears. He never hears what's going on."

"Then something *is* going on," Beamish said. He looked at his wife as though he had told her so beforehand. "Are we going to put the Comanches on the reservation? That would mean I might get field duty." He reached across the table and touched Gary's arm. "Jim, you know I'd keep anything you told me confidential."

"Yes, but you'd tell Hostedder, and he'd only tell his

friend, Lieutenant Beuener, and in three hours the old man would hear of it, and he'd know damned well who spilled the beans in the first place." He grinned. "Then General Cameron would get himself a new aide."

"Yes, you wouldn't want to lose a job like that," Beamish said. The tone caused Gary to glance up at the round, perspiring face, and he realized that Beamish envied him, regarded him as more of a bellwether of information than as a real friend.

Gary did his best to hold up his end of the conversation and tried not to let this new knowledge trouble him, but it did, for he was looking for hidden meanings in everything Beamish said.

Beamish ate hurriedly, as though he had something important to do, and hardly had cleaned his plate, when he got up and excused himself. "I've got to check with the sergeant of the guard." He snatched up his hat and went out.

After the door slammed, Susan said: "Harry takes his work so seriously. He wants a command very badly, Jim."

"Yes, we all do," Gary said, hoping to keep the conversation general. "In time, I suppose, we'll get one."

An inner voice advised him to leave, for it didn't look good, his being there while Beamish was out. Of course, he had been invited, but that tug of uneasiness was strong. Gossip was the easiest thing in the world to start, and the hardest to stop, and he didn't want to get involved in anything, however innocent.

"Your work is so much more important than Harry's," Susan said. "He always said that, if he'd worked harder, got better marks, he might have a job like yours." She reached out and placed her plump, warm hand on his. "You're such a good friend, Jim. We both like you so much."

"Thank you," Gary said, his discomfort increasing. He

55

needed an excuse to withdraw his hand, so he reached for his watch and made a serious study of it. "I'm going to have to be getting back to headquarters. General Cameron is a stickler for punctuality."

When they stood up, she touched his arm, gripping it with her strong hands. "If you could," she said, "would you put in a word for Harry?" Her fingers moved gently, suggestively, like a cat kneading a lap before sitting down. "He feels so left out."

Now that she had come out with what she wanted, he felt better, on more secure ground. "If an opportunity arrives," he said, "I'd do what I could. Thank you for the supper, Susan."

"You're always welcome here, Jim."

Gary left her and walked rapidly toward headquarters.

Cameron was in his office, completing his paper work, when Gary entered. "Mister Gary, would you dash over to my quarters and ask the cook for a small bottle of olive oil."

"Olive oil, sir?"

"Yes, and don't bother my wife about it. Use the back entrance."

Gary went out, and Cameron finished his work, his pen scratching his signature on a dozen documents. He was lighting a cigar, when Gary returned, and he got up to get a glass off the sideboard. He poured some olive oil into the glass, made a face, then held his nose, and drank it.

"God, that's foul stuff," he said. "But it's good for the stomach. Sit down, Mister Gary. After dinner at the officers' mess, all the field-grade officers are invited to a private conference with General Sherman. At that time, policy will be drafted, and the cards laid on the table. This will be your first command-level conference, so be attentive, and also be omniscient. I'm sure you'll conduct yourself properly."

"I'll do my best, sir."

"At the dinner, stand between Sherman's chair and mine. See that his water glass is filled and, if he drops his napkin, make sure you have a clean one handy. Don't run out of matches . . . he's always letting his cigar go out."

"I've already noticed that, sir, among other things."

Tracy Cameron arched an eyebrow slightly, and smiled. "I expect you have, Mister Gary." He patted his stomach and belched. "I don't think I'll ever get over this gas. Until you've experienced it, you'll never know what kind of a constitution it takes to make social calls. You take a drink of whiskey, and pour a glass of wine on top of it, then a drink of brandy, and so on, until you're either glassy-eyed or sick. If you're neither, you may have what it takes to go into politics." He laughed softly. "As soon as the meeting breaks up, I want to have a gallon of coffee ready here in my office. I've allowed myself forty minutes in which to become reasonably sober. We can't offend the ladies at the dance, you know."

Gary took out a small book and made note of this. "Anything else, sir?"

"You might take down anything the general says. It will make a good newspaper story. The public pays the bills, after all, and they're entitled to some gems of the general's wit." He shifted his cigar around in his mouth. "Mister Gary, it strikes me that you'd make a good politician."

"It's the furthest from my thoughts, sir. I'd have no talent for it at all."

"Quite the contrary. I think you have a good talent for it. A straight face, Mister Gary, is not confined to the poker table." He leaned back in his chair and put his hands behind his head. "When I was a much younger man, I wanted combat, a tactical command, but I always drew the attaché posts instead. It's not easy for a man who knows he is destined to be a good leader to spend his years opening the doors of diplomatic carriages, and dancing with the governor-general's wife."

"A man can transfer, sir."

Cameron raised an eyebrow and said: "A request for transfer, my boy, indicates that one does not fit. It doesn't go on the record as such, but no commander wants a man who has transferred too many times. Oh, I'd considered it, and swore many times that I'd do it, but I never did."

"What held you back, sir?"

Cameron thought about it, then said: "Because I was needed, Mister Gary. Because it suddenly dawned on me that I was an important man. Suddenly there arrived a time, a moment in history, when Lieutenant Tracy Cameron could do what heads of state and generals could not. A man can have an ear for music, while another has an ear for talk, the millions of words he has half listened to by the carriages and in the anterooms. The heads of state talked of how much the other side would pay for war damage. And when this failed, the generals talked of surrender. When I stepped in as a last resort, I never mentioned surrender. I spoke only of peace, and, by God, there was peace."

He paused to knock the ash off his cigar. "From that moment on, Mister Gary, I never sincerely wanted to participate in a war. My destiny was cleanly clear, as it is now. I know what Sherman wants. He wants me to be completely responsible, to plan and execute, and, if I fail, my head will roll, not his. And he'll do it that way, too, because it will look as if he's doing me a big favor. But the favor is always questionable. Politicians have to have something to stay in office, Mister Gary. If there's a war on, they get votes by stopping it. If there's peace, they look for a boil to lance, some money swindle, some labor mess to squeeze. The secret of staying alive in this atmosphere is to know when to change sides. Change too quickly, and they'll put you down as a deserter. Change too late...." He spread his hands. "Well, it's just too late, that's all. However, this fence-walking does develop the sense of balance." He tipped his chair forward and placed his slender forearms flat on the desk. "Mister Gary, you're from the Midwest, aren't you?"

"Yes, sir, generally speaking. Do I have a twang?"

Cameron laughed. "No, but your sympathy toward Mister Beamish, who can't seem to release the plow handles, brought to my mind that there must be a similarity of locale or background. You're not the same kind of men at all."

"My father was in the hardware business," Gary said. "Yes, I was raised among farmers, although I'm what they referred to as a town boy."

"I see," Cameron said. He got up and walked to the window and stood there, looking out at the dark parade ground. "Well, the Beamish business is none of mine. The man has offered no hint of any talent he may have, so he can hardly expect a duty more exacting than he has."

He sighed and faced about, leaning his hands on the sill. "In a few weeks now we'll likely be entertaining Senator Chaffee and his Congressional friends. We'll have to set up a buffalo hunt. That's always something they like to take back home with them and brag about . . . a lot of Wild West flavor there, and it's been the rage with politicians for a long time."

"From the tone, sir, I suspect that I'm to squire them around."

"Who else?" Cameron reached for his hat. "Let's go hear what Sherman has to say. Generals always have choice suggestions to make, and the higher the rank, the more suggestions, and the more attention you have to pay to them."

59

Crossing the parade to the officers' mess, Jim Gary kept a proper station behind Tracy Cameron, and he enjoyed trailing two paces, for it gave him a chance to think things over. When Cameron closed the office door and talked like a man, not a general, Gary found his respect deep and boundless. Cameron was top man in a rough, thankless business, and his manner, his methods were all tuned to the job.

Yet there was much more about this man that fascinated Gary. Cameron had what old-line Army men called — "a clear dedication to duty" — and Gary sensed it more than he understood it. Cameron's philosophy was alien to Gary, who had been trained to make war. The concept of spending thirty years in the service without once having engaged in conflict was beyond Gary's understanding. How did an officer distinguish himself? For that matter, what did a soldier do? He felt sure that he was not the only one who pondered these questions.

As soon as they entered the building, Gary could see that Sherman hadn't yet arrived, but that everyone was expecting him. As soon as Cameron took his seat, he motioned Gary closer, and, when the young aide bent over, Cameron said: "Mister Gary, will you call at my quarters and ask the general to join me here? Protocol, you know." He made a wry face and winked, which shocked Gary as much as it amused him.

He was certain that he wasn't supposed to laugh and didn't, until he got outside, then he chuckled as he walked toward Quarters A. One of the servants let him in and directed him to the parlor. Edith Cameron was reading a book, and she started to get up, but Gary said: "Please don't bother. The general's compliments, and he'd like to have General Sherman join him in the officers' mess."

She sent one of the servants with the message and waved Gary into a nearby chair. "You're a very nice young man,

Mister Gary. I want you to know that I appreciate your attention to duty, even if Tracy doesn't seem to."

"Thank you, ma'am."

"These social functions are difficult for him," she went on. "He'll drink too much, of course, but I don't suppose he can help it, although a man his age should watch his liver. Mister Gary, if my husband laughs a bit loudly, it's a sign that the liquor . . . well, I suggest that you politely take the glass from his hand and offer to get him another. He'll understand, and in that way he can drink less without seeming to."

"I'll do that," Gary said. He sat on the edge of the chair, at attention. It would not be proper to lounge in the commanding officer's parlor.

General Sherman came down the stairs, and Gary popped out of his chair as though propelled by a spring. "At ease, Mister Gary," Sherman said, and he bowed over Edith Cameron's hand. "I'm sorry this is stag. I'll miss your charming company." He ran a hand down the front of his blouse to check the buttons, then said: "Later, I assume I have the honor of the first dance?"

"Yes, of course."

He glanced at Gary, as though giving him the signal to go. And Gary hurried down the hall, arriving at the door just in time to open it for Sherman's passage through. He followed the general across the parade ground to the mess room.

The entire assembly came to attention and remained that way until Sherman told them to carry on. Gary went first to the head table and handled the general's chair, while he sat down. Then he took his station and divided his attention between Sherman and Cameron. Throughout the meal, Gary was as invisible as the servants carrying dishes in and out, bringing new bottles, packing away the empties. He lit cigars and provided an ashtray, so neither man dropped a careless ash on his uniform. And he saw to it that they had something to drink, but never too much.

While he performed these duties, he thought of the circus he had once seen, where a man twirled plates on long sticks, swished rings around his feet and hips, and played "Yankee Doodle" on a silver cornet suspended from a string, all at the same time. Perhaps that man had received his first training as a general's aide.

After the meal, Sherman rapped on his water glass, and an instantaneous hush fell over the room. He stood up slowly and paused for a moment before speaking.

"Gentlemen, this has been a most pleasant visit. I've renewed old acquaintances and made new ones. And I'm paying my respects to a new general officer, the first Fort Elliot has ever had for a commander . . . General Tracy Cameron, a man who holds my deepest respect." There was a full round of applause, and Sherman waited for it to die down. He stood and looked at their faces, attentive, rapt even, but all stone-silent. "Gentlemen, I have news for you. As departmental commander, I've been ordered to establish a lasting peace on the Texas plains. As you know, the Kiowas are on the move again and talking war. The Cheyennes talk of joining the Kwahadi Comanches under Quanah Parker. And he talks of driving the white man from his hunting ground. But in spite of all this, we're going to have peace. General Cameron has just come from Washington, where he's convinced certain politicians that peace is easier won than war." He laughed briefly. "Believe me, gentlemen, if I had considered war, I'd have sicced some hot bloods on the job." He waited for the laughter, but there was none. The faces remained stony. Some even presumed to reflect a certain unfriendliness to the speech.

Sherman cleared his throat and spoke again. "But *I* want

peace. Sincerely want it. That's why I've given the job to General Tracy Cameron."

He sat down amid a mere scatter of polite applause, and it wasn't what he expected. Standing behind Sherman, Gary did not attempt to mask his outrage. The speech was a clear stab in Cameron's back, and he wondered what he would do about it.

Cameron stood up and put his glass aside. "Earlier today I mentioned to General Sherman that departmental commanders ought to read fewer reports and spend more time in the field. But the general's aged some since his splendid march, and the rump soon becomes more accustomed to an oak-bottomed chair than to a saddle."

The laughter was spontaneous, and all but Sherman enjoyed the joke. He looked at Cameron briefly, then stared at his drink as Cameron went on speaking.

"Yes, there's sign that the Kiowas are thinking of gathering. We know that. But, gentlemen, through our efforts they have not gathered. We all hear the talk of war, but so far through our efforts there has been none. All right, the fire is banked, the fuel is stacked. Which one of you will be fool enough to light it just to see it burn?"

Major Wringle, whose judgment was often not the best, threw away his chances of making lieutenant colonel by shouting: "Hear, hear!"

This was applauded, and Sherman never took his eyes from his drink. Cameron held up his hands for silence, then said: "Gentlemen, God gave me a choice years ago, and I made it. I would rather go down in history as the man who saved a land, than one who sacked it."

He sat down, while the clapping was thunderous, and Sherman spoke beneath this sound. "How dare you upbraid me this way, Tracy?"

"You made a mistake, General," Cameron said. "I respect you, but I'm not a damned bit afraid of you." He raised his glass. "A toast, gentlemen, to the dove of peace."

They raised their arms, as though they were tied to one string, and the string had just been pulled.

Lieutenant Gary shifted his weight from one leg to the other, because he was tired and his feet hurt.

Chapter Five

At a quarter to ten, everyone left the mess and went to the sutler's place for the dance. Cameron waited until the room was empty, then said: "Help me up, Mister Gary. I'm drunk."

Gary didn't believe it, not even when he heard the slur in Cameron's speech. The mess was foul with the trapped cigar smoke and littered with glasses and whiskey bottles. He took Cameron's arm and helped him stand.

"Let's get across the parade ground without staggering," Cameron said, and seemed to draw himself together like a man about to make a magnificent effort.

But as soon as he got into his office, he slid into his chair and slumped over, his thin hands resting on the edge of the desk. Through the open window, Gary could hear the music and the laughter. The junior officers, excused from the meeting, were having a time of it, flirting and dancing with the senior officers' wives, and Gary wondered how many promotions were cinched that night.

"Close the window and pull the blinds," Cameron said. His eyes were watery and vague, and Gary saw how very drunk he was. Yet he hadn't seemed so in Sherman's presence. "Lock the door, also. Where's that coffee?"

"I'm sure it's in the orderly room, sir. Or else a corporal is now a private."

"Get it," Cameron said, and began fumbling with his buttons.

When Gary returned with the coffee, he saw that Tracy Cameron had struggled free of his blouse and underwear.

They hung slackly about his waist, and he still sat hunched over in his chair, an arm securely braced against an obviously swaying desk.

Gary placed pot and cup before Cameron, who said: "Dismiss the orderlies, Mister Gary."

"Yes, sir," Gary said, and went into the other room. After the orderlies left, he locked the outer door and turned the lamps down, then went back into Cameron's office.

The general was crouched over a cup of coffee, his face flushed, his eyes shining like fresh varnish. He spoke without turning his head. "I'm gosh awful drunk, Mister Gary. And I've got to be sober." He shook his head sadly. "Just can't drink the stuff like some can."

It was amazing to Gary, how Cameron could have maintained a veneer of sobriety as long as he had. He had seemed to hold himself in by will alone, but, when he let go, it was sudden.

Gary poured Cameron more black coffee, and, after drinking some of it, Cameron said: "There are some heavy towels in the closet, Mister Gary. Soak one in a pail of water, wring it out the best you can, and bring it here."

So you have a whopping headache, Gary thought as he wetted the towel and wrung it out. He brought the towel over, and Cameron said: "Whip me with it."

Gary was startled. He thought he had misunderstood. "I beg your pardon?"

With what seemed a great effort, Cameron looked at Jim Gary. "Within a reasonable length of time, say half an hour, I'm expected to appear at the dance and do not want to stagger about the floor. Now lay on the towel."

Cameron lay face down across the desk to provide the best target. Gary still hesitated, for this was somewhat like one's father commanding his son to strike him. Then he slapped

66

Cameron across the bare back with the towel and was told to lay it on harder. Cameron grunted every time he struck. Gary whipped until his arm ached, and he had to switch to the other arm.

There was a sheen of sweat on the young man's face, when Cameron commanded him to stop. The back was lobster-red from neck to waist, but Cameron's head seemed clearer now, and he drank some more coffee. His eyes were red, but the glassiness was vanishing, and there was no slur in his voice.

"This must have come from the guardhouse," Cameron said, indicating the coffee. "Sergeant McCreary's coffee always tastes like India ink." He put the cup down. "Would you hand me a cigar? Thank you. And a light?" He puffed, drank his coffee, then put the wet towel over his head. "I'll be fine in another ten minutes. Then I'll go to the dance and show every officer on the post how impartial I am by dancing with his wife." He slipped his arms into his underwear which Gary held for him.

"I recall some sharp words aimed at Sherman," Cameron said. He glanced at Gary. "Is the general properly angry?"

"He wasn't laughing, sir. Just stared at his drink."

Tracy Cameron grunted softly and slipped into his blouse. "Well, a man's bound to put his foot in his mouth one time or another. Constitutionally, I'm unsuited for boozing. But it's part of the rank. Quite a paradox, Mister Gary. If I didn't drink at all, my officers would swear something was wrong with me. And if I appeared before them drunk, they would say that I lacked control of myself and would lose respect for me." He buttoned up and put on his hat. "Would you have this cleaned up. Better make it tonight. There may not be much time in the morning. I'll have the O.D. post orders for C Company and F Company to be assembled after morning's mess with a week's rations." He reached out and thumped

67

Gary on the chest. "Get some sleep. You'll go with me on patrol."

"Will General Sherman be . . . ?"

"He can stay here and sit on his ass, for all I care," Cameron said flatly.

He went out, leaving the doors open, and walked toward the sutler's place. The music was a bright sound in the night, and along the long, broad porch couples stood and talked and laughed. Cameron's step was sure now, and the cool night air blew the final wisps of fog away from his mind, and he felt that he had survived this bout quite nicely. Visiting generals and many whiskey bottles were the downfall of more than a few commanders. He also worried about what Gary would think, seeing him drunk. Gary was pretty much of an idealistic ass, when it came right down to it, and Cameron wanted the young man's loyalty and respect.

When he was about to step onto the porch, heads turned toward him and talk stopped. He was the center of focus which all commanders know. Lieutenant Garnett, who had been bucking for captain now for nearly four years, thrust his pretty wife into Cameron's arms with the promise that she danced divinely. He went in with her to whirl her about the floor, all the time hoping someone would cut in so he could free himself to find his own wife.

But he was a general, and no officer present was stupid enough to cut in. Cameron silently cursed them as cowards and endured the dance. He smiled politely, complimented Mrs. Garnett on her dress, which he felt sure was three years old, and walked about searching for Edith.

He found her, took her hand, and they smiled at each other.

"How's your stomach?" she asked.

"Afire, but I'll live." He laughed. "I don't see Sherman around."

68

"He's at the quarters," she said. "I'm afraid he drank a little too much."

"I hope he gets sick as hell and throws up," Cameron said. "Care for some night air?"

"Yes, it's quite close in here."

She took his arm, and they walked, smiling and nodding, to the side porch. A few young officers, lounging there, hastily vacated a proper interval, and Cameron sat on the railing, while his wife studied the dark parade ground.

"You're angry with Sherman, aren't you?"

"The man's paying me lip service. He says one thing and means another. All along I've been hoping he'd hold Burley and Miles and the others off, but he won't. I don't think it was his intention to let me know this, but he had plenty to drink, too, and made the wrong speech. I've got my orders to go ahead with peace proposals all right, while Burley and Miles ready columns to march. When the Indians get wind of that, what chance do you think I'll have?"

"That isn't fair," she said. "I want you to tell the senator when he gets here."

Cameron shook his head. "I wouldn't tell a man something he already knows, Edith. Politics is a rough-and-tumble business. I knew the odds, and Chaffee didn't have to explain them to me." He put his arm around her and gave her a hug. "I'm taking two companies into the field for a week, just to find a spot where trouble is not likely to occur. When those Washington politicians get here, I want them to have a good time and go away thinking that the Army is the greatest thing since soap."

She took his arm, drawing his attention to a man, crossing the parade ground. "Isn't that Mister Gary? He's a very nice boy, Tracy."

"He might not appreciate you calling him a boy,"

69

Cameron said. "Why don't you stay here for a while? I want to talk to Captain Evans and Lieutenant Byrd." He kissed her cheek and went back inside.

Captain Evans was in command of C Company. He was a spare, functional man with a restlessness that now and then got him into trouble. Byrd, commanding F Company, was short and blocky and quick to temper. His command was composed of ninety-day-old recruits and a few hardened, non-commissioned officers. He had one of the toughest jobs on the post and was doing well at it.

Cameron found them inside. "Gentlemen," he said, breaking politely into their conversation.

They turned to him, attentive without being effacing. Both had put in years on the frontier and knew their worth without being fat-headed about it. Both men were drinking, and, when they saw that Cameron had none, they set their glasses aside.

"I'm posting orders with the O.D.," Cameron said. "C and F must be ready for the field after morning mess."

"Very good, sir," Evans said. "May I ask the duration of the patrol?"

"A week. Details will be posted with the order." Cameron looked at Lieutenant Byrd. "For new recruits, F Company is shaping up to my liking. I've put you on patrol because the company needs some extended work. C is seasoned and should set a good example."

"Yes, sir," Byrd said. "But F Company will come along."

"I well realize that," Cameron said. "There have been times when I thought your methods a little hard, but the results seem to justify them." He turned his head as though a new, important idea had struck him. "I believe the sutler has a map on the wall of his office, and I saw a light in there when I was on the porch. Would you step over there with me? It's closer than my office."

"Of course," they said together, and left the hall with him.

Adam Greer was doing some late work on his accounts, and he grumbled after Cameron knocked, but, when he saw who it was, his manner changed.

"Just going over my books," Greer said as he let them in.

"I saw you through the window," Cameron said. "I'd like to consult your map, Mister Greer."

"Why, sure, just help yourself." He lit another lamp for Cameron and carried it to the back of the room. He lingered there, for he always liked to know what was going on.

Cameron knew this and said: "I don't want to hold you up from your work, Mister Greer."

Greer was disappointed, but he went back to his office, and, to make sure he didn't overhear, Cameron spoke softly, and Evans and Byrd crowded close to hear.

"A patrol comes and goes from Fort Elliot every three days, but never in double company strength. However, this time I want enough men to split the command and make a big, sweeping circle, meeting in mid-patrol."

Evans smiled. "Sort of cleaning the ground for a buffalo hunt, sir?"

"Rather like that," Cameron admitted. "But, of course, I must assume that these officials are bent on serious business. They want to see the Indian situation first-hand, and make up their minds as to the practical aspects of Chaffee's proposals." He pointed to the map. "I want to swing north from the post, cross the Fort Smith and Albuquerque road, then turn west along the Canadian, past Adobe Walls. Then in a southerly direction, easing into an easterly sweep to Gray Beard's village. That country is being run over with buffalo hunters, and, if there's any Indian unrest, any dancing or medicine-making, we'll turn it up." He looked at each of

71

them as though expecting an opinion.

Evans said: "Gray Beard's a toothless old bastard, sir. There's no trouble in his bailiwick." Then he smiled broadly. "Oh, I see. We're going to cover beforehand the grand tour through peaceful country."

Byrd had a question. "When are we going to split the command?"

"After we pass Adobe Walls," Cameron said. "We'll form a pincer movement. By the way, you know Mister Beamish. I want to use him as a runner. The field experience will do him good."

The two men glanced at each other, but made no comment. Cameron caught this exchange and wondered about it. He even wondered why he'd brought up Beamish's name in the first place, then decided he'd done it for Jim Gary, because Gary seemed to see something in Beamish others had missed. And Tracy Cameron was willing to make a small bet on his aide's judgment.

"I think that covers it," Cameron said, turning from the map. "I'll see you gentlemen after morning mess."

They went out together, but Evans and Byrd held back a little, leaving Cameron to go on to the dance alone. The two officers stood by the sutler's porch with fresh cigars and an intention of discussing between themselves what they would never think of mentioning in front of their commander.

Edith Cameron was dancing with a dutiful lieutenant who could not quite conceal his relief when the general cut in. A moment later Cameron saw him talking earnestly to a young girl, and he understood why.

When the set was finished, Cameron crossed the room to where Sherman was holding court, a devoted crowd of officers around him. Some gave way so that rank could stand shoulder to shoulder.

"By George, I'm having a good time," Sherman said. His eyes were very bright, and he seemed to smile continually and over something that only he understood. "Tracy, you've a gall, posting a field order while your commander is a guest on the post."

"Did the general wish to go on a buffalo hunt?" Cameron asked.

Sherman bristled. "Damn it, no! But you could have consulted me." He waved his hand impatiently. "All right, Tracy. It's your command."

When you considered Fort Elliot the hub of a wheel, with the rim marking a fifty-mile radius in any direction, then you knew you were sitting in the middle of enough trouble to give any post commander fits. This was Lieutenant Gary's thought as he rode along three paces behind General Cameron. Thirty-seven miles due east lay the Texas-Indian Territory border, and another twelve miles farther the Washita River and the spot that had once been Black Kettle's village, which had fallen to the "long knives" on November 27, 1868. *That was two years ago,* Gary thought, *long enough for a white man to forget but not an Indian.*

A hundred miles northeast, across the Canadian, lay Camp Supply and in a southeasterly direction, an equal distance away, Camp Radziminski. But distance on the frontier, Gary had learned, was not measured in miles. Camp Supply was a clean shot, a horse-killing ride from Fort Elliot but no more, while Radziminski lay near the Red River in the heart of the Comanche country, which heightened considerably the risks of travel.

Almost due south from Elliot, Fort Anderson offered the only other gathering of military strength, and it was pitifully small. Adobe Walls was a stronghold, but of buffalo hunters

73

who hated the Indians and disliked the Army. All one could expect from them was trouble.

During the day's march northward, they passed through low-rolling hills and wide stretches of grassy open country — buffalo country. They saw a few scattered herds in the distance, like humped black mounds of freshly turned earth.

In the late afternoon they approached the Canadian, and Cameron ordered night camp made there, with F Company standing back to the river, and C Company drawn in a line across the wide interval of "street."

An orderly made up Cameron's command post at the west end of the camp, and Lieutenant Gary placed his bedding nearby. The picket line was established behind C Company, a long string of ground rope with sentries walking their tour from end to end. This was Gary's first venture into the field, and he was determined not to compile a pyramid of errors. The general had a tent, but he preferred to sleep on the ground like a line trooper, cook everything in his pannikin, and conduct his correspondence out of his small dispatch case.

Since Lieutenant Beamish was the "runner," his bedding was placed near the command post. If Cameron wanted someone summoned, it was Beamish's job to do it. Gary could not see how the man could make a mistake doing that.

As soon as Cameron got squared away, he motioned Gary over. "I want to meet with the company commanders and section leaders in fifteen minutes."

"Yes, sir."

Gary went over and told Beamish, who dropped what he was doing and settled his kepi firmly.

"Jim," Beamish said, "I don't know how to thank you for this. I just don't know."

"Don't be an ass," Gary said, and went back to his place, feeling annoyed. Keeping out of Beamish's way was going to

74

be a problem, for the man was like spilled molasses, soon tracked everywhere. Harry Beamish would start looking for some way to express his gratitude, and he'd be a pest about it.

The four officers arrived and assembled around Cameron's tent.

"Lieutenant Byrd," Cameron said, "at the commencement of tomorrow's march, take your company and proceed along the Canadian in the direction of Adobe Walls. A leisurely pace should do it. C Company will swing north into an arc so as to come down on Adobe Walls. I'll remain with C Company."

They nodded, for there was no need to comment or question this.

"I want an accurate survey of the activity in this sector. Check all the heliograph outposts, and any Indian movement, regardless of how innocent it may appear, must be looked into . . . particularly family migrations, women, lodges, and such like."

"Do you want them turned back, sir?" Evans asked.

"No, but stop them and observe every detail of their gear. It should give a fair indication of how far they've come."

"I understand," Evans said. "Clear to you, Byrd?"

"Perfectly."

"There's quite a congregation of buffalo hunters in the area," Cameron said. "Bivouac near them when possible, a rest stop, or anything you can think of, just for an excuse to talk. Get their opinions, for they're a high-tempered bunch, and it's well to know what kind of trouble we can expect from them. We know for damned sure they won't co-operate." He glanced at each of them. "I believe that's all. Good night, gentlemen."

They turned away and went back to their own commands. Gary started to return to his own bedding, but Cameron motioned him back. From his dispatch case he took out his maps

75

and spread them. Then he moved a lantern closer so there was more light. "By my estimate, we should camp tomorrow night at the heliograph detachment near Crooked River. At that junction, Mister Gary, I want you to take four men from each company and proceed to Tascosa. I have no idea when these Washington politicians will arrive, but they'll likely try to surprise me, thinking, of course, that in that way they can get the true picture before I sweep the dirt under the rug. Sergeant Reed, the signalman, has an ambulance there. Remain on duty, meet every train, and see that they have a pleasant trip to the post." He dipped into his dispatch case. "I've prepared this letter of credit for you, in the event you need to rent another vehicle or some horses."

"All right, sir. Any specific hints on how to make a trip through the heat pleasant?"

Tracy Cameron smiled. "Make each day's march no more than twenty miles, or perhaps a little shorter. And always stop where there's some grouse shooting, or a place to bathe. You'll have to go some out of your way to hit the small creeks, but it'll be worth it." He reached out and slapped Gary on the shoulder. "Buy me a little time, Mister Gary. I want them to be favorably impressed. If they're not, I know an aide that's going to be transferred to the infantry."

He said it lightly enough, but Gary knew that he meant at least part of it. He'd be in trouble if he made any mistakes. "You can rely on me, sir. I guarantee that every one of them will be nursed and coddled."

"Keep that in mind," Cameron said, "and you can't go wrong. It's not always possible to shield a man from danger, but as long as he is unaware that he *is* in danger, you've succeeded."

Gary was dismissed, and he went back to his blankets and sat down to tug off his boots.

Chapter Six

Before the sun was over the rim of the prairie, General Cameron's command was moving in a northwesterly sweep, with C Company making a slow march along the Canadian. The day was going to turn out hot, for the sky was gray, and the sun looked like an orange hanging there, big and soft and unbearably bright.

Shortly before noon, Gary saw movement in the sea of short grass. They were moving through an undulating ocean of rises and valleys where no breeze stirred, and, at Gary's sighting, Cameron swung the company to a piece of high ground and stopped. A mile away a band of Indians, some on ponies with travois trailing and the rest afoot, moved south toward the river crossing.

"A bit of luck here," Cameron said, and rode forward, taking Gary, the bugler, and the guidon bearer with him.

As they drew nearer, Gary could identify the Indians as Kiowas and Cheyennes, old men mostly with wives and children and dogs and their litter trailing behind the ponies. He could not see a male between the ages of fifteen and fifty; they were all over that, or under. Gary's knowledge, gleaned from books, served only to identify the Indians. Cameron's, however, extended beyond that. He spoke to them in Santee Sioux, a language commonly used among the Plains tribes. The bugler, a wizened little man who had spent eighteen years relaying commands through the bell of a C horn, sidled up to Gary and translated.

"He wants to know where the hell the young men are."

The old Indian turned and raised a withered hand to the east. *"Wanasse aya,"* he said.

"He says they went huntin'," the bugler whispered. "It's a damned lie, sir. They don't move their families all over creation, when they go huntin'."

Cameron talked at length with the old men, and the gist of it was that the braves were all hunting, and that was that. Of course, Cameron did not believe it, but he didn't let on by word or gesture. So the Indians went on their way, and the cavalry proceeded toward their evening rendezvous at the heliograph station.

Six men operated the station, and they took pride in their work. A cavalry squad guarded the signalmen in the event there was trouble. With the device he could get a message and an answer to and from Tascosa in an hour, while a dispatch rider, changing horses five times, could only make it in twenty-nine and be half dead, when he got there.

The heliograph did have a built-in weakness. It relied on sunlight, and darkness or an overcast sky knocked it out of operation. The Indians considered it all a part of the white man's nonsense and never connected the activity with their comings and goings. To Gary's way of thinking, the use of the heliograph made Cameron somewhat of a progressive, but one who knew what he was doing — something few progressives know.

When the evening cook fires began to die, Lieutenant Gary made ready to leave the camp. He intended to make a night ride of it, since they had crossed the river earlier in the day, and there was only open prairie ahead.

In his last-minute instructions, Tracy Cameron said: "I'd keep an eye out for those bucks. They're likely somewhere north of here with intentions other than buffalo hunting. I'm not positive of this, but I think I saw White Horse's two young

78

sons and wife with that bunch. If I'm right, he's going to join up with Parker or raise some Cain on his own." He offered his hand. "Good luck, Mister Gary."

"Thank you, sir. I'll see you in ten days, possibly."

"Stretch that into three weeks, if you like." Then Cameron impulsively took some cigars from his pocket and stuffed then into Gary's.

Gary looked down at the brown ends peeping out and said: "But I don't smoke, sir."

"There's nothing like a cigar in a man's mouth to make him look five years older," Cameron said.

"Yes, sir," Gary said, and grinned.

He walked down the company street to pick his men and get going. Beamish left his place and followed after Gary as though he had something on his mind. But Gary was at the picket line with the sergeant, picking mounts. The sun was down, and a gray haze of early evening was spreading rapidly.

The rest of the detail formed, and Gary led them toward the end of the company street. Then he motioned the detail into quicker motion and put the camp behind him.

When his circling movement was completed, Tracy Cameron bivouacked his combined forces along the edge of timber near Adobe Walls. Before his camp was properly set up, Captain Evans left his command post and joined Cameron.

"The buffalo hunters are unhappy, sir," Evans reported. "They said so when I camped early yesterday."

"I suppose they want us to move on?"

"Yes, sir."

"I want them to come and tell me, then," Cameron said, and he sat down with Evans to compile reports.

Within an hour, a spokesman from the hunters' camp

came over. He was a tall man named Graves, a little more articulate than his friends with the hint of a good school somewhere in his background. Cameron invited him to sit down and join them for supper.

"I've already eaten," Graves said. He looked around the camp. "This is quite a patrol, General. To look at it, you'd think you were going out to whip a lot of Indians."

"With a big enough force," Cameron said, "it isn't necessary to whip them. They look at you, count you, and there's no fight. How's the hunting?"

"Getting thin," Graves said. "At the rate the buffaloes have been taken these last ten years, it doesn't pay to hunt. I guess this is my last year. I'll hardly make expenses."

"How many men at Adobe Walls post now?"

"About a dozen," Graves said. He opened his shirt and fanned it against his body. The day's heat lay thick, and, although darkness was growing rapidly deeper, the heat would linger until late. "Mighty hot for the first part of June. You don't expect this kind of weather until mid-August." He looked again around the camp as though the sight of so many soldiers gathered in one spot bothered him greatly. "It's been mighty quiet around here, General. No Indian trouble, and that doesn't seem right, seeing as how every buffalo taken is one an Indian can't eat, or cover his lodge with. The prairie's changing, that's all."

"Men have to change with it," Cameron pointed out. "Next year, there won't be anyone at Adobe Walls station. It'll start crumbling."

Graves laughed. "That's prophecy, all right. We're pulling out in a few days. Going south about a hundred miles. Heard there was some buffaloes down there."

"Some Comanches, too," Cameron said, "but don't provoke anything, Graves. The Army protects the Indians, just as it protects the hunters."

They talked some more, of the weather and of the possibility of getting an early rain. Then Graves went back to the post, and Cameron told the orderly to bring him some supper. Beamish was off somewhere, on some fairy chase instigated on Byrd's order. Cameron thought about asking Byrd to ease off a bit but decided not to. Byrd's methods were hard, but it took a hot fire to make steel out of scrap iron. And, too, he couldn't say anything without playing favorites.

Byrd joined them. He wore only his trousers and underwear; his sweaty shirt had been washed and hung to dry.

Evans asked: "Where's Beamish?"

"Gathering buffalo chips," Byrd said. He mopped his face with his neckerchief.

"Hell, he'd have to hunt an hour to pick up an armful," Evans said.

"So? The stooping will reduce his waistline." He glanced at Cameron. "Hot day today, eh, sir?"

"Hmm," Cameron said. "No new reports from heliograph?"

"No, sir," Byrd said. "White Horse is still on the loose, and the bunch we saw has moved on south of the post, giving it a wide berth." The orderly came with the food and Byrd shifted his stool around, so the folding table could be set up. "I suppose the hunters had a list of complaints, sir. Every time I talk to them, they're either sore because we're not around when the Indians are, or because we're sticking our nose in when there are no Indians."

"You can't please everybody, Charlie," Evans said.

"Graves was enlightening, though," Cameron said. "They're vacating Adobe Walls and moving south. That may be bad in one way and good in another."

"I don't follow that, sir," Evans said.

"Well, they're cleaning the prairie from here to Dodge City," Cameron said. "Hide-hunting will eventually be ending. The number of buffaloes isn't infinite. The Indians want the prairie clear of hunters, and it may satisfy some of them. At least, they won't be anxious to join Quanah Parker, when they already have what they want." He ate some of his stew. "Of course, Parker will object to the hunters moving south, and there may be a fight over it."

Byrd shook his head. "There goes three years of work, sir. A man can't want peace, when he fights."

"But he can want peace so badly he'll fight to get it," Cameron said. "We'll complete our patrol, gather reports from heliograph, and, after evaluating them, send our patrols south, saturating the Comanche country with them. Indians somehow don't like to do anything, when they're being watched, and, by golly, we'll watch them from now on, closer than ever. At least at Adobe Walls, though, we can concentrate our patrols a little better and get better results."

"Won't Parker object to an increase in patrols, sir?" Evans asked.

"Yes, if we struck a war-like posture," Cameron pointed out. "But we're not going to do that. We'll go on with our general way of equipping patrols lightly, for speed and not for war. Parker will see that more troops will only mean a closer watch. No Indians are to be bothered. That order has not changed and will not be."

"Well," Evans said, "there's one thing you have to say about Parker. He's always done his damnedest to stay clear of white men, and so far he's never really locked horns with the Army. The trouble is, that's been good on one hand and bad on the other. We haven't had to fight him, but it's also left the Comanches strong in force. No wars to kill off their braves."

"He loves his people," Cameron said. "Loves them

enough not to fight. I think the man loves them enough to make peace. He's half white anyway. A push . . . the right push . . . and he's gone the whole way."

"It's something to hope for," Byrd said, and ate his supper.

This was a summer of change for the Kiowas and the Cheyennes, the final changing summer in a string of changing summers. The beginning was a bad peace, with the long-knife leaders, Chivington and Custer, destroying villages along the Washita River. Some, like White Bear and Lone Wolf, who had no choice, went the white man's way. But some, like Kicking Bird and Woman Heart, with small bands following them, fled to the Staked Plains to join the Kwahadi Comanches. But even then they were doomed to fail. Parker had turned from the Cheyenne and Kiowa leaders for many years. Now his heart was beginning to thaw again, and there was hope among people who had forgotten what it had been like.

Life had never been easy, since the bad peace, and evil times fell upon White Bear. He was jailed and released, but the times did not improve. Many buffalo hunters came and killed off the herds, and the soldiers at the fort increased in numbers, and the medicine men danced and wore paint constantly, but the buffalo herds grew thinner and the enemy stronger. Amid this, Quanah Parker remained aloof, firm in his resolve to stay clear of all white men. The Comanches, he swore, would never go on the reservation as the Kiowas had done. But he was not blind. He could see the white men, coming in ever stronger numbers, and the buffalo herds growing smaller, and he knew that he could not wait much longer.

Always the soldiers watched, and their little lights blinked across the prairies, but the war never came. For a time Parker thought the soldiers were afraid of war, but he knew now that this was not so, for they rode where they willed, without fear, and he did not want to start trouble, when the enemy was so strong. He waited for the challenge to fight, but it did not come from the soldiers. They were not afraid; still, they offered no challenge to Parker, gave him no excuse to fight. Many times he had seen them near his camp, riding past as though it were not there, and his pride was stung by this. Still his people knew peace among the enemy, and it was a precious thing he would not thoughtlessly destroy.

Runners passed in and out of his camp with news. The hunters had left Adobe Walls. They were moving south in search of the great herds that remained. This was a sad thing to Parker's ears, and he decided then. His word went out — we must fight against the hunters or go on the reservation.

This meant a great council, and Quanah Parker invited all the free Kiowas and Cheyennes. So the trek began, from every corner of the prairie, to a place near the mouth of Elk Creek on the north fork of the Red River. It promised to be the greatest medicine dance on the plains, a harbinger of doom for the hunters, a prophecy that the buffalo would soon return.

Quanah Parker had known war, and he had no fear of it, but it was not his way of life. He had a wife and sons, and he wanted to live his own life and take his sons hunting and to look across the reaches of prairie and know he had no enemies there. He did not consider this a very big dream for a man to have, but it would never be a reality until the hunters were gone, and the soldiers were gone.

Lieutenant Jim Gary arrived late in Tascosa. All the stores were dark, and even the saloon was closed up. He stabled the horses, told the men to bunk down in the loft, and sought out a hay-strewn spot to spread his own blankets.

The next morning he checked the telegraph office but found no messages there. Sergeant Reed, who was in charge of the heliograph station, passed on the report that Gary had arrived and was waiting.

During the next four days Gary did nothing but wait, and he was at times hard-pressed to keep his men out of trouble. Civilians liked soldiers only on occasion, and four days of them hanging around town began to stretch tolerance on both sides.

Gary put up at the hotel, and on the evening of the fifth day Sergeant Reed came with a wire. Senator Chaffee and his party were on the Wednesday train, which meant they ought to arrive in Tascosa early Thursday morning.

All along Gary had been counting on more of a warning. He had expected them to wire before leaving Washington. So this was going to be a surprise visit, after all, he thought, and wondered how he could get word to General Cameron. If he waited until tomorrow morning, the senator and his party would be here, and he wouldn't have time to send a message.

He glanced at Sergeant Reed and said: "I wonder what the general would say, if we sent him word tonight?"

"The general would be damned surprised, sir," Reed said. "And so would I."

"I've thought of an improvement on your heliograph, Sergeant. What kind of a mechanic are you?"

"Good," Reed said. "What's on your mind, sir?"

"Let's go to your office," Gary suggested, and picked up his hat.

They walked to the edge of town to a small shack past the railroad tracks. A sixteen-foot tower had been erected on the east side, and from this elevation the heliograph operator could signal the next outpost.

"I want a lantern small enough to fit inside the instrument after you remove the mirror," Gary said.

"If the lieutenant is thinking what I'm thinking, it won't work. It's been tried, sir."

"Let's try again," Gary insisted.

With some reluctance the sergeant began to dismount the reflective mirror, and Gary unwrapped a polished disc and a four-inch glass from a bull's-eye lantern. "I took this reflector from behind the wall lamp in the hotel," Gary said. "The bull's-eye I bought. Now, I believe that, if the lantern light is reflected into the center of this concave reflector and then shot through the center of the bull's-eye, it will be bright enough to be seen at the next station. It's worth a try. See what you can work up. I'm going back to the hotel."

He wanted to stay and help Reed, but it wasn't the way things were done in the Army. An officer gave the order and kept clear of the matter, until it was finished.

He slept for a few hours, then Reed woke him gently. Gary went back to the signal station and climbed the ladder to the tower. He could tell by the way Sergeant Reed lit the lantern that he didn't think this would work, and Gary wasn't sure, either. It was just something he thought he'd try.

Reed spent some minutes adjusting the mirror to reflect light directly into the center of the bull's-eye, then Gary said: "All right, Sergeant, let's send a message."

"I don't think anyone will be watching, sir."

"Send your call letters anyway."

This was an order from an officer, and that was the only reason Reed went along with the whole thing. He flashed for ten minutes, while Gary stood there and gnawed his lip and wondered if Reed was right, if the whole idea was useless.

"All right, that's enough. Send this message. Light a lantern . . . put it in sending instrument . . . and acknowledge."

•

86

This message was repeated, and then Reed stopped sending. "Mister Gary, if they're receiving that, they sure ain't . . . what the hell was that? Did you see that, sir? It looked like a light. Right out there. See? Damn it, anyway, it's so faint you just can't make it out."

Gary felt like shouting, but he restrained himself. "Reed, tell them to place a polished mess tin behind the lamp. That ought to build the power a little."

The message was sent, and almost immediately the reply came back, a clear, flashing light, only a winking pinpoint, but it could be read. Gary laughed and slapped his thigh. He recalled the lectures at the Academy which drummed home the necessity for an officer to be calm in victory and stoic in defeat.

"Here's the message I want sent, Sergeant," Gary said, and wrote it down. "Pass that along with the instructions on how to rig the lantern and reflector. I'm going to bed."

Walking back to the hotel, he let the feeling of accomplishment fill his lungs and body with a tight pleasure. He could imagine the surprise of each signal sergeant out there as a light winked out a message. New things always took people back a little.

He undressed and settled into bed, wondering what General Cameron would say, when he received a message sent after sundown. Probably he wouldn't say much, because Cameron didn't scatter praise too freely. But he'd be pleased, and that was enough.

A full flood of sunlight awoke Gary in the morning, and he got up, realizing that he had overslept a bit. Sergeant Murphy of F Company had already routed out the troopers because regulations said so. He came to the hotel, bearing a can of coffee and a tin cup.

He knocked with the toe of his boot, came in without an invitation, and said: "I'm sure the lieutenant would like some coffee."

"Thank you, Murphy," Gary said. "Any message from signal?"

"Yes, sir. From the old man . . . congratulations." He grinned. "That's as good as a medal, sir."

"I guess it is," Gary said. He drank some of the coffee and finished pulling on his boots. "Sergeant, we'll leave this afternoon, even if the hour is a bit late. I don't expect we'll gain much by hanging over in town another two days while they rest up." He smiled. "If they get used to the feel of a bed, they'll just find more room for complaint on the way to Fort Elliot. I want the ambulances ready and extra canteens filled. Be sure to stow the bathtub and three barrels of water. I'll attend to the extra rations myself. But keep the men out of the saloons today. I want everyone in smart shape. Do you understand?"

"Perfectly, sir. Every man will be shaved, if I have to do it myself."

"We'll assemble on the main street," Gary said. "I think five o'clock will be about right. Give them a chance to eat a decent meal and clean up. Lord knows, though, it'll be useless. They'll collect enough dust during the first five miles to plant a crop of potatoes."

Murphy returned to his duty, and Gary went to the downstairs dining room and had a big breakfast. Afterward, he went to the stable to inspect the ambulances. He left orders that the wheels all be greased and that all nuts and bolts be tightened. The last thing he wanted to happen would be a breakdown on the prairie. That wouldn't impress the visiting dignitaries at all. All harness was minutely inspected, and the mounts selected carefully.

At the store, he ordered some canned goods and a side of ham. He was privileged to sign in script for anything he needed. He told the clerk to have the provisions ready. A trooper would pick them up later.

Because of the guests, he had a camp stove brought along, and a box of pots and pans, and a few other things a trooper can always get along without. But the best Gary could offer would seem crude, he knew, and he tried to raise the standards of comfort as high as possible.

He went back to the hotel and, borrowing pen and paper, spent an hour writing to his mother and sisters. He told them that his duty was grand and that there was no danger from the Indians and not to worry about it. It was his duty, he felt, to assure them that he was well and safe, and that his profession was as honorable as any other. They knew nothing of soldiering. The fact that he had become a soldier still baffled them, for they could not understand the seed in his lineage that had induced him to take up wandering ways so far from home. His father had not lived to see him graduate, and Gary regretted that. He'd been in his third year, almost finished with it, and after the funeral he returned to his studies, instead of taking over the hardware business. It had been a decision almost beyond his mother's forgiveness.

Because he wouldn't give up the Army and come home to run the store, they sold it, leaving them with a comfortable nest egg, but Gary thought it was a foolish move to settle for a lump sum, instead of making a living out of it. Which was why he always enclosed a generous share of his pay each month, to help carry them along until the girls grew up and got married.

He posted his letters at the dépôt — they'd go out quicker that way — then he walked up and down the street for a while, looking into the windows and watching the citizens of Tascosa going about their business, wondering what it could be. He was not suited to civilian life, and it always amazed him to find that people accomplished anything without a definite directive. Routine was a part of his life, and he could not imagine living without it. Right now at Fort Elliot there would be a sense of order about everything. About this time Sergeant-Major Karopzig would be hastening toward the infirmary, the sick book tucked under his arm, or perhaps going for the contract surgeon's report. The guards would be moving about mechanically, and the squad sergeants would be drilling troops. At the farrier's the big forge would be going, while a detail at the remount stable broke horses to cavalry duty. Everywhere there would be a definition of purpose completely lacking among civilians.

Before train time Sergeant Murphy brought the men to order at the dépôt and made "ready to receive," as the military always put it. Jim Gary stood in the shade of the porch, where he could look far down the tracks, prepared to wait with a soldier's trained patience.

The sheriff came down the street, a tall man, teetering along on spiked-heel Mexican boots. He came up to Gary and said: "Where's the brass band, sonny?"

"I beg your pardon," Gary said. He looked at the sheriff, trying to remember his name. He'd heard it a few times but had paid little attention to it.

"How come the Army has to make a fuss over everything?" The sheriff took out his hunting-case watch and popped the lid. "You've got fifteen minutes, give or take a few hours." This joke seemed to amuse him, and he chuckled. Gary's expression remained smooth and indifferent, and the sheriff stopped laughing. "You're Gary, aren't you?"

"Lieutenant Gary, yes."

The sheriff made a surprised O of his mouth. "My, excuse me. I keep forgettin' that all you people got handles on your names. Sort of like ears on jackasses."

Gary put his hands on his hips. "Did you come here to pick a fight, Mister . . . ah . . . ?"

"McCabe. Guthrie McCabe. If you want to be formal, sonny, you can call me Sheriff McCabe, although we ain't such sticklers as you in that regard. No, I'm not here to pick a fight. I had my fill of that in the last year of the war. I killed two Yankees."

"How splendid," Gary said. "I'm sure your commanding officer took you off the manure detail for that."

Guthrie McCabe's heavy face broke into a sudden grin, and he slapped his lanky thighs and guffawed. Then he wiped his eyes and said: "Well, you ain't stupid, anyway."

"A blessing we all do not share," Gary said.

McCabe frowned. "I took one of your jokes. Don't tire me."

"Excuse me," Gary said. "I didn't know you had a thin skin."

"Mister Gary," McCabe said, "we're not going to get along for sour swill, but I like you." He looked past Gary as a train whistle sounded faintly in the distance. Still several miles away, the engine belched dark smoke and huffed along the tracks toward the town, sitting in the middle of the prairie. McCabe said: "Well, I'll leave you to your politicians. I stay out of another man's business until it becomes mine."

"A wise course to follow," Gary admitted.

McCabe frowned. "I don't know how to take that."

"It'll give you something to think about, won't it?"

McCabe laughed. "One of these days I'll have to pin your ears back. That'll be something to think about."

He walked back toward town, and Gary waited for the train to arrive. It was a coal-burner, and, even before it drew into the station, he knew what a dirty ride the passengers had

had. The soot and cinders came through every crack and cranny, and a six-hour ride was enough to make the strongest man swear off trains forever.

There were three coaches behind the baggage car, and Gary kept an eye out for the conductor, who dismounted with his set of steps. Gary moved over to the train in time to hand down a young woman. He took her arm briefly and tipped his hat. She was pretty, slender, and shapely, with dark eyes and a manner remarkably composed after so hot and dusty a journey. Gary helped her to the cinder platform, and turned as a portly man in a tight coat huffed his way down.

"Senator Chaffee?" Gary asked.

"I'm Congressman Bennett," the man said, and motioned behind him. "Chaffee's coming along." He stood aside as two more men got down and looked around as though they had suddenly been dropped off in the middle of perdition and wanted to know why.

Chaffee pressed forward and offered Gary his hand. "Are you our escort?"

Gary came to attention. "Lieutenant Gary, sir. Aide to General Cameron."

Bennett grunted as though he really didn't give a damn, and turned to someone still inside the coach. "Let me help you down, my dear," he said, and Gary groaned inwardly. Not another woman!

She was fifty or so, a little plump and very prim, and she kept raising her handkerchief politely to her nose as though faced with some odor she couldn't ignore.

"This is my wife," Bennett said. He reached back and drew the third man forward. "Congressman Eastland."

All this time Gary was bowing and shaking hands. He was relieved when he came to the last of it.

Then Bennett turned him half around so that he faced the

young woman. "This is my niece, Miss Elizabeth Rishel."

To know that he had two women to look after was a shock, but somehow it evaporated when Elizabeth Rishel smiled and offered her hand. "I'm so happy to know you, Mister Gary."

"An honor, I'm sure," he said.

A gesture brought Sergeant Murphy and his detail into action. With splendid efficiency, the luggage was picked up and stowed in the ambulances, and Gary could see that Bennett appreciated this kind of treatment. From the baggage car, a pile of additional trunks awaited loading, and the troopers descended on it so suddenly it looked as though they were attacking it. In one swoop, the trunks were loaded into the second ambulance.

"Most efficient," Bennett said. "Well, let's get started, my boy. I could do with a bath and a shave before having dinner with your commanding officer."

The meaning did not fully descend on Gary for a moment, then he said: "I'm sorry to disappoint you, sir, but Fort Elliot is a three-day ride in an ambulance."

Chaffee and Eastland seemed resigned to anything, but Bennett's eyes looked like glass beads thrust into the face of a pink pumpkin. He said — "Good God!" — and let it go at that.

Glancing at Mrs. Bennett, Gary was sure she was going to burst into tears, and he felt sorry for her, much as he felt for all women who followed their men to the frontier. He said: "Madam, may I suggest that you go to the hotel and rest for an hour?" He tried to sound experienced and worldly in these matters, as though he had met a thousand trains, a thousand important people, and had handled each with diplomacy and aplomb. "A bath and a nap will refresh you, I'm sure. We won't start for three hours yet. Traveling is much better in the evening, for there's a breeze, then."

"Good thinking there," Bennett said. "Mister Gary, we accept."

He took them to the hotel, where the clerk was a little taken aback by this deluge of guests, but Gary handled the matter efficiently. He signed the register for all of them, took charge of the keys, and one by one he saw them to their rooms.

Bennett paused in his door and said: "I understood that Elliot was close to Tascosa." He said it, as though he expected someone to rush out and move the post in closer.

Gary said: "Out here, sir, *close* may mean a hundred miles. I'm sorry for the inconvenience."

"Oh, to hell with it!" Bennett said, and slammed the door.

Gary started to puff his cheeks, then remembered Elizabeth Rishel was standing there, waiting to be let into her room. He caught himself in time and moved on down the hallway.

When he unlocked the door, she said: "You're thoughtful, Mister Gary. Were you trained in the diplomatic service?"

His face took on color, then he made a joke of it. "If a man can please the Army, he can please anyone."

"I expect you're right. When you arrange for the baths, make mine hot."

"All right. How many degrees does Congressman Bennett like?"

She was amused by the implication that Gary had already fathomed Bennett's peckishness. "About a hundred and thirty, Mister Gary."

"Fahrenheit or Centigrade?"

Her laughter was like a chord struck on delicate bells. "Make it Centigrade, Mister Gary. It won't hurt Uncle Albert to boil a little." She regarded him seriously. "You're not awed by him, and he senses it."

"Well," he said, "perhaps it's because I'm not seeking anything. It'll be another four years before I can seriously think of promotion, so the congressman and his party become merely a responsibility that I take very seriously."

"Oh, I'm sure you do," she said. "What's your first name, Mister Gary?"

"James Mayhew," he said. "It really won't sound very impressive until I can put captain in front of it."

"You may put colonel there someday," she said, "if you don't allow rashness to spoil it." She stepped inside and partially closed the door. "Don't forget . . . hot."

"Shall I have the boy knock, or slip the tub under the door?"

She made a wry face at him and closed the door. He stood there for a moment, and then went on down the hallway, taking the stairs two at a time.

Chapter Seven

An hour before they were scheduled to leave Tascosa, Lieutenant Gary had the ambulances parked in front to the hotel and the detail ready to form at a moment's notice. He waited on the porch. The first to appear was Senator Wilson Chaffee. A razor had cleared his face of beard stubble, and bathing had left his round cheeks shining. He had a cigar in his mouth and was enjoying it. His focus was drawn to Gary, when the young man came to a heel-clicking attention.

"Ah, my boy, at ease there, or whatever you do in the Army." He patted the tight drum of his stomach. "Bless me, it doesn't cool off much in the afternoon, does it? But the heat seems drier than in Washington. A man could get used to this." He took a long puff on his cigar and blew smoke toward the ceiling of the porch, and in the undisturbed air it hung there. "Have you served long on the frontier, Gary?"

Gary hesitated, wondering what he should say. If he told him that he hadn't been out here a year yet, Chaffee might get the idea that he was in inexperienced hands. Yet he didn't want to lie about it, so he said: "Long enough to know how to handle myself, sir."

Chaffee laughed softly. "What more can a man ask? When I was elected to the Senate, I was the youngest man ever sent from my state, and in two years' time I was on three committees. Think of that . . . three committees!"

Gary was sure that must be a splendid record, but it didn't mean a thing to him, although he tried to hide that fact from the senator. There wasn't anything he could say without revealing his abysmal ignorance, so he smiled and made a slight nod with his head.

It was enough to satisfy Chaffee, who liked best the men who listened instead of talked. "Seventeen years in the Senate," he said. "And I'm proud to say, seventeen years of unselfish service. I, too . . . I'm a soldier, Gary . . . part of an army of men fighting to preserve and expand our wonderful country. You have your service record, my boy . . . I have my voting record. And each will tell what a man is." He reached out and tapped Gary with his finger. "Be proud to serve General Cameron, for there is no more divine a cause than peace."

"I am, sir, and I'll give him my best."

"The general has many detractors, Gary, but he also has a record beyond argument. While all the other commanders have had trouble and some casualties, Cameron has had none. His Indians fare better than those on the reservation. God, if the Interior Department and the War Department ever got together on the reservation situation and let Cameron run the Southwest, the Indians would be eating better than I do. Given a chance, and a little money, he'd end all this trouble in a hurry."

He leaned a bit closer to Gary. "Congressman Bennett is a tight man with a dollar. He wants to cut the military appropriation. Eastland is a fence rider, but he's a strong man in his party. Convince him, and you've carried a majority party vote in Congress. Convince Bennett that you're saving money, and my committee can put through our expansion program without opposition. Gary, I tell you this because I want both Bennett and Eastland to enjoy their stay here." He frowned and gnawed his cigar. "This three-day jaunt to Elliot comes as a surprise to me. I understood that it was no more than a day away."

"Yes, sir, for mounted men who push a little."

"Let's not have too much of that," Chaffee said quickly. "Bennett has been complaining about the primitive train conditions, as it is. I shudder to think of what it'll be like in the ambulance."

"I'll make every attempt to insure their comfort, sir," Gary said.

"Of course, of course. Cameron wouldn't send a boy on a man's errand." Then he chuckled. "This damned hot climate agrees with me. I've been eating like a horse. We all brought along rifles. I hope there's some shooting to be had." He slapped Gary on the shoulder. "We'll be starting soon. Remember, you're the captain of the ship, Mister Gary."

Gary touched the beak of his kepi and watched Wilson Chaffee go into the hotel. He was wondering who the captain was really going to be.

An hour and a half out of Tascosa, Jim Gary began to get an idea of how things were going to go. First, Albert Bennett wanted to change seats. This meant stopping the detail, while he moved to the rear of the ambulance. He seemed quite happy there, but his wife complained of getting too much sun, and they had to stop again while they traded back.

Gary could see that his rôle of guide, protector, and entrepreneur was not going to be easy. During the four-hour march to sundown, Gary had a chance to study them in some detail, particularly Albert Bennett. He chose Bennett because he figured he would have more trouble with him than with anyone else, and he wasn't far wrong. At first, Gary had put Bennett down as a pompous ass who couldn't get along with anyone, but he changed his mind. Bennett was merely a man accustomed to considerable comfort, and now he was put out because he was denied it. Gary didn't begrudge the man his complaints, for there were times in his own life when he felt like complaining. Only he had always held it back, while Bennett continually displayed his disappointment. He was rather like a child, pestering his father to hurry up so they could get home, all the while they sat in the middle of the road with a sheared buggy wheel. Bennett would not believe that matters could not be improved upon.

Gary stopped by a creek to set up the night camp, and his detail did an efficient job of it, erecting the tents and the stove and getting the meal going. Bennett's wife, Gary noticed, was one of those long-sufferers. He supposed she had been doing this all her life, composing her lips until her face assumed a naturally sour expression. It was her natural rôle to suffer in silence for her husband, his career, the public. Now, Gary suspected, she was suffering for him, for all the nasty little orders he gave, for having to sleep in a tent and eat off a tin plate, and ride across this lonesome prairie in an ambulance with the heat and dust a constant irritation. Senator Chaffee seemed to enjoy himself — by every gesture he was bragging about his adaptability, his ruggedness. He wasn't enjoying it a damned bit, Gary knew, but, if Chaffee wanted to go on with the pretense, Gary wasn't going to stop him.

The meal was the best ever prepared on the prairie, but Mrs. Bennett took one look at it and acted as though she were suddenly ill. She wanted to retire, to succumb to the blessed morphia of sleep, as she put it, but she was bothered now by the thought of prowling Indians. Gary reassured her at length that she was entirely safe, and, just as he was congratulating himself on his powers of persuasion, she brought up the subject of rattlesnakes. This fear was not so easily put down, but Gary did it by assuring the congressman's wife that he would post a "rattlesnake guard" around the camp all night.

He was glad, when they all took their blasted baths and

went to bed, and he went over to the dying fire to sit a while and ponder his military career. He still had the cigars Cameron had given him and thought that he might find comfort in one. He peeled the wrapper off it and was bending over to light it, when Elizabeth Rishel spoke softly from behind him.

"I didn't think you had any bad habits, Mister Gary." She came around and sat down on a camp stool. She wore a heavy robe tightly belted about her, and her hair was hanging in twin braids down her back.

"I also sing tenor, while I'm in the tub," he said, and smiled. "Busy day, huh?"

"Better busy than not," she said. She leaned forward and hugged her shoulders. "Jim, how long do you live here before you stop feeling lost?"

"Some never do. It's big, isn't it?"

"Vast," she said.

He studied her a moment, then said: "I've been watching you."

"Well, I'd have been insulted, if you hadn't," she said. "A pretty girl likes to be watched."

"What I meant was, you take the bad in stride. The heat and dust are irritating, I know."

"Irritating, Mister Gary? It's unbelievable! Doesn't it ever rain?"

"When it does, the sky just opens up," he said. "Every depression turns into a raging river, and two hours later the sun's baking it dry again. But the prairie gets to you. I like it."

"You're joking," she said.

"No, I'm not. I had the notion you liked it."

She looked at him solemnly a moment, then laughed. "Mister Gary, I loathe every foot of the place, every grain of dust that's blown into my hair."

He was taken aback by the forceful sincerity, taken aback because he had misjudged her so completely. For a moment he could think of nothing to say, and she waited for him to speak.

When he didn't, she went on. "If I seem not to be bothered by this discomfort, Jim, it's because I'm twenty and nothing really bothers me. Call it the adaptability of youth, if you want."

"Why did you come with your uncle?"

She shrugged. "It was an adventure, and it will soon terminate, so I'll endure without complaint these frontier inconveniences."

"I see," Gary said. "My mistake."

"Which is . . . ?"

He shrugged. "My thinking was that you were a woman who had found something here, something she could live with."

"I don't know what you're talking about," Elizabeth said. "Are you sure that *you* do?"

"No," Gary said. "I guess we'd better forget it."

She shook her head. "If we do that, it will be unsettled and can be brought up again. I don't want it brought up again."

"Then it won't be," he said.

"How can you be sure?"

"Because I say so."

"It isn't good enough for me," Elizabeth Rishel said. "I'm quite accustomed to having single men think of me as a possible wife. Generally, I'm flattered by it. Now I'm not. I'm irritated to think that a man would even remotely consider my wishing to share his life in Texas. I find the landscape ugly and military duties uninteresting. I don't want to hurt you, Jim, but I've got to speak plainly."

"That's plain enough," Gary said, an angry tone in his

101

voice. "When I first talked to you, I thought that here was a woman with some strength of her own. Perhaps you have the strength, Elizabeth, but I think you'll waste it. Like you say, you'll put up with the inconveniences out here just because it'll make good conversation back in Washington. It's too bad. You could give something to this country."

"Why would I ever want to?" she said, rising. "We'd better not talk any more, Jim, or we'll really be angry with each other. Men always take rejection badly."

He stood up, also, and looked at her. "What makes you so spoiled?"

"Men. Fathers, brothers, sweethearts. Men, Jim. Good night."

He broke camp an hour later than was customary, and even then Albert Bennett complained about the ungodly hour. Congressman Phillip Eastland seemed to be wearing well. He wasn't having a good time, but he believed strongly that while in Rome, a man should do as the Romans do.

Breakfast was served, and, after the tents and gear were packed, the detail got under way. It was nearly eight o'clock, and Gary hoped that didn't go on his record. He never slept that late on Sundays.

During the morning Bennett insisted that they stop while he got out his hunting rifle, an enormous .50-125 Express. Gary was quite happy to leave the rifle stowed in the luggage, but he gave in to Bennett, thinking that perhaps just carrying it in his hands might soothe him a little, something like giving a child his toy, although there was no place at the moment to play with it.

At the noon stop Bennett approached Gary with a novel idea. "Lieutenant, I bought this rifle from Abercrombie and Fitch."

"A splendid firm," Gary said politely.

"Yes, but I want to shoot a buffalo with it." He said it as though he expected Gary to be surprised. Phillip Eastland sat nearby, and he looked at Bennett.

"Albert, why don't you put that damned cannon up? You can see there aren't any buffalo."

"A good hunter never lets the scarcity of game deter him," Bennett said. "Lieutenant, you haven't heard my plan yet." He placed his hand in a fatherly fashion on Gary's shoulder, as if to say: *Now I'm going to tell you something politely, and, if you don't agree, I'm going to knock your block off.* He went on. "You can spare a few men to forage out and find me a buffalo. Drive one in close to the ambulance, and I'll get a trophy for my den."

Gary stifled the urge to come right out and say that this was pure foolishness, but he couched his response in more polite terms. "Sir, that would be ill-advised. Buffalo are dangerous and unpredictable and, with the ladies present, even the slightest risk is too great."

"He'll be a captain before he's thirty," Eastland said, and considered the matter closed.

But Bennett wasn't so easily put off. "Good heavens, Gary, I'll stop the brute. And I think the ladies would rather enjoy it."

A firm note was creeping into the man's voice that Gary didn't like. In a minute there would be a dispute over authority, a test of strength, with a residue of bruised feelings, and this Gary couldn't afford. For himself it didn't matter, but for General Cameron it might be enough to throw future relationships into a cocked hat.

"I don't want to disappoint you, sir, but. . . ."

"Then don't," Bennett said quickly. He laughed pleasantly. "You want to bargain, eh? Meet you halfway, then.

103

Nothing's fairer than that, is there?" He placed the rifle in the crook of his arm. "Suppose we sight a small herd. Rather than send the men out, why couldn't you swing the whole outfit over there, so I could get my shot?"

"There's still the danger, sir, and. . . ."

"I'm getting a little bored with all this danger business," Bennett said flatly. "I was a soldier during the war, decorated, too. And I'm a crack shot. Now I've given in to you, come a little your way. You come some to me. I'm not asking much, am I?" He took Gary by the shoulder and shook him gently. "You wouldn't begrudge a man some fried tongue, would you? I've heard it's delicious."

"Like eating soap, sir."

"That won't spoil my pleasure," Bennett said. "There's something satisfying to a man to eat a meal killed with his own hands." He looked at Gary. "I understand you have your duty to do, but let's not overdo it. Well? Is it a bargain?"

Gary didn't hesitate too long, and afterward he supposed that he should have, but he knew Bennett wanted an answer now, that was the way the man was. "All right, sir, but on a condition." Bennett frowned, but Gary had made up his mind. "I know the prairie, sir, and I'll pick the herd."

"All right," Bennett said. "But I want my shot today."

"Well, I don't know, sir. We may not run across anything small. . . ."

"Then we'll take what comes. Lieutenant, I've agreed to your terms . . . the bargain's been made. If you see a herd and pass it up, then it's your gamble that we'll see another, a more suitable herd before sundown. I know you won't disappoint me, because I don't like for a man to go back on his bargain."

He took his rifle and went back to the ambulance, leaving Gary to consider this new mess he'd gotten into.

Eastland said: "No one really ever outargues Albert. He

gets his way, one way or another." He got up and came over to Gary. "You talk with Albert for five minutes, and he leaves you feeling a little battered. I don't think it's the deals themselves a man is forced to make that bothers you so much. It's just that you always feel, afterward, that you were forced to make them." He helped himself to some coffee. "What are the chances of sighting buffalo?"

Gary shrugged. "You see a small herd from time to time. They've been just about hunted off, though."

"Well, let's hope you find some. He's going to be hell to put up with, if he doesn't get his damned fried tongue."

When they moved on into the afternoon, Gary pondered Eastland's statement and didn't doubt for a moment that he was entirely right. Bennett would be a fright, if he didn't get his fried tongue.

Around three o'clock the lead ambulance driver saw dust and pointed it out to Gary, who dismounted to study it through his field glasses. It was buffalo all right, a small herd of cows with two or three calves, and he made up his mind then and there.

He ordered the line of march altered, and, within an hour, they drew near the herd, taking care not to get them running. Gary halted the detail and advised Bennett to dismount for his shot so as not to frighten the team. That buffalo Express rifle was going to make a big noise, when he touched it off.

Bennett used a shooting crutch for the fourteen-pound barrel, took his time about setting up. He downed a calf with one shot. The range was a good three hundred and fifty yards, and it was a fine shot in any man's language, but Bennett spoiled it by acting as though he couldn't have missed with a slingshot.

The rest of the herd scattered, and Gary told the sergeant to get a fire ready while he and four others went out to the downed calf. Bennett wanted to drive the ladies out to see his kill, but his wife wouldn't go, and Elizabeth had no desire to see a dead buffalo. This seemed to be a disappointment to Bennett, but he managed to live with it and go along to watch the tongue being removed.

The sight of it dampened his appetite a bit, but he'd made his brag, and he was a man who lived up to every one he made. Sergeant Murphy took charge of the cooking; buffalo tongue was one of his specialties.

Gary could see no need to proceed farther, so he ordered the picket line set up and the camp made for the night. There was no water nearby, but they had the barrels, enough for their baths. He moved around, supervising the small details of night camp, seeing that the tents were properly pitched, the cots set up, and the stove erected. Mrs. Bennett and Elizabeth wanted something to eat that was not buffalo tongue.

A good three hours until sunset, Gary estimated, as he looked at the sky, and rather a disgraceful hour for a patrol to be making a night camp. But as the general had advised, he was taking his time, although it was unmilitary and aroused feelings of guilt.

A plume of dust aroused his curiosity, and he got his field glasses to have a better look. Then he called Sergeant Murphy over. He handed him the glasses, and, after Murphy made a brief study, he said: "I guess about thirty, sir."

"And moving directly toward us," Gary said. "Sergeant, quietly now, bring the men in off their details and have them casually pick up their arms."

"Too many to make a fight of it, sir," Murphy said.

Gary smiled thinly. "The general doesn't want us to fight. We'll see if we can't face this out."

"With the odds three to one, sir? Indians don't face down unless it's the other way around."

106

"Shall we try, Sergeant?"

This stung Murphy, and his complexion reddened a bit. His fingers touched his hat brim. "Yes, sir." He trotted away to carry out his orders.

Albert Bennett came over, still carrying his enormous rifle. "Are those Indians friendly, Gary?"

"Absolutely," Gary said. "I suggest, sir, that you put your rifle in the tent, out of sight."

"Why?"

Gary felt like telling him — *Because I said so, that's why.* — but he refrained. "The rifle is a buffalo gun, and the sight of it always reminds them that white men killed them off. I'm afraid I must insist, sir."

Bennett grumbled, but he put the rifle away. The women came out of the tent and stood there, watching the Indians draw closer. Murphy had his men in a line, dismounted, but holding their horses.

Gary wished the women hadn't come out, and he walked over to them. "Ladies, would you please go back in the tent and wait?"

"Why?" Elizabeth asked.

He bit his lip and wondered if this particular question wasn't a civilian curse. "Because I told you to," he said, "and because I haven't the time now to explain why."

Mrs. Bennett presented to him her stern expression. "Mister Gary, I've noticed a tone in your voice at times that I don't like, especially from the lowest-ranking officer in the service." Then a new thought came to her, and she expressed it. "Is there danger?"

"I'm sure there's none," Gary said, making his lie smooth and digestible.

"Then I don't see why I can't stand here," Mrs. Bennett said firmly.

He opened his mouth to speak, then looked at Elizabeth Rishel, and found her smiling faintly. This angered him and frustrated him, and he wheeled away to join Sergeant Murphy.

The Indians were close enough now to be recognized, and Murphy said: "That's White Horse, sir. You met his kin a while back."

"Mount the detail, Sergeant. We'll hold this line."

"We'll try, sir," Murphy said. "Preee-pare to mount! Mount!"

Gary watched the Indians come on, and once turned his head to see what was going on behind him. Bennett, the brave hunter, was standing with his arm around his wife. Chaffee and Eastland stood a short distance away. They were very still, like two historical statues about to be moved to distant city parks.

Murphy spoke, and Gary gave him his attention. "Well, they ain't wearin' paint. Guess that's something in our favor."

"But they've seen the women," Gary said. "I don't like that."

"You want to know the truth? . . . I don't like none of it." Murphy paused to spit. "You put the advantage on an Indian's side, sir, and you got some pretty haughty Indians."

White Horse halted his band a hundred yards from the camp and came on alone, trotting his calico pony. He was a short, broad man with a flat face and dark, darting eyes. He carried a repeating Evans rifle and a bandoleer of .44-40 cartridges, and Gary wondered where he had come upon these items.

With regret he realized that White Horse, in coming forward alone, was getting a good look at everything — their strengths and weaknesses. *I made a mistake in not going to him,* Gary thought.

White Horse saw the downed buffalo calf, smelled the tongue cooking, and said: "Buffalo belong to me. Why you kill?"

Gary felt like telling him to take it and get out, but he knew he couldn't without having it interpreted as a sign of fear. *Best not even to answer him,* he decided. "What do you want here?" he asked.

The Indian ignored him. "Why you kill buffalo? Not yours. Mine." He waved his arm at the parked ambulance. "Got food. Got blankets. No need buffalo to eat. No need skin for lodge. Why you kill?"

The argument was as profound and unarguable as any Gary had ever heard, and he wondered what Bennett was thinking. Or was the man still clinging to his opinion that a white man had certain rights over an Indian and his property? Still, Gary knew, he couldn't just sit here and let White Horse lord it over him. And he didn't want to argue, because that was a bad thing to do with Indians. They had their own narrow spheres of thinking and were unresponsive to logic. Everything was medicine to them, and they acted accordingly, depending on whether the medicine was good or bad.

"There were many buffalo in the herd," Gary said. "Only one was taken, a small one whose skin would not make more than a blanket for a woman. Does White Horse want a woman's blanket?"

"The buffalo is mine. I take now."

"No," Gary said. "The buffalo belongs to the man who killed it. Even among your own people, this is so."

"Buffalo mine," White Horse said again. "When Indian take horse of white man, he must give back or pay. It is the rule of the chief at the fort. My buffalo. You take. You pay me."

Gary was losing his argument, and it galled him and worried him, because this was his second mistake and a most serious one. He said: "If you want meat, take what you need. That is payment enough."

White Horse struck his chest with the flat of his hand. "You have many bullets. We have few. Give us bullets, and we let you go in peace."

"No bullets," Gary said. "If you had enough bullets, there wouldn't be any peace."

"It is a white man's way to have all the bullets," White Horse said. "The Indian must fight with a stick against bullets." He waved his hand to include all the camp. "I can take bullets. Women and wagons, too. Give me bullets, and we go now."

This was, Gary was sure, the showdown, and what he did next would determine whether they lived or died. He sat erect in the saddle and spoke firmly. "White Horse speaks of the Indian fighting with sticks. We do not need bullets to keep what is ours. There will be no bullets, no women, and no wagons, White Horse."

"I can take!"

Gary wasn't sure whether this was a bluff, brag, or threat. He could count eight or ten rifles among the braves, waiting out there, but he was doubtful as to how accurate they were with them. It could be that he might repulse a charge with squad fire, but he didn't want that. He didn't want to be the one who ruined Tracy Cameron's chances.

"White Horse, do I speak to a woman or a man?"

The Indian was deeply insulted and shook his rifle at Gary. "You speak with leader, pony soldier!"

"Then I will test your courage," Gary snapped. "Sergeant Murphy, order carbines slung." The sergeant stared in disbelief, but he waved his hand, and the troopers hooked their carbine rings onto their saddles. The Indian watched this with a blank expression on his face, and Gary said: "We have no bullets now, White Horse. You see our line. You see what you claim is yours. Come past us and take it."

"We have guns," White Horse said.

"Do you need them to show your bravery? Do you lead women?"

From behind him, Albert Bennett said: "Gary, what the devil are you doing?"

"Shut up, sir," Gary said. "Well, White Horse, I wait. Will you ride away in peace?"

Gary knew what the answer would be, and he was willing to gamble on carrying this off. He had a few things on his side that even the Indians didn't understand. It had been three years since they'd taken a shot at a white man, especially a soldier, and they were out of the habit. They would hesitate before opening fire, or attacking, and, if he could just buy one more day of this, they'd hesitate even more the next time, and the next time, until the day came when they just wouldn't want to fight.

With an angry whoop, White Horse wheeled away from the camp. Gary glanced around in time to see Bennett come out of the tent with his rifle. There wasn't time to argue. Gary flung off, ran over, and grabbed the barrel.

Bennett hung on with a characteristic stubbornness, and Gary brought into play some of the things he had learned on the Academy wrestling team. He threw the congressman over his shoulder. Bennett struck solidly and grunted, and Gary gave the rifle one whirl over his head and sailed it clear of the camp.

Then he went back and mounted his horse, feeling that he had lost anyway. Bennett would never forgive him for this humiliation. Murphy was sweating, and Gary spoke to all of them, mounted there.

111

"They'll try to break our line. Don't give an inch. Use your fists, if you have to, but turn them."

He had hardly finished, when White Horse and his band charged, bunched up like the head of a maul. They rode, yipping and screaming, directly toward Gary's detail, and the men waited, erect in the saddle, holding their ground like planted fence posts.

The dust rose thickly in a screen, and it seemed that the Indians would smash full tilt into the waiting cavalrymen, but they held, and the Indians broke, wheeling, milling around, then charging back for another go at it. The dust cleared, and Gary had his men straighten their line slightly. He was sweating now, and the dust was turning to mud in the cracks of his flesh. "They'll come into us the next time," he said. "Stand your ground."

He knew they would, yet he felt compelled to give the order, for saying it aloud firmed up the resolve tottering within him. *Damn,* he thought, *it's difficult to be brave, difficult to do the right thing.*

He'd bought a test of courage between the Army and the Indians. White Horse and his braves would come as close to collision as they dared, trying to make the troopers give way. Gary didn't fool himself. There wasn't a coward among White Horse's band, and, before this was over, a few Indians and soldiers were going to taste dirt.

The second charge was more ferocious than the first, and this time they didn't pull up as short. Two troopers went down, but the Indians fared worse, for the troopers knew how to use their fists. When White Horse pulled free, he had five men down, five riderless ponies trotting away to be picked up later. The two troopers regained their saddles in time to present a still solid row to White Horse, and with a yell of rage he wheeled his braves back for another try.

112

They didn't understand what a mounted wedge was, and Gary was grateful for that. With hardly a pause, the Indians wheeled and stormed across the brief interval of prairie. The two forces met with a rush, horses whinnied and milled, and the dust rose in a dense, choking screen, but the Indians were forced to draw back. Gary was pinned under his horse, and half the troopers had to remount. White Horse's band was dismounted, except for a handful of braves who had been in the rear and had not really mixed into the hottest part of the collision. Some blood had been started in that round. The downed Indians nursed broken noses and teeth, where the hard fists of the troopers had landed.

Murphy helped get the horse off Gary, so that he wouldn't be mangled as the animal struggled, and Gary hobbled on one leg, sure that the other was broken.

"Mount!" he shouted. "Get mounted!"

They all went into the saddle and reformed their line and sat there, waiting, watching White Horse try to gather enough men for another charge.

But there wasn't any. The Indian rode forward, and Gary was pleased to see a discoloration over his right eye. Someone had gotten in a good one there, and it made the shooting pain in his own leg more tolerable.

"It is enough," White Horse said solemnly. "The pony soldier has strong medicine with him."

This was, Gary knew, as close to an admission of being licked as White Horse would ever make. The Indian had his face to save, so he turned his horse, gathered his band, and rode away, faced with the time-wasting chore of catching up the loose ponies.

"My, God!" Murphy said. "We out-cold-nerved 'em, sir."

"And without firing a shot," Gary said. "Dismiss the men to their duties, Sergeant."

"Yes, sir." He watched Gary's tight expression and said: "That leg bad, sir?"

"Sprained, I think," Gary said and swung down. He set his weight gingerly on it and found that it would support him. He turned and hobbled over to the fire, beating dust from his clothes with his gauntlets. Someone had knocked over the frying pan, and the congressman's buffalo tongue was on the ground. It made Gary indescribably happy to see it there, to know that Bennett wouldn't be eating it, after all.

Chaffee was the first to reach Gary. He thrust out his hand and said: "Mister Gary, if you are an example of General Cameron's officers, I don't think he can lose."

"Thank you, sir," Gary said. Then Albert Bennett pushed Chaffee aside. He did it cleverly by putting his hand on Chaffee's shoulder and swaying him a little, just enough to let him know that he was in the way but not enough to offend. *Oh, you're a subtle bastard,* Gary thought.

"Mister Gary," Bennett said, taking both of Gary's hands, "rarely does a man get to witness such a display of courage. By God, Wilson, I'm going to make this boy a first lieutenant the minute we hit the post. And I can do it, too." He put his arm around Gary's shoulder. "This is an example, Wilson, of what I've always argued for . . . seasoned, experienced officers on the frontier, men who do the right thing by instinct and training." He laughed. "I suppose I owe you an apology of sorts, for taking up my rifle as I did, but you *are* young, Gary, and I thought . . . well, it doesn't matter what I thought."

He looked around the camp. "The dust made a mess of it, didn't it? And my buffalo tongue is ruined. Well, perhaps I can shoot another of the beasts tomorrow."

On the excuse of overseeing his men Gary got away from Bennett. He limped to the edge of camp and stood there, massaging his leg.

114

Elizabeth Rishel came up from behind him and spoke. "You're a modest man, Jim."

He turned his head and glanced at her. "I thought that I was presumptuous and dictatorial and too big for my britches."

"I suppose I deserve that."

"Is there any doubt?"

She was shocked by the directness of his honesty, and it forced aside her own pretenses. "No, there isn't, Jim. I'm sorry."

"So am I. We deserved a better start than we got."

"Is your leg badly hurt?"

He shook his head. "Wrenched, that's all. It will be all right, if I walk on it a while."

"You made a great impression on Uncle Albert, and I think he was serious about promoting you."

Gary laughed. "He's full of hot air. In the Army we're promoted on seniority, and I'm 'way down the list. He can't do a thing for me."

"Well, you could pretend to be grateful," Elizabeth said.

"I don't like to pretend," Gary told her. "And I'm grateful all right. Grateful that I had the luck to turn White Horse away without a lot of guns going off." He turned to face her. "I haven't had this duty long, but I've got a commanding officer who knows what he's doing. That's why we stood our ground, instead of unlimbering carbines . . . because General Cameron wanted it that way. I shouldn't have let your uncle kill the buffalo, and he's not going to kill another, at least not until after we reach the post. The general can organize a hunt, if he wants."

He held up his fingers and counted off the points, as he made them. "My first mistake was when I let him kill the buffalo. The second, when I dickered with White Horse. The

115

third, when I let the whole thing get so far out of hand it almost came to shooting."

"You're being unduly critical of yourself," Elizabeth said.

"No, I'm trying to look at it as General Cameron will. A man gets into a mess like this because of a lack of basic leadership." He took her arm and turned her back toward the tents. "You'd better stay near the fire. It'll be dark soon."

Chapter Eight

As soon as he received the message from Jim Gary, announcing their arrival time, General Tracy Cameron made plans to receive the politicians in a proper social setting. He had the sutler's hall decorated gaily, the officers' mess hung with bunting and Japanese lanterns, and Quarters A turned out for a reception.

Cameron's planned festivity was echoed at Quanah Parker's camp at the mouth of Elk Creek on the north fork of the Red River. The dance lasted a day and a night, for they were making big medicine, bigger than they had ever made before. It was all right to dance a little for rain, or for victory in a minor raid, but now they danced for what was life to them, the strong medicine to bring back the buffalo.

Quanah Parker sat and watched the dancing, and the Kwahadi medicine man placed himself in close attendance, for Quanah was near the spirits and would need guidance. The medicine man was called Isatai. He was an old man, very wise, and his words held truth to all the Comanches.

"I have talked with the spirits of sun and wind," he said, and Quanah listened to him with attention.

"What did the voices tell you, medicine-maker?" Quanah asked.

The old man made a sign. "They have taken pity on your people, Quanah. The voices say we shall be strong in war, and we shall drive the hunters away. The buffalo will come back, and there will be full bellies in every lodge."

"You have heard a good voice," Quanah said. He was tall

117

and slender, and in his veins ran the blood of a white woman, his mother. But he was a Comanche, with a Comanche's way of thinking. By no indication of gesture or feature did he show his white blood.

"There is more," Isatai said. "I have learned a very strong medicine from the voices, Quanah. When I make this medicine, you and all who follow you will turn away the hunters' bullets." He bent closer. "Had White Horse my power he would not have been turned away by the pony soldiers."

"They did not shoot," Quanah said. "There were no bullets to turn away."

"My medicine will make their courage leave them," Isatai swore. "I have not spoken of this power, Quanah, for the medicine-makers of the Kiowas and Cheyennes are full of envy. They wish to make medicine of their own and claim it is stronger than mine, and, when victory comes to you, they will say that it was their medicine that brought it. I have served faithfully, Quanah, and you will know that it was my medicine that brought power to the Comanches."

"You speak wisely," Quanah said. "Tonight, at the feast, you will speak of this power and make the medicine."

Isatai said nothing more. He had won his point, and, no matter which way this turned out, he would not appear less in Quanah's eyes. For if they attacked the hunters at their new camp and killed them, he would be praised, and they would sing songs about him. And if the fighting went badly, he would claim that the Kiowa and Cheyenne medicine men had conspired against him out of jealousy. Isatai had no power, heard no voices, but he was a little smarter than the next man, quick with his wits, and he had a politician's natural flair for drama and showmanship, and for forty years it had brought him a good life. He never worked, never hunted, never stole a horse, or exposed himself to danger in battle, and he did it all

118

by making himself too valuable to lose. When winter came and his buffalo robe began to look a little shabby, he just looked around the camp to see who owned the best one, then he'd drop some heavy-footed hint that the spirits had talked with him, and that the owner of that robe was about to lose his power in the hunt, if he didn't do something right away.

Isatai was very free with his medicine, and there never was a hunt or raid that he did not mix up a whole batch, but there never was enough to go around. So he'd endow only a few with his strong potions, and, when a few were killed, he'd cover himself by stating that they hadn't received his medicine because of some past sin. He played this game successfully, because he never announced which ones had received the medicine until after the battle and then claimed the survivors had been blessed. After the dancing went on a while, Isatai had no trouble getting braves to stand up and swear his medicine had made their arms stronger, or their aim straighter, or that their rifles just would not run out of bullets. He was a first-class snake-oil salesman who had never seen a bottle of patent medicine.

During the feasting, Isatai made his medicine in a way that impressed even his Kiowa and Cheyenne competitors. He spoke of his power, now so strong that it would turn away bullets, make brave men out of cowards, and bring back the buffalo. He claimed that at his word every buffalo would turn into two, and every two into four, and to demonstrate this ability he took a long belt of leather, put a half twist into it, and sewed the ends together. Then before their startled eyes, he sliced it all around, down the middle, and instead of having two pieces, he had one, still sewed together, but twice as long. Amid the exclamations of wonder, he did it again, in case anyone hadn't been suitably impressed before. It still remained in one piece, again twice as long as before.

Quanah, seeing how impressed everyone was, announced that they would go south and attack the new hunter camp before they had time to build another Adobe Walls. Lone Wolf of the Kiowas disagreed. He felt that the pony soldiers should be the first to go. To bolster this claim he maintained that, if Isatai's power was truly strong, they had nothing to fear.

Quanah Parker didn't have an argument for this, but one of the Cheyennes, still a little goggle-eyed over Isatai's demonstration, said that he thought attacking the hunters was best. The Great Power might be displeased, if they asked for too much help all at one time.

This settled the matter. Quanah would make all the plans and lead the raid with the Comanches, while Lone Wolf and Stone Calf led the Kiowas and Cheyennes. Outlining his plan simply, Quanah meant to attack the southern camp of the hunters, making one fell swoop of it, with the Kiowas and Cheyennes pressing on each flank as the Comanches charged. Everyone liked the plan, except that each wanted to charge, while the others flanked. They argued that for the rest of the night.

Upon arrival at Fort Elliot, Lieutenant Jim Gary turned his guests over to Major Bassett, who took proper charge of them and saw them to suitable quarters. Murphy dismissed his men, and Gary turned to headquarters to make an immediate report to General Cameron.

The orderly opened Cameron's door for him, and closed it. Gary stripped off his gauntlets and took the hand the general offered.

"Sit down, Jim," Cameron said. "You've got a limp there."

"Not as bad as it was yesterday," Gary said. "Did you get

120

my last report, sir? I sent it at the first heliograph detachment I came to."

"Completely," Cameron said. "Perhaps you'd like to read *my* report." He reached across his desk and handed Gary his latest dispatch. Three paragraphs glowed with praise of Gary's action — most men hoped for a line, their names merely mentioned.

Gary said: "That ought to move me one notch up the promotion list, sir." He smiled, when he said it, because he didn't want Cameron to think that was all he had on his mind.

"With two congressmen and a senator present, probably closer to three or four notches," Cameron said. "You may be a first lieutenant by twenty five." He took the dispatch back and studied Gary. "What is your opinion of that little affair between you and White Horse?"

"I hardly know, sir. He wanted a quarrel, and I suspect a fight. Still, he couldn't quite make up his mind whether to make it or not." He rubbed a hand across his unshaven cheek. "General, I had to get over being scared about it before I reached any conclusions, and that was some hours later. White Horse has been a reservation Indian, and he's smarter than most. Right off, he argued about the buffalo calf Bennett had shot, but that didn't seem to be his point."

"What was his point, Jim?"

Gary shook his head. "I don't know, sir. I'd have to guess."

"I'll listen to it."

He squirmed in his chair, trying to ease his sore leg. "Well, sir, he wanted cartridges. Now most of the Indians know our carbines are Forty-Five-Seventy and our ammunition won't fit their repeaters. Some years back, when troopers were getting killed right and left, carbines were picked up, and Army ammunition had a value. But not any more. The whole thing appeared to be just another jangle, sir. Kind of like he was testing his strength." He shook his head again. "General, there were thirty Indians in his band, and he could have wiped us out, but somehow he didn't seem sure of that."

Cameron slapped his hands together, and paced up and down the office. "By golly, are they losing their knack for war? It can happen, you know. Happen fast. Do you see what we have gained by not locking horns with them? By not testing our strengths all the time? Could it be that White Horse doubted his ability for a moment?" He chuckled. "Then you faced him down, boy. Faced him down without firing a shot. If he had doubts before . . . just one small one . . . he now has a bigger one, driven in a little deeper, a little firmer. That's good. Very good."

"Yes, sir, but he wasn't just wandering around the prairie, sir."

"No, of course not. Were they traveling light?"

"Yes, sir."

"Well, then it means he's joined Quanah and was working out of his camp." He stroked his chin. "That could mean there's trouble brewing somewhere. It would be a hell of a time to have anything happen, with the congressmen here. Well, we've got a bill of goods to sell. I've got capable officers on patrol who'll keep an eye out on things."

Gary got up, and Cameron put his arm around the young man's shoulders. "I hesitate to bring up the social activity you're in for. Bathe and shave and get into your parade best. You're to squire the congressman's niece at the dinner and ball tonight."

"Thank you, sir."

Cameron laughed. "Thank you, hell. Now get out of here. I've got some damned calls to make. You can't keep a politician waiting . . . they won't stand for it."

He held back until Gary left the office, and then walked over to Quarters A. He knew Edith would be taking care of the visitors. The servants would be attentive to their comfort, and he'd given them enough time now to wash off the dust and put on their happy faces, whether they felt like it or not.

Cameron's wife was in the hallway, giving one of the servants an order. She turned to him and kissed him briefly and said: "My, this is a busy place. I've got the three gentlemen upstairs in the guest rooms, and the ladies in the back. Oh, I hope it's all right. This is so important for you."

"Don't give it a worry, old girl. Pour me a drink. I've got a full schedule and need something to help me stand up to it."

He went into the parlor with her, and she handed him a glass as he sank in his easy chair. "I haven't received a dispatch from Sherman since he left. I suppose he's at Fort Union now, making plans of his own with Miles and Mackenzie."

"You rather deserted him, Tracy."

He laughed and tossed off his drink. "Sherman knows me too well to expect me to play nursemaid to him. He did what he came here to do, so there wasn't any use of playing poker with him and taking him bird shooting." He put the glass aside and closed his eyes. "Have you any olive oil left? I'm going to pour a lot of whiskey in me between now and midnight, and I need something to keep my stomach from being eaten up."

"Mister Gary never brought the bottle back from your office," she said as she sat on the arm of his chair. Idly she stroked his hair. "Missus Bennett is wishing she hadn't come along . . . I can tell. We want to make her stay pleasant, Tracy. After all, a wife can argue with her husband, when someone else can't."

"I'm well aware of that," he said. He turned his head,

when a man's step sounded on the stairs. Wilson Chaffee came into the room, a broad smile on his face. Cameron got up.

"General, it's pleasant to see you again so soon." He glanced at the whiskey decanter and raised an eyebrow. "Could you sneak me a shot of that? Thank you, Missus Cameron." He raised his glass in a toast. "Here's to what I consider a most informative trip. A bit close out there on the prairie, but, once we saw how that young fellow, Gary, was going to handle himself, we all felt secure." He took Cameron's arm. "I'd like to give you a report of that, sir, before Bennett does. He colors everything quite emotionally."

"Mister Gary gave me his report yesterday."

Chaffee frowned. "What? You're joking? He was on the prairie yesterday." He looked at Edith as though he expected to find a clue in her expression. When he didn't, he looked at Tracy Cameron. "How the devil did he do it?"

"Heliograph."

"I saw no heliograph," Chaffee said.

"We have outposts on the prairie," Cameron said. "All the positions are underground. Gary simply knew where they were, came near one, left the column for a half hour or so, and sent his message. Mister Chaffee, we've been baffling more than a few with this method of communication."

"Bennett's going to pop a button. He's been dying to tell you the details, sir. He likes to bear news, if you know what I mean." He finished his drink and handed the glass back. "Did Gary include in his report that part about disarming Bennett by throwing him over his shoulder?" Chaffee laughed. "I know it isn't funny, and Bennett certainly didn't think it was. I know he won't tell it, but it's too good to keep."

"Mister Gary said in his report that he had to physically

124

disarm the congressman," Cameron said. "I had no idea the incident contained humorous overtones."

Wilson Chaffee laughed. "There's an honest young man for you, telling on himself. You should have seen the look on Bennett's face, when he hit the ground." He stopped talking as the sound of footsteps came from the stairway. Albert Bennett and Eastland came into the parlor.

"Don't let me interrupt your conversation, gentlemen," Eastland said.

"We were talking about Albert," Chaffee said. "Gentlemen, I'd like you to meet General Cameron and his wife."

There was a flurry of handshaking and bowing. Bennett said: "Talk about me all you want, Wilson. Good or bad, I don't care, as long as you mention my name." He laughed heartily. "Learned that from my wife's father. He was active in public life." His glance touched Tracy Cameron. "I expect you've heard of him . . . Governor Todd. Spelled with two d's."

"That's pretty impressive in itself," Cameron said dryly.

"What is?"

"Two d's," Cameron said. "Considering one was enough for God."

Bennett stared at him, and both Chaffee and Eastland roared with laughter. Eastland slapped Bennett on the back, and said: "Be glad you don't have him on the floor of Congress, Albert."

"May I pour you a drink?" Cameron asked.

They nodded and sat down. When they had their glasses in hand, Chaffee proposed a toast. "To the last shot fired in anger."

They drank to it, but Bennett was the first to put his glass aside, and Cameron knew that he had a contrary opinion to express.

"General, I don't mind telling you that was a harrowing experience out there on the prairie. With your permission, I'd like to write up an account of it for the papers."

"It will have some publicity value," Eastland said dryly.

"Well, why not?" Bennett snapped. "It happened, and that's all there is about it." He shook his finger at Cameron. "Now, it's a fact that, but for the courage of one man, Lieutenant Gary, we might all be dead and scalped at this very moment."

"Oh, come now, Bennett," Chaffee said. "Let's not overdramatize it. They wanted ammunition and the wagons. I doubt that they would have taken your life."

"Let him tell it his own way," Eastland said. "It makes a better story."

"Good story or not," Bennett said, "I got a close look at Indians, and I'm not overly impressed with their peaceful intentions. General, a campaign for peace is expensive. The Indians will have to be placed on reservations, agencies established, payrolls met, schools set up. It all costs money, and I for one do not intend to throw away a penny of the government's money on a lost cause."

Chaffee said: "You wouldn't be the first who had, Albert, and got himself reëlected on it, too."

"Senator, you're very funny," Bennett said matter-of-factly. "General, I can assure you that I'm going to look the situation over most carefully. Chaffee here has painted a rosy picture, but it may that he has his colors mixed."

"Now, I didn't put it that way," Chaffee insisted. "I said that we have two alternatives on the frontier, and that it was better to spend money in an attempt to achieve peace than to make war."

"To quote a little history," Bennett said, "the Carthaginians were completely destroyed at one time, and since then they haven't given anyone any trouble."

"Do you want the papers to print that statement?" Eastland asked.

"Hell, no!" Bennett snapped. "This is a private conversation." He placed his hands on the arms of his chair and pushed himself erect. "I think I'll look in on my wife and niece. If you'll excuse me, gentlemen . . . Missus Cameron."

They waited until he went out before speaking, then Chaffee said: "Albert's not an easy man to do business with, General. He'll take some convincing. The incident on the prairie was unfortunate in a way, yet it contained some hidden blessings. Mister Gary's action was singular enough, and I'm not trying to detract from the man's gallantry, but, after considering the whole thing objectively, I've come to the conclusion that the Indians did not really mean us great harm. Physically, Mister Gary held them back, but they were restrained in addition by some other force." He looked at Eastland. "Do you agree?"

"I believe I do," Eastland said. "I think you've summed it up nicely, Wilson. If Gary had not stopped the Indians, we'd have been roughed up, I'm sure, but not killed."

"Mister Gary and I came to that precise conclusion when he returned to the post," Cameron said. "Gentlemen, we've been conducting a campaign of non-reprisal. When an Indian steals a horse, we go and get the horse back. He isn't punished or cursed or accused. We say nothing, just enter their village, and recover the animal. No debate, no question of right and wrong, no force of arms. When we first began this a few years ago, we all knew some genuinely trying moments. Until you've taken a patrol into a hostile village to recover some property or other, you can hardly realize the sinking feeling in the stomach. They didn't understand why we didn't come in shooting. I don't think they will ever under-

127

stand the Christian concept of turning the other cheek. But it cast a doubt into their thinking. It's strong enough to make them wonder whether firing the first shot would be wise. Those are the seeds of peace. Now we've got a cultivating job to do."

"Chaffee believes they're ready," Eastland said. "Do you think so, General? We're well advised on general conditions in this area. Parker, the Comanche leader, is a thorn in the side. He's never made any indication that he wants to take the white man's road."

"We'll lead him," Cameron said.

"Can you do that, General?" Eastland asked.

"I know I have to try," Tracy Cameron said. "I think we all must try." He took out his watch and glanced at it. "Gentlemen, if you'll excuse me, I have some official duties to take care of before the dinner this evening."

They shook hands, and Cameron left them and walked rapidly across the parade. The low sun was making long shadows, and the heat of the day lay still and dense over the land. He couldn't help but wonder how many votes in the committee Chaffee had in his hand. Two? Possibly three? Certainly Bennett and Eastland had a few, or they wouldn't be out here, looking around. Nine men to decide the issue. Chaffee was one, and, for safety's sake, Cameron assumed that he controlled two more. Eastland was a big man, an old-time party politician, so Cameron gave him three, with a possibility of four. That was enough right there to block any move Chaffee made.

But he felt that Eastland was on his side, so far, at least. Bennett was the one he'd have to win over, convince so thoroughly that not even Sherman or Miles could upset his plans. Bennett was the smoking-room bull, all right. He was a hard-fisted, old-line ward man who believed a blow below the belt felled a man as quickly as one to the chin, and you didn't have to reach so far to deliver it. From the man's manner, Cameron knew he liked to run things, and he made a mental note to pay special attention to Bennett.

Promptly at six, Lieutenant Gary called at Quarters A for Elizabeth Rishel, and she made him wait thirty-one minutes, which irritated him to no end. He sat in uncomfortable silence in a straight-backed chair, and several times Mrs. Cameron passed in and out of the parlor. She smiled at him each time, and finally stopped and said: "Mister Gary, when they feel sure of you, they no longer do this to a man."

He laughed, and she left him. A few minutes later, Elizabeth Rishel came flouncing down the stairs in a gown whose splendor would certainly dazzle every man on the post and make every woman hate her on sight. She gave Gary her hand and said: "I hope I haven't kept you waiting."

"You have," Gary said pleasantly. "But I understand that it's part of the male rôle, until you feel sure of me."

She was taken aback by this directness, then she laughed. "Some woman has been talking to you . . . a man would never figure that out for himself. Shall we go?"

"Yes. We'll have to walk the long way around, where there are walks, or you'll get your gown dusty. I had Sergeant Gail lay down planks, so we could cross to the officers' mess."

"Why, Mister Gary! That was very thoughtful."

"I have a few good points," he said, smiling. "Thoughtful, kind, thrifty, punctual. . . ."

"Now, let's not start that," she said, and took his arm.

They walked along the row, and at the end he made her go ahead of him across the planks. He held her by the waist in case she started to lose her balance. She laughed, when they reached the walk on the other side. Then they turned into the mess building.

Gary sat at the head table during the dinner. He listened to some jokes told by Bennett and Chaffee, and afterward he made sure that Elizabeth was properly introduced to everyone. It was a trying chore, boring and a bit exhausting, for, if he slighted anyone, even by accident, he'd hear about it later. Gary realized that, as the general's aide, he needed to be in the good graces of all the officers. He was particularly careful in his dealings with them.

I'm sort of a politician myself, he thought, and started to look around for an escort for Elizabeth. It was getting toward nine o'clock, and he had a scheduled meeting with General Cameron. At ten, Cameron was meeting with Chaffee and the others, which gave Gary about half an hour with the general and half an hour to get Elizabeth back to Quarters A.

Rather like running a railroad, he thought, and collared Lieutenant Fry, a tall, red-headed man with a slow way of speaking and a pleasant smile. He did not have to talk very hard to get Fry to take Elizabeth's arm, and Gary excused himself and ducked out, right on schedule.

Hardly had he reached Cameron's office, when he saw the general crossing the parade. Cameron came in, closed the door, and said: "I saw that maneuver, Jim. You're getting clever." He waved Gary into a chair. "I asked you to come here because there likely will not be time after the meeting to talk, and there are some things that should be settled."

He went around his desk and sat down, "Bennett's talk disturbs me. He's not at all convinced that the Indians want peace, or would welcome the suggestion of it. I've got to get my foot in the door with Quanah Parker. I know that, if I can sit down and negotiate with him, I can reach terms."

"Suggest that, sir, and he'll want to handle the parley himself."

Cameron laughed. "He'd like to dictate terms, all right. But we can't have that. I've got to kill two birds with one shot here, so I'm going to send you out with a twenty-man detail to escort our visitors on a tour south for some bird shooting while I make a broad sweep with a company to see what Parker is up to."

He pulled around a sheet of paper and made a few notes. "I would say that two ambulances and a supply wagon would carry guests and enough provisions for their comfort to last a week. You might aim the detail so as to spend a day or so near Gray Beard's village. He's probably the most peaceful, lazy Indian in Texas, and from his camp the guests might get a glimpse of contented, aboriginal life." He smiled. "Of course, you'd be a fool to let on that Gray Beard has been a tame Indian for many years. Let them think that here is a savage tribe, being weaned of their blood-letting ways."

"I understand, sir."

"I knew you would," Cameron said. "And I'll try to locate the Kiowa-Cheyenne camp, although I suspect it's damned close to Parker's, and disband them with peaceful means, if possible. Now, Mister Gary, I want your little field trip to be disguised as a patrol to investigate Indian tempers. Perhaps if you somehow created, by posting point and outriders, a sense of imminent danger, Bennett might more readily accept the elements of peace you'll find. And, incidentally, take along a keg of cigars for Gray Beard, and some sacks of salt . . . it won't hurt to come bearing gifts, since it worked successfully for the Greeks."

"Yes, sir," Gary said. "Kind of sneaky, though, isn't it?"

"Probably, but it's always cheaper to repaint the old barn than to build a new one. You might go as far south as the river

131

but don't let them talk you into crossing it. There are some quicksand bogs there, and I don't want to run the risk of trouble."

"Shall I select the detail, General?"

"I'll have Byrd do it," Cameron said. He frowned a moment, then added: "Jim, I don't want to sound as if I'm loading you unduly, but I want you to take Mister Beamish along." Gary opened his mouth as though to protest, but Cameron waved his hand. "Now, I know you have a complaint there, but I have my reasons. Beamish is making an ass of himself . . . to be blunt about it. Of course, Byrd rode him quite hard, and Beamish is angry about it. He's blamed it on you, Jim, and the damn' fool never knows when to keep his mouth shut."

"Blamed me! For what?"

"Does there have to be anything?" Cameron looked steadily at Gary. "I want him to accompany you and, while you're out there, settle this for good. Now that's a direct order. I don't care how you do it, but it must be done. If you find no solution, I'll have to transfer Beamish, and it'll be on his record." He stood up and came around to sit on the corner of his desk. "You've got ten or fifteen minutes. Why don't you go and have a talk with the man before you take Elizabeth Rishel home?"

"What the devil will I say?"

Cameron shrugged. "Jim, within most men there is an area of compromise. You can establish some terms of association with the man that will put an end to this nonsense."

"All right, sir, I'll try." He saluted, feeling a little put out that the burden of this rested so squarely on him. Then he reasoned that he'd started it, and it made sense to finish it, if he could.

When he returned to the festivities, Gary relieved Lieutenant Fry of Elizabeth Rishel's company and took her to the punch bowl. She said: "I wouldn't like to think that I was deserted for anything but official business."

"Strictly that," Gary said. "Each moment away was an hour."

"Now you're lying," Elizabeth said. "Be honest with me, Jim. So few men are. You didn't think of me once, did you?"

"No," he said, and sipped his punch. "Seems like there's some rye whiskey amid these varied fruit juices." He smacked his lips. "The sutler's brand, I think. From the brown bottles."

"Are there other kinds?"

"Clear bottles and brown bottles," Gary said. "The brown bottles are sold to the enlisted men for a dollar. The clear bottles cost a dollar seventy-five. You pay for the privilege of seeing what's in them." He drained his glass and set it aside. "At the dance, I'm going to have to excuse myself. The general has a meeting scheduled, and as his aide I'm expected to. . . ."

"You won't be missed," she said lightly.

"Now you've hurt my feelings," he said.

She regarded him seriously. "Jim, I couldn't hurt your feelings, because you don't care a whit about me. And that bothers me."

"I like you," he assured her.

"Yes, I know, but I'd be more flattered if you were a little in love with me."

He shook his head. "You're too spoiled, and I haven't the time to straighten you out."

This aggravated her so much that she almost stamped her foot, and he laughed softly. Then a smile broke the severity of her expression, and she said: "Jim Gary, I hate you."

"Hate and love, they say, go. . . ."

"Oh, no, you don't. You're not going to get me to cry when I leave here." She laughed and patted his arm absently, putting him in his place.

Chapter Nine

This was the fourth day on patrol for A Company, Captain Paul Einsman commanding, and he had swung south, making a big circle of it, until they reached the buffalo hunters' new camp. Had Einsman been given a choice, he would have stayed clear of the buffalo hunters, but it was his duty to observe closely their activity, so he made a night camp within easy walking distance of theirs.

The hunters were building another trading post, but they hadn't made much progress on it — the wall was barely three feet high in spots. Einsman could see at a glance that it wasn't squared up properly. Any dirt farmer would have had the walls up by now, but the native laziness of the hunters slowed them to a crawl. They liked to hunt and drink and run down Indian women and fight, but they simply were not builders.

Graves, who bossed the hunters, came over to Paul Einsman's camp after the evening meal. He sat down by the captain's fire and took out a pipe. After he filled it and got it going, Graves said: "How far south do we have to go before we lose the Army?"

"The Gulf of Mexico," Einsman said dryly. "But then you'd have to contend with the Navy." He looked at Graves. "You're going to go broke here. Can't you see that?"

"The buffaloes will come back," Graves said. "There's a big herd in the south."

"The buffaloes are gone," Einsman said. "It's only fools like yourself and the Indians who won't admit it. So why build here and stir up the Comanches? Take what profit you have and quit the game."

"I haven't any money," Graves said. "You know how it goes after a month or two in a town."

A hunter came into the soldiers' camp then and approached Einsman's fire. He said: "I've got to talk to you, Graves."

"Talk then," Graves invited.

The hunter glanced at Einsman, then said: "Maybe it don't mean anything, but there's a heap of Indians out there."

"Out where?" Einsman asked.

"To the northeast and the northwest," the man said. "Maybe two miles. A couple of the men took a scout, and they both spotted the camps."

Graves's expression was serious. "Get all the men inside the wall. Split them into three shifts, a third on guard at a time." His glance touched Einsman's. "Now, here's your chance to earn your pay."

"My pay isn't enough for you to bother with," Einsman said and stood up. He snapped his fingers and brought a sergeant over on the double. "Sergeant, inform the two section officers that we're moving into the shelter of the walls. Graves, I'll take charge of your men and post them as I see fit."

"Like hell you will!"

"You're in my camp," Einsman said quietly. "A whistle would make you a prisoner. Now . . . is it on my terms . . . obeying my orders?"

Graves thought about it, but he didn't take too long. "All right," he said. "You're the boss."

"Good. I don't believe the Indians will move until dawn, if they move at all. However, we'll move our mounts within the shelter of the wall you've built. How deep is your floor?"

"About three feet below ground level."

"Well, that's enough protection," Einsman said. "Your men can sleep, Graves. We'll stand our own guard."

"I won't object to that," Graves said. "Come on, Jake, let's get back to camp."

As soon as he left, Einsman began to move his company to the shelter of the wall. The buffalo hunters did not like this intrusion, and the way they were crowded back. But Einsman was a firm man with a no-nonsense way of doing a thing, and he got the job done. Within an hour the guards were posted.

While waiting for his section officers to arrive, Einsman gave his problem some serious thought. He didn't dare to assume that the Indians were gathered for any other reason than to make war against the hunters, and his sympathy was with the Indians not the hunters. This was what Cameron had always feared, that the Indians would weary of an undecided program and start a fight. Peace or war — they had to have one or the other.

Lieutenants Butler and Skinner arrived, and Einsman spoke to them softly. "We may have to break the old man's record in the morning, lads."

"It's a damned shame," Butler said.

"The hunters could be lying," Skinner offered.

Einsman shook his head. "Graves knows me better than to think he could play a joke on me. The soldiers have been itching for a fight with the buffalo hunters for a long time, and all I'd have to do would be to give the word, and there'd be the damnedest free-for-all you ever saw in your life." He stopped talking and stood there, a faint surprise on his face. "What did I say?"

Butler volunteered to repeat it, but Skinner hushed him up. "What are you thinking of, sir?"

"I just thought of why the Indians are out there in the first place."

"Because they want to run the hunters out," Butler said.

Skinner said: "Luke, if you don't shut up, you'll never make first lieutenant." He gave his attention to Einsman. "You have a new idea, sir?"

"One that I think may get us into some trouble," he said. "However, I'll make two copies of a statement exonerating you of all responsibility . . . there's no sense in ruining two promising careers. Gentlemen, I can only see two choices here. We either defend ourselves at dawn, kill some Indians, and shoot down General Cameron's hopes for a full peace. That'll not only be bad for the general, but for the Indians and for the settlers who haven't even come here yet. On the other hand, we might remove the sore . . . lance the boil, so to speak . . . and run the hunters out. We'll have to do it on a trumped-up charge . . . something like infringing on Indian grazing rights or some idiotic thing. Of course, it won't hold water, and I'll be court-martialed for removing them bodily, but it'll clear the air, stop the fight, and give the general some time."

"The hunters will put up one hell of a fight, sir," Skinner said.

"Yes, and we'll have to take them by complete surprise. We outnumber them to some extent, and we'll wait until around one o'clock in the morning before making a move. It'll have to be quick and decisive, because before dawn I want to be on the march with the lot of them bound hand and foot. And we'll march them right through the Indian camps to let them see for themselves that the hunters are leaving."

"God," Butler said softly. "This is going to make a stink, sir."

"To high heaven, I'm afraid," Einsman admitted. He

138

sighed. "Well, we'd better work out the details. Butler, we'll take your section first. Tell your sergeant what we're up to, and have him pick the men to make the assault. We'll hold what few remain in reserve. The hunters will use knives or anything they can get their hands on, so we can't be gentle about this. Carbines and pistol butts will be the order of the day on any man displaying a weapon." He gave them each a slap on the shoulder, and they went back to their sections.

Then Captain Einsman sat down and wrote out two orders for Butler and Skinner, and he hoped they wouldn't lose them, for it would clear them at their courts-martial.

There were no fires that night, and for this Einsman was grateful. As the time drew near, he consulted his watch often, lighting matches so he could read the hands. At the appointed time, Butler and Skinner appeared and reported that the guards had quietly been called in. All was ready.

Each man knew his position, and, at Einsman's signal, all began to move silently about until each was standing by a sleeping hunter. Carefully, rifles and pistols and knives were picked up and passed along, hand to hand, like a bucket brigade, and placed under a four-man guard. The largest share of weapons was gathered this way, but Einsman knew that they hadn't gotten them all.

He gave the signal by lighting a match, and instantly the camp was turned into bedlam. The hunters, pounced upon in their sleep, fought desperately, and Einsman supposed they thought that the Indians had somehow infiltrated into the camp.

With the element of surprise the soldiers were at an advantage, and they had their own ambitious licks to get in, which made the treatment rough for the hunters. Fists were used with belts wrapped about them, and pistol barrels raised lumps, but the struggle began to die down, although not without some damage to the troops. Three troopers were hurt, for not all the knives had been taken. Einsman ordered the lanterns lighted. One trooper had a deep gash on his side, and another had been stabbed in the thigh, while the third had lost a finger after grabbing the blade in desperation.

But the hunters were all military prisoners. The horses were gathered and ropes brought out, and they were loaded, some face-down, and tied that way. Skinner got the company to order and mounted, and they moved out, with the prisoners on lead ropes, and bunched together, surrounded by the Army.

As soon as they were moving in column, Einsman rode back a bit and sided Graves, who rode with his head tipped forward, bound hand and foot. For a moment Graves didn't realize that Einsman was beside him. Then he turned his head without raising it and said: "I'm going to kill you for this, Captain."

"I hate to say this, but it's for your own good."

Graves laughed and raised his head, and even in the dark of night Einsman could see the smear of dried blood around his nose and mouth — someone had hit him hard. "When we get through talking, Captain, they'll take you out and shoot you."

"Likely they'll just kick me out of the Army."

"Then I'll be waiting to shoot you," Graves said, and he added: "All my supplies . . . the Indians will take 'em."

"Yes, they probably will," Einsman said.

"You're not worried, and you should be."

"I keep it all inside me," Einsman said, and started forward.

"Wait!"

Einsman eased back.

140

Graves was looking at the stars. "We're going toward the Indian camps!"

"I believe we are, at that," Einsman said, and returned to take his place at the head of his company.

Well, he'd kept up a good front for Graves's benefit. Perhaps it would worry him enough to calm him a little. Still, Einsman didn't hold out much hope for himself. Seventeen years in the service and he had a wife and three children at the post. He'd taken all that and just thrown it away. But a soldier did that sometimes. It was part of being a soldier — to be expendable, to die in battle and have someone take your place, or to surrender to a cause and know that, even though you are through, the system will go on, and you'd made it a little better by what you'd done.

The dawn would come early, and he gauged his rate of march to meet it. It had been after two by the time they cleared the hunters' camp, and they were moving very slowly, so he calculated that they would reach the Indians' positions as the sky turned gray. The Indians wouldn't be sleeping, either, not if they were planning an attack.

He wondered what their reaction would be. Surprise, surely, and anger, too, for he was cheating them out of some blood-letting, a favorite Indian pastime. He considered the fact that they might become so riled that they would try and take the hunters from his custody. That would be a fine affair, getting war from both sides. This was a strong possibility, for the Indians had been doing some dancing and working themselves up to a frenzy. They always did that before they made war.

Well, it was just something else he'd have to put up with when the time came. Positioning in his mind as best he could the two Indian camps, he tried to steer a course that would let him pass between them, within sight of both and just out of

141

reach of either. He'd better maintain a brisk rate of march, to keep the closure distance from becoming dangerous. It would also show that he had his business to go about and that he wasn't going to be fooled with. The Indians were easily impressed with boldness and decisiveness.

Still, there'd have to be some parley, to let them know that the Army was still running things and would handle their troubles. He'd have to do this talking himself, simply because he didn't want to trust anyone else with it, or waste anyone else in case it turned out badly.

He called Lieutenant Skinner forward and told him how it was going to be. Skinner would take command as soon as Einsman cleared the column, and there'd be no argument about it.

After Skinner returned to his section, Einsman thought about his wife and family. This wouldn't be easy for them — all the publicity — and there'd be plenty of that, all of it bad.

In time, the sky began to turn gray, and, with visibility increasing, Einsman saw that his direction had not been as exact as he would have wished. He was within rifle range of one camp, or would be as the column passed it. But he couldn't wait — the Indians had seen him. He turned in the saddle, motioned for Skinner to come forward, then spurred his horse, and rode toward the knot of mounted warriors waiting on the prairie.

Chapter Ten

Jim Gary put up a camp half a mile from the village of Gray Beard, and he took care to occupy a position to windward, but, even so, the area was reminiscent of the Chicago stockyards. Albert Bennett was all eagerness to go in and look the Indians over, but Gary tactfully restrained him. Proper conduct around Indians was always a touchy thing, almost as touchy as it was with congressmen, and Gary didn't want bruised feelings on either side.

It was Gary's intention to brief Bennett, Chaffee, and Eastland on certain rules of procedure before going into the village, but this had to be postponed, when the supply wagons arrived from Tascosa in the company of the sheriff. Gray Beard and his followers were not strictly reservation Indians, for this wasn't reservation land, and there was no agent in charge. But Gray Beard had made his deal with Cameron. No more trouble as long as the groceries came in regularly. So Cameron paid the bill, and once a month Ray Kline drove out from Tascosa with flour and salt and sowbelly.

Gary didn't think it was wise to explain this to the politicians, since Cameron's appropriations were to be spent on military matters, not to help feed sixty-odd Indians. He was sure that Chaffee would understand the true purpose of this expenditure — that it was always cheaper to feed the enemy than to fight him.

Ray Kline and Sheriff McCabe wasted no time in paying a call to Gary's camp. They saw the tents and knew this was no ordinary patrol. Gary was expecting this and walked forward to meet the two men on the fringe of the camp.

McCabe smiled, and said: "What you got there, sonny, a tent show?"

"I suspect you gents came over to say hello," said Gary. "Well, I'll consider it's been said, so I'll say good day."

"That's unfriendly as hell," Ray Kline said. He was a slender man, rather small, with a thin face and a pointed chin. Years of bargaining had formed a hard, demanding tone in his voice, and he had a merchant's natural sense of the direction in which the profit lay. Kline didn't particularly like the Army, Gary knew, because he'd never been able to pad his bills for more than freighting costs. He did business with the Army because he needed the trade, but it wasn't "make money fast" trade.

"Ain't you going to ask us to share supper with you?" McCabe asked. "Lieutenant, I treat the soldiers pretty good, when they come to Tascosa. I could slap 'em around a little when they get drunk, but I don't. I just put 'em in jail until they sober up." He placed his hands on the saddle horn and smiled at Gary. "Now, if you think that's a threat, you'd be right. Scrub my back, and I'll scrub yours. Ain't that a good way to be?" He nodded toward the tents. "I hear you have some politicians on the grand tour. Now, I've a few ambitions myself. Suppose you introduce us."

"Gentlemen, I wouldn't press my company on this party, if I were you," Gary said.

"What you got to hide?" Kline asked.

"I'm not going to debate it," Gary said. He heard someone approach from behind and knew who it was before he turned his head to look.

Albert Bennett smiled and said: "Callers, Mister Gary? I'm Congressman Bennett, Sheriff. I didn't catch your name."

Join the Western Book Club
and GET 4 FREE* BOOKS NOW!
A $19.96 VALUE!

—Yes! I want to subscribe — to the Western Book Club.

Please send me my **4 FREE* BOOKS**. I have enclosed $2.00 for shipping/handling. Each month I'll receive the four newest Leisure Western selections to preview for 10 days. If I decide to keep them, I will pay the Special Members Only discounted price of just $3.36 each, a total of $13.44, plus $2.00 shipping/handling ($19.50 US in Canada). This is a **SAVINGS OF AT LEAST $6.00** off the bookstore price. There is no minimum number of books I must buy, and I may cancel the program at any time. In any case, the **4 FREE* BOOKS** are mine to keep.

*In Canada, add $5.00 shipping/handling per order for the first shipment. For all future shipments to Canada, the cost of membership is $16.25 US, which includes shipping and handling. (All payments must be made in US dollars.)

NAME: _____

ADDRESS: _____

CITY: _____ **STATE:** _____

COUNTRY: _____ **ZIP:** _____

TELEPHONE: _____

E-MAIL: _____

SIGNATURE: _____

If under 18, Parent or Guardian must sign. Terms, prices, and conditions subject to change. Subscription subject to acceptance. Dorchester Publishing reserves the right to reject any order or cancel any subscription.

"McCabe. This is Mister Kline, a merchant from Tascosa."

"My pleasure," Bennett said, and shook hands. "Mister Gary, why haven't you invited them in?"

"They haven't time, sir."

"Well, now, we'll take a little time," Kline said. "Ain't that so, Guthrie?"

"Right," McCabe said. He dismounted and handed the reins to Gary, grinning as he did it. Then he took Albert Bennett by the arm and walked over toward the tents. "Born and raised in this country, Congressman. I know every buffalo wallow, every clump of grass for miles around. You want to know anything, you just ask me."

"I'm sure we'll have some questions," Bennett said. "I also want you to meet my associates." He took McCabe to meet Chaffee and Eastland. Gary observed this, then took the two horses to the picket line.

Sergeant Murphy was there and he said: "You need McCabe, sir, like you need a rattlesnake in your blankets. He's got a big mouth and an opinion on everything."

"I'd better get back," Gary said, and shook his head.

When he returned to the tents, McCabe was spinning a drawn-out tale of his exploits, and he had an appreciative audience. "And there we were, sir," McCabe was saying, "myself and a handful of others, and out there a whole passel of savages. For three days the fighting raged fierce, but we held. Licked 'em proper that time. But I guess I've bored you with the details."

"Not at all," Bennett said quickly. "Of course, we're familiar with newspaper accounts of battles with the Indians, but we would never get the flavor of it without a first-hand telling. Right, Chaffee?"

"Definitely," Chaffee said, and moved over to stand near

145

Jim Gary. He glanced at Gary, but did not speak.

Gary said: "McCabe, I think your mare's about to throw a shoe. If you want to take a look at it, I'll have the sergeant fix it."

"Well, all right," McCabe said. "Excuse me, gents." He walked away with Jim Gary.

"You tell them a few more windies like that, and they'll put you down as the biggest liar this side of the Canadian," Gary said. He was far enough away from the others so as not to be heard, and now he stood still. "There's nothing wrong with your horse, Sheriff. I just wanted to say something."

"Make it nicer than that last remark you made," McCabe advised. "Things like that rile the hell out of me."

"You're going to boil then," Gary told him. "McCabe, I've got a job to do, a bill of goods to sell, and I don't want anything to come up to ruin the sale. Now, you tell them all the lies you want, but we're going to come to an understanding."

"Such as?"

"Such as the fact that you weren't in any battles with Indians. And you're about as big a hero as I am. But you can have your fun, if I get what I want."

McCabe glared at him. "What do you want?"

"I want to hear you tell about how friendly all the Indians are around here. And if you even hint that Parker's cooking up trouble with his Comanches, I'll damn you for a liar. McCabe, I'm beginning to understand you. You want to be a big man, and it would break you to have anyone even suggest that you're not a big man. So it wouldn't make any difference who proved his point, would it?"

For a minute Guthrie McCabe stood there, slapping his leg. He then pointed at Gary and opened his mouth to speak, but he changed his mind and let that withheld word go.

146

"You've got all the instincts of a horse thief," McCabe said.

"But there'll be no bargaining here," Gary pointed out. "You do it my way, or you'll make your excuses now to everybody and light out."

"Or you'll make a fuss?"

"You know it."

McCabe nodded, then grinned. "Well, I've got a story about cattle rustlers that makes interesting listening. There's a chase in it, clear to Mexico."

"Where you capture them all single-handed?"

"Hell, yes," McCabe said. "What's a lie, if it ain't a good one?" He reached out and gave the beak of Gary's kepi a tug. "You're pretty good at this lyin' business yourself, if you convince those politicians the Indians out here want to plant corn and pay their taxes."

"You've fought Indians," Gary said. "Do you want to do it again?"

"Not particularly," McCabe admitted. "Well, it's a dull subject, and they're waiting for me to come back and tell 'em all about my glamorous life. Gary, always tell people what they want to hear. It saves a lot of time."

"You're one hell of a man for sheriff."

McCabe didn't argue the point. "It's better to have a little crook in office than a big one." Then he turned and walked back to the tents.

Jim Gary had duties that occupied him until supper, and, when he came to get his meal, he found he was late — they were all having coffee. McCabe was spinning a good yarn, for Gary saw how enthralled they appeared. He could understand it well enough, for McCabe was a big, handsome man, and he wore a pearl-handled pistol in a way that suggested that it could fairly jump out of the holster to defend a woman's precious name. *Put him in a cutaway suit,* Gary thought, *and he could run for Congress.*

Bennett and the others were huddled together, and he waved Gary over. "Sit down, my boy. Pull up that stool. Sheriff McCabe has been relating to us General Cameron's exploits in taming the Indians."

"I'll bet that was exciting, sir," Gary said ironically, and then thought that maybe he was going a bit too far.

Chaffee smiled, but the barb did not penetrate Bennett's hide, who said: "Not exciting at all, but methodical. Very methodical. I'm, indeed, impressed by it. Naturally, I'd read reports and heard him speak, but I read a lot of reports and hear a lot of speeches. I have to put most of it down to boasting or hogwash."

"You can believe the sheriff," Gary said. "He has a reputation for honesty and factual reporting."

"I'd hardly go that far," Chaffee said. "But I know what good work Cameron has been doing here. Good heavens, Bennett, you've seen his theories in practice. When Gary and his detail turned those Indians away, he did it without firing a shot. Now, I ask you, how many officers would have done that?"

"That's a theoretical question," Eastland said. "I don't think it can be answered. Let's assume you're right, Wilson. What are we really buying here?"

"A long-range program for the Indians," Chaffee said. "Surely we must have learned by this time that we can't merely negotiate a treaty and then let the Indians shift for themselves."

"There are reservations," Bennett said. "Last year I voted on the appropriation committee, and it was a substantial sum. Now they're in business at the agencies to handle Indians and their problems. When a tribe surrenders, it's logical to ship them to a reservation."

"People don't like to move from their homes," Chaffee said. "Albert, there's no reason a reservation can't be created in this very area, and after a peace treaty the Comanches can live as they've always lived, in Texas. When I return to Washington, I'm going to recommend approval of this program and request that the appropriation be set aside for a ten-year trial."

"How big an appropriation?" Bennett asked.

"A half million dollars," Chaffee said.

"That's a shocking amount," Eastland said. "How would you handle it? Through what agency?"

"We'll establish one," Chaffee said. "General Cameron would head it. Gentlemen, we'd teach the Indians to read and write, to work at white mens' jobs. In a few years they'd no longer need us. It's better to spend the money now than to support agencies year after year for God knows how long."

"That's a point," Eastland said. "Well, I'll reserve my opinion until tomorrow, when we go into the Indian village. If they look and act as bad as they smell, I'm afraid there isn't much hope. You do throw rotten apples out, Wilson. You don't make a pie with them."

"To adopt an Army policy of Indian extermination is unthinkable," Chaffee said.

"Throwing away money is also out of the question," Bennett said firmly. "But like Eastland says, I've still time to decide."

Jim Gary had remained clear of this conversation, for he could have added nothing of value, and he was glad to hear them discuss it, for it gave him an insight into their thinking and a gauge with which to measure the success or failure of his position.

When he finished eating, he took his tin plate to the cook.

Then he stood at the edge of the camp and looked toward Gray Beard's village. While he waited there, a small band of Kiowas approached from the north and rode into the Indian camp. They did not stay long, and he watched them ride away, thinking that this was a strange thing. He couldn't see that they came to beg provisions, for they seemed to carry off no more than they'd brought. And they hadn't stayed long enough to eat.

His curiosity was aroused, and he went to find Murphy. Within five minutes, ten men were saddled and ready to mount, and Gary swung away from the camp and struck out in the direction the Kiowas had taken. There was still an hour and a half of daylight left, and he could see their dust. They were not traveling fast, but they moved right along.

For a time the Indians were not aware that they were being followed, and, when they discovered the cavalry, Gary had closed the distance to a little less than a mile. The Kiowas began to step up their pace, forcing Gary to spur harder. This went on for ten minutes, then the Indians began to slow. He could not immediately understand why, until he and his men drew up to them and formed a ring around them.

Their ponies were lathered, for they had ridden hard to get to Gray Beard's village, and were not up to another long chase. A few of them carried rifles, mostly Evans .44-40 repeaters. Gary disarmed them before forcing them to dismount for personal search.

Murphy and three others handled this detail, and they found that each Indian had six boxes of .44-40 cartridges on his person. These were stacked on the ground, and Gary motioned for them to get on their horses and get going. He kept their rifles.

Forty-eight boxes of cartridges, he decided, with fifty to a box, made up a lot of shooting. "Murphy, pack that ammunition and mount your men," he said.

He sat his horse and thought about the coincidence. Ray Kline, making his delivery on schedule, and then those Kiowas showing up like that, as if they knew all about it. As far as he was concerned, there wasn't any possibility of the Kiowas carrying that much ammunition on them, with only a few rifles among them. And he'd seen those Evans rifles before, that day they were marching from Tascosa to the fort.

By the time Murphy had finished, Gary had made up his mind and was writing a message.

Commanding General
Fort Elliot
 Have seized two hundred and forty rounds of Forty-Four ammunition off small Kiowa band. Suspect Gray Beard is using village to distribute ammunition. Suspect Kline selling it. Will await your orders.

           Gary

He gave the note to Murphy. "There's a heliograph detachment about six miles east of here. Have this sent as quickly as possible and wait for a reply. We'll remain in camp."

"Yes, sir," Murphy said, and trotted away.

Gary then turned the detail back and made a slow ride of it. He thought about Guthrie McCabe and wondered if he was in on this with Ray Kline. McCabe had never made any bones about liking a dollar, and he wasn't as honest as a lawman should be. Gary knew, of course, that he couldn't just go into the Indian village and search it for ammunition. If the congressmen got wind of that, Chaffee's hopes would go out the window. *This will have to be done quietly,* he decided, and he began to plan how he would do it.

Chaffee and Bennett were waiting for him, when he returned. Bennett said: "You left in a hurry, Gary. Is there some trouble afoot?"

"No, we just wanted to talk to the Indians," Gary said. His glance touched Chaffee, and in it was a plea for understanding. "Tomorrow," he went on, "I'd like to take you on a conducted tour of the village, but I should make some form of preparation."

"Like what?" Bennett asked.

Gary smiled, then said: "Well, sir, they have some very interesting dances that I'm sure you'd find entertaining. And they're great wrestlers, sir."

Bennett laughed. "Going to amuse us, eh? All right, my boy. Do whatever you like."

"Thank you, sir. I'll go over tonight and see if I can get Gray Beard to co-operate. It'll take some time, so I may not be back until late. They like to talk and bargain." He made some mental calculation and added: "I think four guards here will be enough. Indians are always impressed with a certain amount of show, sir. That's why I want to take as many of the detail as possible."

"We'll leave it to your excellent judgment," Chaffee said.

They returned to their tents, and Gary stood there in the darkness, thinking that this had been easier than he had expected. Or perhaps he was getting so glib that he just carried these things off easily.

A movement in the shadows startled him, then Guthrie McCabe said: "You've got a good line of bull there. You almost make me wish I could stay and see the dancin'."

"Are you leaving?"

"Kline wants to get back," McCabe said. "He was in a hurry to get here, and now he's in a rush to get back. That's not my way . . . rushing all the time."

"Why did you come in the first place?" Gary asked. "It's not your job."

"He pays me for it," McCabe said. "Ten dollars each way. What's it to you?"

"Nothing in particular. McCabe, do you want to go over to the village with me?"

"There's nothing over there for me," McCabe said. "There's dung on the lodge floors, slop in the cook pot, and lice in the blankets. So you come away stinkin', sick, and scratching." He shook his head. "Thanks, no. I'll make a night ride of it, when it's cool."

"This won't take long," Gary pointed out. "You're not worried about anything, are you?"

"Why should I be?"

"When a man's reluctant, he has a reason."

"I told you my reason, so drop the subject," McCabe said. He gave Gary a light punch on the chest. "I'll see you in Tascosa."

When he turned to walk away, he exposed his right side, and, before McCabe knew what was happening, Gary snatched his .44 from the holster and cocked it. McCabe turned back and found it pointed at him.

"Now this is a joke . . . it's got to be. So you just put it back, and we'll forget it."

"No joke," Gary said. "We're going to the Indian village."

"Hmm," McCabe said. "All right, you play your game . . . but, when it's over, I'm going to teach you one."

Gary took him to the picket line where the troopers were camped. A wave of his hand brought Corporal Turner over, and Gary handed him the pistol. "Keep the sheriff quiet. Where's Mister Beamish?"

"Sleeping, sir."

Gary woke him, and Beamish sat up. "What's the matter? Oh, it's you, Jim."

"Leave the four on guard here," Gary said. "Assemble the others quietly. We're going over to Gray Beard's village, dismounted. Side arms only."

"That's a strange way to. . . ."

Gary's voice was hard. "Damn it, Beamish, I'm not going to debate the matter! Now get on with it, or I'll put you on report!"

"What a temper!" Beamish said, and put on his hat. He acted like a small boy who had been whipped for something he hadn't even known he'd done. Gary was a little sorry he'd snapped that way, but he'd felt it had been necessary. Beamish was a strange man. So far he'd done his job and stayed out of the way, but like a child he'd conduct himself properly for a while then think that it had earned him some special privilege.

Gary went back to the picket line. McCabe was still standing there with his own pistol pressed into the small of his back. He said: "If this hokey-pokey isn't real good, I'll bet I've got enough pull to get you cashiered to the manure pile."

"Yeah," Gary said. "And if it is as good as I think, you'll be on the rock pile."

"What rock pile?"

"At the state penitentiary," Gary said.

"Hey, that's not very funny at all," McCabe said.

One of the guards came up and said: "Sir, Mister Kline's eager to leave. He wants to know whether Mister McCabe is ready or not."

"Tell Kline that McCabe's staying over," Gary said.

The trooper walked away, and McCabe looked after him for a minute. Then he said: "Am I under arrest or something?"

154

"I don't know for sure yet," Gary admitted. "But I figure it this way . . . I'd rather have Kline on the loose than you."

"So what have I done? Just tell me that."

Gary hesitated, then called Corporal Turner over. "Corporal, fetch the goods we took off the Kiowas. A couple of boxes will do. And bring a lantern with you."

Presently the corporal came back, and Gary took the wooden ammunition boxes from him. He slid a lid open and dumped the cartridges on the ground. Guthrie McCabe stared at them.

"I don't get it," he said.

"Then I'll spell it out to you, McCabe. Those shells were taken off a band of Kiowas that had just paid Gray Beard a visit. I've got forty-six more boxes just like those. Kline delivers more than flour and salt, Sheriff. And I think you already know that."

"Why, I'll kill that son-of-a-bitch!" McCabe roared.

"Keep your voice down," Gary snapped. "You're going to have to convince me a little better than that."

"Convince you? How the hell can I?" He raised a hand and wiped his mouth. There was a genuine worry now in his eyes. "Oh, what a sucker I've been. And for twenty dollars a trip. Sure, he wanted me along. Who the hell would stop him with the county sheriff along?" He let his hand drop. "Gary, I can't prove he and I weren't working together, but you take that gun out of my back, and I'll tear his arm off and beat him to death with it."

"It's no good," Gary said. "We're going to the village. Maybe I'll know then who was in on what."

"I'll go, and no fuss," McCabe said sincerely.

"You keep your mouth shut. One peep out of you and Turner will bend that gun barrel over your skull. Have you got that, Turner?"

155

"Yes, sir, bend the gun barrel."

"Jesus, you don't trust anybody, do you?" McCabe asked.

"I don't trust big-mouthed Texas sheriffs," Gary assured him.

Beamish formed the detail, and they left the camp in a double-line formation, with Gary at the head and McCabe marching beside him, the pistol still covering him. He didn't say anything for a while, but he wasn't a man who could endure silence long.

"Gary, I'm innocent."

"We'll see," Gary said, and refused to say more.

Yapping dogs greeted Gary and his men as they neared the village, but they walked on in, for Gray Beard was accustomed to visitors, especially soldiers. The lodges were shabby. It had been two years since Gray Beard's followers had stirred from this spot. Now and then they moved a few lodges, when the dung piles got too high, but they no longer hunted buffalo. They only sat and waited for what the white man brought them, and often that was wasted. Tracy Cameron had once sent a dozen tents, and even showed them how to put them up. But a week later, the poles had been chopped into firewood and the canvas cut into robes and blankets.

The appearance of the soldiers created no particular excitement, and Gary stopped near the fire. A motion of his hand was a signal for the others to move around, to deploy themselves and wait for his order. Guthrie McCabe remained by Gary's side, the corporal standing back of him, still holding the pistol.

Gary said: "You can put it away now, Corporal. The sheriff's going to behave himself. Isn't that right, McCabe?"

"You'll get no trouble from me," McCabe said. "I just want out from under this mess."

Gray Beard came from his lodge, an old, half-naked man who couldn't have seen much worse days. He had a soiled blanket over one shoulder and wore moccasins with the seams split. He gave Gary's hand one pump, which was his way of passing along a greeting and a few lice.

"Me friend of soldier," Gray Beard said, and smiled. "Me friend to all people."

"Yes," Gary said. "We saw some of your Kiowa friends earlier this evening. We saw the gifts Gray Beard gave them."

"I am poor man, soldier. No ponies, few blankets." He spread his hands in a helpless appeal. "What gifts have I to give?"

"The Kiowas have ponies and blankets," Gary said. "They want rifle bullets, and that is the gift you gave them." He raised his hand and snapped his fingers. "Take the camp apart, piece by piece! On the double!"

For an instant, Gray Beard was too dumbfounded to speak. Then he opened his mouth to give an order, but Gary drew his .45 revolver and pressed the muzzle just under the Indian's rib cage.

"Make one sound . . . one move of resistance . . . and I'll blow you in half."

This was Gary's bluff, for he had no intention of shooting the old man and starting a war, but he was sure Gray Beard didn't know that and wasn't going to take a chance on whether this was bluff or not.

The soldiers were rousting everyone out of the lodges, tearing them apart in their search, but they weren't finding anything, which caused Gary a bit of worry. He felt certain that there was more ammunition than what the Kiowas had taken. There had to be. Ray Kline was in this to make money, and there was no profit in half a case of shells — at least not the kind of profit Kline wanted.

For fifteen minutes, Gary stood there, his gun on Gray Beard, and he knew that, if they didn't find the shells, he'd be in one hell of a spot. Cameron would have him cashiered out of the Army for this stunt.

"Gary," McCabe said, "you must have made a mistake. A bad one."

"I don't think so," Gary said.

The corporal from Beamish's section came up. He said: "Sir, we turned out everything, but there's nothing."

Gary could see how thoroughly the job had been done. The camp was a shambles, and there just wasn't anywhere else to search.

The corporal said: "Do you think they buried the stuff, sir?"

"Indians don't like to bury things," Gary said. "Wait a minute. Corporal, round up all the women and bring them over here."

"Yes, sir."

He moved away, and McCabe spoke. "I don't understand why you ain't dead, Gary." He swung his head from side to side and looked at the men in the camp, looked at their bright eyes and dark faces and saw the hate there. "What's holding them back?"

"The ammunition," Gary said. "It's here . . . I'm sure of it."

The soldiers herded the women near the fire. Gary looked at them for a moment, then said: "Corporal, take them one at a time and strip them."

"Naked, sir?"

"As much as necessary," Gary said. He took Gray Beard by the throat. "Am I right, friend of the soldier?" He didn't think the man would answer, so he nodded, and the corporal ripped the sack dress off the first woman. She tried to run, but

158

there was nowhere to go — two soldiers blocked her way.

She stood there, breasts sagging, bony-hipped, her eyes dark with anger. Around her waist she wore a thong, and tied to this were four boxes of rifle cartridges. The corporal cut the thong with his knife and said: "She's just a skinny one, sir. I'll bet we run eight boxes to the fat ones."

"Never mind the humor," Gary said. "Get on with it."

Each woman was stripped, and each one carried ammunition hung from a thong about her waist. One of the women carried a baby in a back cradle, and a trooper made the joking remark about how that the little fella was sure husky. It stabbed the rawness of Gary's keen suspicion, and he ordered the baby removed, and the cradle upended. That netted twelve boxes right there.

In all, they found three cases, a hundred and fifty boxes. At ten dollars a box — bootleg price — it wasn't a bad profit for Ray Kline.

Gary said: "You may discontinue the search, Corporal. I want all weapons removed from this camp, every pistol and musket you can find."

"Yes, sir."

Gary looked at Gray Beard, and he shook the man slightly and squeezed a little on his throat. "You've eaten the food the soldiers brought you. You've slept in the blankets they gave you, and pretended to be a friend. You're no friend. You're a liar, a man with no honor. Now, you take these people and you start moving back to the reservation. You'll be watched all the way, and, if you stop for more than water and rest, the soldiers will come down on you."

He gave Gray Beard a shove that sent him sprawling, and a murmur ran through the Indians watching. This was a supreme insult, and they expected their leader to rise and kill this bold soldier. But Gray Beard stayed on the ground.

Gary pulled his men away, and they walked back to their own camp.

McCabe asked: "What about me?"

"Give him back his pistol, Corporal," Gary said.

McCabe slipped it into his holster, and addressed Gary. "How could you be sure I had nothing to do with it?"

"When I accused Gray Beard, he never even glanced your way, which suggested to me that he did not connect you with the ammunition."

"That's shaving your judgment pretty fine," McCabe said. "Suppose he had looked at me?"

"You'd be under arrest," Gary told him. "I want to get this straight right now, Sheriff. When you get back to Tascosa, don't arrest Kline. We don't have anything on him that would stand up in court."

"Who the hell says he's ever going to get to court?"

"None of this pistol justice," Gary said. "The general wouldn't like it." He stopped and faced McCabe. "Gray Beard isn't going to say anything against Kline. In the first place, he knows what the general's policy is . . . take the bad toys away but don't punish. Gray Beard's not in serious trouble, and he knows it. He'll move on, like he's been told to do, and he'll dawdle at it, hoping to get word to Kline to come with some more shells. Gray Beard's caught between two forces, the Army on one side and the Kiowas on the other."

"You want to catch Kline with the ammunition, right?"

"Right," Gary said, and walked on.

Albert Bennett was waiting for him, and he was in a poor humor. "What was all that hullabaloo at the Indian settlement? From here, it looked as if you were tearing the place apart."

"That's it, precisely," Gary said. "I'm afraid we'll have to move on in the morning, sir. Perhaps we could go farther

160

south, for some bird shooting. Might even find you another buffalo."

"Don't be impudent to me," Bennett warned. "Blast it, I want an answer. Why did you create a disturbance in the village?"

"Tell him," McCabe said sourly.

"This is a military matter," Gary warned. "You keep out of it."

Bennett looked at Guthrie McCabe. "If you know anything, I charge you to tell me. Sheriff, I've met the governor of Texas on several occasions, and I. . . ."

"So have I," McCabe said blandly. "We used to get drunk together about ten years ago, when we were stealing horses from the Mexicans."

For a moment Bennett just stared, then he snapped: "General Cameron had better clear this matter up for me." He wheeled and went to his tent.

"He sure gets hot, don't he?" McCabe said. He laughed. "He was going to dangle something in front of my nose, wasn't he? I wonder what he would have offered?"

"You should have listened and found out."

"Oh, I don't want the man to be beholden to me," McCabe said. "Everybody owes me favors, as it is. It's getting so that a man can't spend a dollar. Why, if I want a meal, I just sit down and eat, and, if money is mentioned, I kind of polish my star a little, and they smile and forget it. Haven't bought a drink or a meal since I've been in office."

"What a crook," Gary said.

"Sure, but I have my charm. Hell, admit it. You didn't want to believe I'd sold the ammunition. You like me, Gary."

"I'd rather stand next to a pickpocket than have you around," Gary said. "You can go on back to town now, if you want. No hard feelings?"

161

"Naw," McCabe said, and stuck out his hand.

Gary glanced at it, a natural thing to do, and McCabe hit him then, nailing him squarely with a left hook. Gary went back, arms flailing to get his balance, and he struck the ground hard.

"McCabe," he said, pushing himself up, "you made a mistake."

"Let's not have a fight over it," McCabe said. "You had that coming for riding me so hard. I figure that squares us for me standin' with my own gun in my back." He raised his hand to the brim of his hat in mock salute. "I guess I will go back. Your jaw's going to start achin', and you'll think about putting a lump on mine."

He walked toward the picket line, and Gary got up and brushed off his clothes. He couldn't quite work himself up to an anger, yet he wasn't in the frame of mind to forgive Guthrie McCabe, either. They were, he decided, like two boys with sticks. They just couldn't stop poking each other. *We'll either be the best of friends,* Gary thought, *or the damnedest enemies imaginable.*

Beamish had the guards on duty, when Gary sat down on his blankets and tugged at his boots. Everything seemed in order, and he was rather proud of Beamish. Although the responsibility was small, the man had taken it seriously, which was a good sign and worth mentioning to General Cameron.

It was very late, when Sergeant Murphy returned and woke Gary.

"The general's 'way to hell and gone south, sir, approaching the buffalo hunters' camp," Murphy said, handing Gary the message. He struck a match and held it while Gary read:

Well done . . . use best judgment . . . make no arrests without secure evidence admissible in court . . . keep Bennett and all happy.

Cameron

Jim Gary tore the message into minute pieces, thanked Murphy, and told him to roll in for the night. After Murphy went away, Gary lay back, hands behind his head, and enjoyed the good feeling men know when they've used good sense. Tomorrow he'd start writing a detailed report, and would send another rider out with a message to be relayed on by heliograph. The Fort Elliot patrols would pick it up and ride herd on Gray Beard's bunch clear back to the reservation.

It was a hard thing to do to the old Indian — reservation life was in no way as soft as the agents led everyone to believe. The rations were always lean, and there was no work and no hunting, nothing to do but sit around and quarrel among themselves and think about all the good old days that were gone.

Gary listened for a while to the sounds of the Indian camp a mile out on the prairie. They were gathering up everything, packing it for the long walk. *God damn people like Kline! . . . they couldn't let a thing be.*

Presently he heard someone approaching and sat up. Albert Bennett spoke. "Are you awake? Good. If you hadn't been, I'd have woke you." He hunkered down. "Mister Gary, I've just had a very interesting talk with Mister Beamish."

"Mister Beamish is a very interesting fellow, sir."

"Damn your impertinence!" Bennett snapped. "What gives you the right to treat me like a fool? Beamish told me why you went to the village tonight."

"Mister Beamish doesn't know," Gary said. "He remained in camp."

"He got it from the soldiers that were there," Bennett said. "Don't try to lie out of it . . . you discovered a cache of ammunition there."

"Yes, sir. The Indians were naughty, sir."

Bennett swore. "All right, Gary, play your game, but I'm wise to it now. I know what's going on now. General Cameron is trying to sell a bill of goods, but I'm not going to buy it. Peaceful Indians, my ass! I haven't seen a peaceful Indian except in front of a cigar store. They're all war-like, all waiting for the chance to rise and murder a man in his bed." He stood up and lowered his voice. "You're wasting your time on me, Mister Gary. I'm a man with his eyes open at last."

"Sir," Gary said, "the bearing of arms is not an indication of war. Believe me, the Indians want rifles more for the symbolic value than to actually use them."

"Is that a fact?" Bennett laughed sourly. "Mister Gary, I wouldn't be inclined to believe you, if you were under oath and swore on a stack of Bibles."

"That's too bad," Gary said. "I thought you were a man smart enough to see the truth, when you bumped into it."

"I see the truth," Bennett said flatly. "Damn clearly, too. Cameron's got an axe to grind, and he's trying to use me to sharpen it. Well, it's not going to work."

He turned then and stalked off to his own tent, leaving Jim Gary to wonder where all that good feeling had gone to so suddenly. He couldn't make up his mind whether to kill Beamish now or wait until morning.

Chapter Eleven

General Tracy Cameron's scouts detected the smudge of dust on the horizon just as the first bleak light of dawn spread across the prairie. Cameron pulled clear of the patrol to use his field glasses. He was too distant yet actually to make out the details, but he could identify the forces, Indian and cavalry. They would come together before he could reach them.

He pulled forward into position at the head of the column and made the signal for an increase in speed. The light grew stronger, as he grew nearer, and then a bronze rim of sun appeared in the east, and the day was newly arrived. Cameron could only hope to reach the two forces before they met. The Indians were converging on both sides, at least a hundred strong, but part of the cavalry in advance was able to pass through and came toward him. He could make them out clearly, a twelve-man detachment of cavalry with a group of buffalo hunters.

They met on the prairie, and a perspiring lieutenant saluted. "Prisoners, sir. Captain Einsman's in trouble!"

"Carry on, Mister Butler," Cameron said. "We'll relieve Mister Einsman." He waved his command forward, at a gallop now. Einsman's force was completely surrounded by Indians, and from the milling and the waving of weapons they were an unhappy lot.

Cameron did not slow his force but threatened to run the Indians down, and they broke and let him pass through. Einsman's face was bleak, the color gone, and Cameron didn't blame him, for it was like a sickness, this fear that came to a man when he needed more courage.

There was no time to get the straight of the story, no time to be brought up to date on events. A man played a thing like this by ear and prayed that he wasn't deaf. Cameron's presence alone had a calming effect on the Indians. Here was the soldier leader who could speak for all of them. Three Indians rode forward, but with no friendliness in their manner.

The Kiowa and the Cheyenne were known to Cameron; the third was a Comanche, a stranger. Nonetheless, Tracy Cameron felt he knew who the Comanche was, and it made his heart race a little to face Quanah Parker for the first time.

Parker was tall and straight on his horse, and he had a rather handsome face. He wore few ornaments and only a blanket and breeches. His rifle was a repeating Evans with brass tacks decorating the buttstock. He was a man fierce of eye and bold in manner, and one glance was enough to mark him as a powerful leader.

Parker said: "So, you're the soldier leader. My eyes have not seen you before. We will speak now, you and I. All others will be silent." He made a turn of the head, and the Indians grew still. Even a horse that insisted on stamping was quickly quieted.

"What do you wish to say?" Cameron asked. He wanted to risk a glance at his command and at Einsman, but he did not. His field of vision gave him some clue to their manner. They sat their horses, alert, yet not displaying their weapons.

"The buffalo hunters are the enemies of my people," Parker said. "We do not make war with the soldiers, only with the buffalo hunters."

Cameron flogged his mind for something to say. If he'd only had a few minutes with Einsman to come up to date on developments, to understand the circumstances that led to

166

this parley. But he had nothing, not even the barest vestige of an argument.

Captain Einsman spoke up sharply. "We've arrested the hunters, taken them from your land. What more do you want?"

"I did not ask you to speak!" Parker shouted. He was furious at the interruption, but Tracy Cameron was grateful. Einsman had spoken at considerable risk and had said just enough to give Cameron a clear picture of what had taken place. Obviously the Indians had meant to attack the hunters. Einsman had arrested them instead, marching them off to avert a shooting war. By God, that was thinking!

"He will not interrupt again," Cameron said sternly. He then stepped from the saddle. "Stand on the ground and speak with me, Parker." He wasn't sure, from the way he hesitated, that Quanah Parker would do it. Then Parker flipped off his pony. Cameron said: "Let all dismount. I will have fires built, and you will eat our food."

He put it that way because it was Indian hospitality, and he knew that Parker would not be likely to refuse and run the risk of an insult. Again the Comanche hesitated, then he waved his hand, and his band dismounted.

"Captain Einsman, tend to the cook fires. I think pancakes, side meat, and coffee will do. Use the full salt and sugar ration, if you have to."

Cameron squatted and invited Parker to do the same. "For many months I've wanted to speak with you, Parker. We have much to say to each other."

"My words are few," Parker said. "I will eat your food, then go, for the hunters are mine to punish."

"The hunters will be taken where they won't bother you," Cameron said. He offered Quanah Parker a cigar, always a delicacy to an Indian, and then lit it for him. "It is useless to fight the hunters, Parker. It's a fight no man can win, especially the Comanches."

"We have strong medicine," Parker said. "The hunters' bullets will be turned away."

"Ah, yes, the subject of bullets," Cameron said. "Parker, you will grow old, waiting for the bullets your Kiowa friends are supposed to bring." He watched the Indian carefully, and even Quanah Parker could not keep the surprise from his eyes.

Play this casually, Cameron told himself, *as though you know everything.* With great unconcern he said: "Since our medicine is so strong, we looked into the hearts of the Kiowas you sent to Gray Beard's village and saw that they carried bullets sold by the Tascosa trader, Kline." He turned his head. "Captain, let's not waste time with those fires."

"Yes, sir."

Parker remained silent for a time, then he spoke. "It is far to Gray Beard's camp. You speak of a thing, but you do not know it."

"I know it," Cameron assured him. "Kline came to Gray Beard's camp with two wagons, as he always does. And in the wagons he had bullets to fit your rifles. We saw all this and took the bullets from him."

"No medicine is so strong," Parker maintained. "If you have taken the bullets, let me see them."

It was a natural request, one he was sure Quanah Parker would make, and he believed he could get around it — with luck.

"Would you show me how to make your strong medicine" — he smiled — "that can break the spell of bullets?"

"You have no bullets."

"Then how did I know, Parker? You know I speak the truth. A band of Kiowas went to Gray Beard for bullets. They should be here by now. But they're not here. How do I know

168

these things unless I speak true?"

It wasn't a question Parker wanted to answer without consulting his medicine man, so he called Isatai to his side and went into a long-winded conference in Comanche. Cameron didn't understand too much of it, but he caught the gist from Parker's expression. Isatai had some bleak news.

When the old medicine-maker went away, Parker said: "You have strong medicine."

"And yours has turned a little sour," Cameron pointed out.

"Our medicine is powerful . . . it was not turned away by yours. We have angered the gods. A Kiowa killed a rabbit without Isatai's permission, and the gods grew angry."

It was, Cameron knew, an Indian's way of excusing all things bad, but he wasn't going to try to persuade Parker that it wasn't so. "We are too old for war, Parker. Would your gods be angry, if you spoke of peace?"

"There is only one god for peace, but many for war."

"We have only one God," Cameron said, "and He is for peace."

"Then why do you make war?"

"We make no war, Parker. Did you see guns in the hands of my men? Your braves carried guns in their hands."

"The hunters were here on our land."

"The hunters are gone . . . taken away by my soldiers," Cameron said. *Come on,* he thought, *talk to me, argue with me. If you keep talking, I'll get you in a corner.*

"They will come back," Parker insisted.

"My soldiers will keep them out."

"That is a promise you will not keep. You make war."

"How many times in the past three years have soldiers shot at an Indian?"

"Many times."

169

"How many lodges were empty in your village? How many wives sang the death song and threw ashes on their hair?" He pointed his finger like a gun. "Give me the name of one brave who was killed by a soldier. One name only."

Quanah Parker had none to give, and he surrendered the argument. "I have no name to give, Cameron."

"That's because we desire peace. We desire to live, Parker. If it was death we sought, we could die here. Now. My soldiers could draw their guns, and your braves could draw theirs, and we would shoot each other as we sit. All would die, Parker. There would be no more talk of war, no dream of peace. We'd all be dead. But what would we gain?"

"The Comanches will not be slaves to white men," Parker said.

"We weren't speaking about slavery, although you should know about it. You've been keeping slaves for years."

Parker thought about this, then said: "You speak of peace as a child speaks of a piece of meat. It is not a light word, Cameron. It will take much talk, much thought. It will take much truth."

"Then we must talk and think, Parker. The truth will show itself, if we speak."

"Many words," Quanah Parker said. "A lie cannot remain hidden for long, when words are spoken." He waved his hand at the prairie. "Will we sit here until we are old men and talk?"

"We must know each other better, Parker," Cameron said. "In a month, I'll come to your village, and there we'll talk of peace."

"What is this thing . . . a month?"

"Before the moon is again as it is now," Cameron said. "And after we talk, you will come to my house at the post, as

170

my guest, and we will talk some more. The truth will be known then."

"By two moons all will be said," Parker agreed. "It is good. But what of the hunters?"

"There will be no hunters until the truth is known to both. We will have war then, Parker, or a peace." He glanced around and found Einsman nearby. "Is the meal ready? Good. Bring over a couple of plates and see that our guests are served."

Cameron remained behind with his command four hours on the prairie, then he went one way, while the Indians went another, and he could not quite decide which of the two was the more relieved. When he mounted his augmented command, he struck out in a direction calculated to overtake the detail that had been proceeding all this time, accompanying the buffalo hunters. After six hours of forced march he hailed within signal distance of them.

Graves, the leader of the hunters, was in a lather of fury. He shouted at Cameron and demanded to be released immediately, and Cameron motioned for Skinner to come over.

"Have they been giving you trouble, Mister Skinner?" Cameron was peeling off his gauntlets, and he could tell just by looking that Skinner was more interested in what had happened back there with Quanah Parker. *Well,* Cameron thought, *let Einsman tell it. It was really his show.*

"A most obstreperous bunch, sir," Skinner said. He turned as Captain Einsman came up, his face taut with worry.

He saluted and said: "General, I'm afraid I've put the fat in the fire."

"Indeed?" Cameron smiled. "Rather, I'd say you'd pulled it off, nicely toasted. A bit of a touch-and-go there, eh, Einsman?"

"Yes, sir. Your arrival was most timely, sir. Quanah Parker is too proud a man to deal with a captain. Only a general would pacify him." He glanced at Skinner, then seized his hand and pumped it. "A good job of getting away. I'll see that it goes into my report, with the general's permission."

"It seems that a round of kudos is in order," Cameron said. "What charges are you going to prefer against the hunters, Einsman?"

"I hadn't thought of anything specific, sir."

"We'll work on it back at the post," Cameron said.

"General, I wish to assume full responsibility for this," Einsman said. "My junior officers only followed orders."

"I see," Cameron said. "Trying to hog all the credit?"

"No, sir . . . the blame. I don't believe, sir, that we can justify the arrest of civilian hunters."

Cameron raised an eyebrow. "Can't we now?" He chuckled. "When I get through mislaying papers, filing petty charges, blocking writs of dismissal, and finally get around to charging or releasing them, we won't give a damn what they do." He slapped Einsman across the chest with his gloves. "You never fired a shot, Captain. I'm proud of you!"

Then he walked over to where the prisoners were herded together. Dried blood made dark splotches on Graves's face, and it gave him a ferocious appearance. Cameron's tone was infuriatingly jocular.

"Well, what have you been getting into, Graves?"

"I'm going to fix the god-damned Army. I promise you that!"

"Well, men have been trying to fix it since Washington's time," Cameron said. "Why do you insist on riling the Indians, Graves? Can't you behave yourself?"

"Don't talk to me like I was a snot-nosed kid," Graves said. "I demand to be released."

172

"I've never heard of anyone demanding anything of a general," Cameron said seriously. "I'll have to consider it. Wouldn't want to establish a precedent, you know."

"You haven't got anything to charge me with, Cameron."

"But I may think of something," Cameron said, and went back to where his officers waited. "Captain, mount the men. We'll go right on into the post. The quicker those hunters are placed in the guardhouse, the better off we'll all be."

"Yes, sir," Einsman said.

"And Mister Skinner, send a runner to the nearest heliograph and see if you can pick up Mister Gary's whereabouts. I want him back at the post, also." He squinted at the sky. "There may be enough daylight to relay the message."

He stepped into the saddle then and put the column into motion.

Late that night he ordered a five-hour stop and a meal made before they began their march again. Then he went on through the next day, now and then breaking the monotony of the march by housekeeping stops. He got his message through and learned that Gary had already turned back to the post. He would be waiting, when Cameron arrived.

Late in the day he raised the dark smudge of post buildings in the distance, and in two hours he was passing his command through the main gate. The prisoners were taken to the guardhouse and locked up. Cameron went to his office, bone-weary, but understanding that certain things would have to be attended to before he could rest.

The orderly met him inside and said: "General, Mister Chaffee and Mister Bennett both want an immediate audience with you."

Cameron sighed. "Very well, notify them that I'm in my office. I'll see them both now."

"I'm sorry, sir, but they want separate appointments."

"All right then . . . send Chaffee in."

"Mister Bennett insisted on being first, sir." The orderly was beginning to sweat, and Cameron's exasperation grew more evident.

"Very well, Corporal. Summon Mister Bennett then."

The orderly swallowed. "I'm sorry to say, sir, that Mister Chaffee has also insisted on being first."

Tracy Cameron took a deep breath and held it for a moment. Then he said: "Corporal, I'm not conducting an opera house. I have no time for prima donnas. Inform Mister Gary that I want to see him in my office, and, after he arrives, I don't want to be disturbed for an hour."

"Yes, sir."

Cameron went on in and kicked the door shut. He stripped off his gloves and neckerchief and shirt and washed at the sideboard. He needed a shave badly, but that would have to wait. Gary's lengthy report was on Cameron's desk, and he glanced at it and thought a bit guiltily that perhaps he should read it, since Gary had obviously spent hours writing it. It wouldn't be wasted, for the report was official, part of the record. Cameron wanted opinions now, and that would only come from the young aide in conversation.

Gary arrived with his usual promptness, and, even as he saluted, Cameron waved him into a chair and poured two drinks. Gary wasn't a man for whiskey, but he tossed it off with no more than a little eye watering.

Cameron said: "You're getting older, faster."

"How's that, sir?"

"An idle comment," Cameron said. He put a match to a cigar and offered one to Gary, but the young man shook his head. He continued: "What's all the furor with our great white leaders? They both want to see me at the same time."

"I'm afraid, General, that they have a long list of complaints." Gary went into a detailed account of the affair at Gray Beard's village, and he described the sacking of it without sparing himself the full responsibility.

When he was finished, Cameron sat still for a moment, his brow wrinkled in concentration. "You made no attempt to arrest Kline?"

"No, General. I don't think I could have convicted him on the circumstantial evidence. And I didn't want to display my hand too quickly."

"Good thinking there. What about McCabe?"

"I think he'll hold his peace," Gary said. "I don't understand the man, and we don't get along at all, but I believe I like him. And I think he'll go along with me."

"Well, it's a point in our favor," Cameron said.

A small disturbance in the outer office took their attention, then the door burst open, and Bennett and Chaffee both crowded in. They were angry men, and Bennett glanced at Gary as though to say: *Get out of that chair. I want to sit down.*

"Gentlemen, you're interrupting a private meeting," Cameron said. "But no matter. I'd as soon listen to three complaints as one."

"What does he have to complain about?" Bennett demanded, nodding toward Gary. He pulled a chair around and dropped onto it. "General, I want to tell you that this damned hoodwinking has gone far enough."

"Albert, don't get so excited," Chaffee said. "This can be settled by peaceful discussion."

Ah, Cameron thought, *so Chaffee's anger was directed at Bennett. That's something, anyway.* "I don't know what you're talking about," Cameron said. "Suppose you tell me, Mister Bennett."

"I'm talking about these peaceful Indians who are being supplied by a gunrunner from Tascosa." He shook his finger at Cameron. "And don't tell me they're going rabbit hunting."

Cameron's glance came to Gary and rested there, and Gary said: "Mister Beamish, sir. He turned into a fountain of information."

"Yes," Cameron said, and scratched his beard stubble. "The incompetent Mister Beamish again." It was a bad bit of news for him, but he wasn't a man to brood over his misadventures, or the bad luck that fell his way. He leaned back in his chair and folded his hands across his lean stomach. "All right, Mister Bennett. We'll admit that there are certain Indian factions who want rifles for war-making. What do you conclude from that?"

"What do I conclude? Why, you're trying to sell me a bill of goods with no value."

"Am I now?" Cameron smiled. "That's true . . . I am trying to sell you something, but, when you say it has no value, you only demonstrate how loud you can talk through your hat." This insulted Bennett, but Cameron went on before he could reply. "It's been my observation, sir, that certain criminal elements in our society arm themselves for the purposes of illegal activity. Do you condemn society for that? Is it your claim that we're all unlawful?"

"You're talking nonsense," Bennett said scornfully.

Tracy Cameron smashed the flat of his hand on his desk so hard that they all jumped in surprise. His voice was like the honed edge of a saber, and he skewered Albert Bennett with his eyes. "Mister Bennett, you're talking to a general in the United States Army, not some damned lackey, holding your horse. Now I asked you a question, and you'd better give me an answer. I'm not going to put up with your mule-headedness, or your condescension. I'm offering you an opportunity to become a partner in an undertaking fraught with

176

the milk of human kindness, and you sit there like a petulant fool, too self-centered to understand it."

"How dare you talk to me that way?" Bennett said, deeply shocked.

"There are some men who need a periodic cussing out," Cameron said. "You're one of those men. And you'd better understand this. For three years I've poured my thoughts and my soul into the quest for a just peace between the white man and the Indian. With or without you, I will continue to seek that peace. I need your help, yes. God knows, I need it desperately. But if it's denied me, it won't lessen one whit my determination, or dim a bit my dream. Now you can do as you damned please, Mister Bennett. I run my post the way I see fit, and *I* decide what's vital and what is not. Now I've said all I'm going to say on the matter. I'm not compelled to explain every nuance that occurs within the sphere of my command."

"Are you foolish enough to throw away a career on this dream, General?"

"Perhaps I've already done so," Cameron said. "Now, if there's nothing more to be said, Mister Gary and I would like to get on with Army business."

Albert Bennett was still fuming, when he and Chaffee left the office, and Chaffee took his arm, saying: "Come on over to the sutler's place, and I'll buy you a glass of beer." He felt the resistance in Bennett and pulled him a little, making him give way. Bennett would have preferred to have his drink in the officers' mess, and Chaffee knew it, but he ignored it.

The sutler's bar was crowded. Chaffee bought a pitcher of beer, carrying it and two glasses to a corner table. Bennett was already seated, and, as Chaffee poured, Bennett said: "I don't know what to think, Wilson. I'm just damned sure Cameron wouldn't cast his career aside so casually."

"Why wouldn't he?"

"It goes against the basic greed in all men," Bennett said. "I wouldn't go out on a limb for him. Neither would you."

"I like to think I would," Chaffee said. "But I don't know, Albert. Essentially, I'm an opportunist. So are you . . . all politicians are to a large extent. Now, I'm not saying that is bad. But because it isn't bad, doesn't make it good, either."

"Your point is beyond argument," Bennett said softly. "Damn it, Wilson, I'm a patriot. I love this country, and I defended her with a musket once. I'd do it again."

Chaffee smiled. "Yes, I've heard your Fourth of July speeches. But I feel the same way. Let no man attack her by word or deed." He paused to drink some of his beer. "I suppose that's a weakness, Albert, the way we think. How many soldiers in this room do you think hold the country and grand old flag in the esteem we do?"

"They're soldiers," Bennett said. "Soldiers are famous for their patriotism. Ours are, anyway."

Chaffee shook his head. "Don't cite me a slogan, Albert. And stop telling them to yourself. We're patriotic all right, so damned much so that we can't bear to hear a criticism of anything pertaining to this great and glorious country." He smiled. "The words sound a little foolish out here, don't they, Albert? But back in Chicago, at a rally, they'd be just the thing."

Bennett refilled his beer glass. "Cameron does insinuate, doesn't he? He makes a man feel that the job he's doing is not good enough."

"Well? Is it? Albert, I believe in the man. Can you honestly say that you don't?"

"No, I can't say that," Bennett admitted. "But he'd do well to watch that iron fist once in a while."

"He's a deceptive man," Chaffee said. "You never see the steel in him until you're hit with it. And Jim Gary's turning

178

into a chip off the old block." He chuckled for a moment. "Albert, why don't you go and talk to Cameron again? I'll go with you. It won't kill us to admit that our anger stemmed from Gary's presumptuous manner after that Gray Beard affair."

"Do you want to lay it at his door that way?"

"Why not? His pride's a bit more flexible than ours. Purely a matter of age."

Bennett nodded in agreement, and drained his beer glass. The officer of the day came in, saw them sitting there, and walked over. He saluted and said: "I'm sorry to intrude, gentlemen, but I've been searching the post for you."

"What's wrong?" Chaffee asked.

"A group of civilian buffalo hunters have been arrested and locked in the guardhouse. They want to speak to you both."

"Damn it!" Bennett said sourly. "Well, all right. Coming, Wilson?"

"They're voters, aren't they?" Chaffee smiled thinly. "By instinct, we'd never neglect a voter."

The officer of the day went along, striding on ahead, and, when they reached the guardhouse, the guard officer was waiting. "I trust," he said, "that you're unarmed. No weapons permitted in the cell blocks." He made a motion with his hand. "If you'll step this way, gents."

Graves got up off his cot, when he saw Chaffee and Bennett. He came up to the barred door and gripped it as though he intended to spring it off the hinges.

"Get us out of here," Graves said. "Cameron will listen to you."

Chaffee said: "That matter is largely in doubt. What have you done?"

"Not a damned thing," Graves said. "We were setting up a

179

new camp, when the Army arrived. During the night they jumped us. And here we are. We want out, and, by God, we're going to Dodge to get ourselves a good lawyer."

"Cameron wouldn't confine you to the stockade without a reason," Bennett said firmly. "I don't agree with the man, but I have faith in his fairness. However, I'll see if I can't arrange a hearing for you tomorrow."

"Tomorrow? What's the matter with tonight?"

Bennett shook his head. "Believe me, Cameron is in no mood to listen sympathetically to anyone right now. But I'll speak to him and get the hearing set up."

This wasn't what Graves wanted, but it was the best he was going to get, and he knew it. He turned and sank back on the cot, and the two men left the guardhouse.

Bennett paused outside, and said: "I have a strong feeling that I shouldn't meddle in this, Wilson."

"Then don't."

"I'm trying not to. If I can set up a hearing, I can back out then and let Cameron handle it."

"He would anyway, hearing or not." He yawned and stretched. "I'm going to read a while and then go to bed. Are you going to headquarters now?"

"Yes, and get it done with."

They went separate ways, and this time Bennett knocked before entering Cameron's office. When he heard the general's invitation, he stepped inside. Gary was still there, and the room was dense with cigar smoke. A half-empty whiskey bottle sat on the desk; each man held a glass.

"General, I've spoken to one of the hunters. He feels that he's been unjustly arrested."

"Any petty thief would feel the same way," Cameron said. "But I'm not going to turn them loose so they can go south into Parker's country again."

"Are you planning a hearing?"

"In a week or so," Cameron said mildly. "Mister Bennett, this is a military matter . . . strictly."

"Yes, I realize that." He had something more to say, but he thought better of it. "All right, General, I won't press the matter. It's your responsibility."

"It has been all along," Cameron said. He studied Bennett briefly. "Your humor has improved in the last half hour, I'm delighted to say. Perhaps now we could discuss the matter in a calmer vein, if there's anything you wish to add."

"I can think of nothing," Bennett said. "My anger was primarily directed at Mister Gary and his perfunctory manner after the affair on the prairie. After all, I'm a lawmaker, a man of some judgment. I resent being ordered about by second lieutenants."

"Indeed, that must have been humiliating," Cameron said, glancing at Gary. "Congressman, it may ease your bruised feelings to know that I will mete out a suitable punishment to Mister Gary."

"That isn't necessary," Bennett said quickly, but Cameron waved his hand.

"Mister Gary, in the morning will you saddle a splendid horse and make a fast ride to Fort Dodge. General Sherman is there, and I have some important confidential papers that must be in his hands no later than Wednesday. I realize you've just returned from a strenuous patrol, and you face a long, brutal ride, but, when your back aches and your urine turns to blood, you may recall it later and have more respect for a man's position."

Albert Bennett glanced at Gary, then at Cameron. "Good night, General." He turned to the door and hurried out.

After the outer door closed, Cameron leaned back and said: "I believe he was genuinely horrified. Here, have another drink, and don't take too literally what I just said. We must impress the tourists, you know." He downed his drink and sighed. "I'll brief you early in the morning, Jim . . . you'll have to convince Sherman that I need more time now. I'm not asking you to try. I'm telling you that you *must*. And while you're gone, I'll try to take care of Kline . . . if he can be found . . . and the buffalo hunters. Perhaps I can even find out where the Indians are getting the money to pay for the rifles and ammunition."

He stood up, corked the whiskey bottle, and then slid it across desk to Jim Gary. "Take it along with you. It never hurts a man to get a little drunk once in a while."

Chapter Twelve

Lieutenant Gary bathed and shaved and had his breakfast an hour before dawn. He then walked to headquarters to keep a scheduled appointment with General Cameron. The light from Cameron's office window was a beacon, the only light showing on the post.

Cameron motioned for Gary to come in and close the door, then he said: "This is a hell of an hour for a conference, Jim, but it will assure us of being undisturbed."

He had managed to shave, but he hadn't caught up on his sleep, and his eyes were puffed and red-rimmed, and there was still a fuzziness in his voice from all the whiskey he had downed to keep him going. He picked up some papers from his desk and gave them a shove toward Gary. "These were waiting for me . . . communications from Sherman. Quite simply, he's getting cold feet and wants to make a three-column thrust into the Comanche country and subdue them by force. At Camp Supply, General Miles is ready to march. Colonel Ranald Mackenzie is waiting at Fort Griffith, and both commanders from Fort Sill and Fort Union want in on the push. Sherman wants me to argue against this, and that's why I'm sending you to Dodge . . . to argue for me."

"Sir, you could do much better. . . ."

"Of course, I could," Cameron said. "And I mean that kindly, Jim. But I don't dare to leave now. Not with the situation simmering. Boy, you've got to convince Sherman that I need time. Get me that much . . . enough so I can meet again with Parker." He slapped his hands together and rubbed them briskly. "If I can make the peace with Parker, let those glory hunters march, and they'll end up on one big snipe hunt."

"I believe I understand, sir," Gary said. "I'll present every argument in your favor."

"I was confident you would," Cameron said. "Jim, I'm going to see if I can round up those small bands of renegade Kiowas and Cheyennes who've been using those rifles." He brushed another stack of reports. "These are from Fort Griffith and other trouble spots. They're having one raid after another, and, of course, they feel this should be stopped. I have peace in my bailiwick, but actually it's rather an illusion. You see, these renegade bands are going south and west to raid, then coming back here and pretending to be good Indians. I take away their stolen horses and guns, and Kline sells them more."

"To buy and sell costs money, sir."

"Yes," Cameron said, rubbing his chin. "And I'd like to know where the devil they're getting the hard cash." He pushed himself erect and walked around to Gary's chair. There he put his hand lightly on Gary's shoulder. "A bad habit of mine is saving the worst for last. I'm afraid I'm going to have to ask you to escort Elizabeth Rishel to Dodge. She wants to go back East immediately."

Gary groaned, then nodded. "Very well, sir. I trust she'll be riding side-saddle?"

"You'll have to insist on it," Cameron said. "I believe she wants the comfort of an ambulance and a tent. But I can't give you that much time, Jim. It's important that you see Sherman in four days."

"Has Miss Rishel been informed that I'm leaving at dawn?"

"Yes, and it didn't seem to inconvenience her much. She's

184

young and resilient. I suppose it's a bit improper to send a young woman out with a handsome man, unchaperoned, but as Bennett might say in one of his idiotic speeches . . . 'This is war, and we must make sacrifices.' " He gripped Gary by the shoulder and shook him gently. "Assure Sherman that within thirty days I'll have Stone Calf and his renegade raiders rounded up and on their way back to the reservation. That might lessen Miles's thirst for another war."

"In thirty days, sir?"

Cameron laughed softly. "See, it impressed you, and you know it can't be done."

"General Sherman may know it, too."

Cameron shook his head. "I may have Stone Calf cornered for all he knows. He'll just have to take a chance, that's all. We're all taking a chance, Jim. Now that we've cut off the ammunition and food supply, Stone Calf is going to have to change his tactics . . . come out in the open a little more. I'll get him then, and I'll march him back to the reservation in disgrace, just as Gray Beard was marched. Incidentally, I haven't received word yet whether they arrived or not. Well, no matter. It'll be a nice bomb to drop in Sherman's lap, while you're with him. He's always impressed by these dramatic moves."

Cameron gave Gary a pocketful of cigars and a bottle of whiskey, then shooed him out of the office. He stood at the window and watched Gary cross the parade ground. The dawn was a rose blush in the east. The day was going to be bright and hot. Gary and the girl would have a sweltering ride ahead of them, but Cameron wasn't worried about that. Albert Bennett might hit the ceiling, when he learned that they were traveling alone, without escort, but Cameron had no intention of mentioning it. He had sufficient troubles without asking for more.

185

Bennett wouldn't understand that without escort and ambulance they would travel faster and with less chance of running into difficulties. The country north of Dodge still held a few roving bands of Kiowas and Cheyennes, but they were not as dangerous as most men imagined. With the reservation near, six or eight of them could break away for two days, have their fling, and get back before the authorities missed them. Cameron didn't want Gary and the girl to be plodding along with an ambulance and four mules. Mounted, they were more mobile, and time was of importance to Cameron.

A good move right now, Cameron decided, would be a dinner party, some affair whose format was familiar to the politicians. They were drifting away from Cameron, forming opinions on their own, and that was bad. He held to the firm conviction that no politician should be allowed to think for himself. He'd have to woo them back to his side and without delay. Eastland was a retiring man who wasn't feeling well. Cameron made a mental note to have the contract surgeon call and give him an examination. Eastland had been rather neglected, and this bothered Cameron, for he knew better than to neglect anyone.

The tightrope on which he walked was beginning to hurt his feet. *I'm getting tired,* he thought. He needed a long leave so he could enjoy the company of his wife. They'd go somewhere the Army wasn't, and just take walks together, or talk before they lost the art of conversation. A man, Cameron decided, could just give so much to his job, then it had to end because there wasn't anything left to give.

Jim Gary and Elizabeth Rishel crossed the Canadian under the bright heat of the noon sun. After Gary paused to pour the water from his boots, they moved on. He wanted to make the Elk Creek heliograph station by late afternoon, and he figured he just about could, if they didn't dally.

Elizabeth Rishel was a good horsewoman, and she was strong, strong enough at any rate that she could endure the pace without complaint. When Gary stopped for cold rations, he helped her down, shared some dried beef and hard biscuits, and made no effort at conversation.

The silence must have bothered her, for she said: "Are you angry at me, Jim?"

"No, not at all."

"Well, you haven't said a dozen words to me since we left the post."

"I don't have anything to say," he told her. "And I'm bone-tired."

She shook her head. "Then think of something."

He took a swig from his canteen. "You seemed to be in a sudden hurry to leave Fort Elliot."

"I was growing bored," she said frankly.

"I can show you a hundred soldiers who're bored," Gary said. "You should have said something. I'd have gone out and burned the stable down or something."

"That wasn't a nice thing to say." She smiled at him. "I'm not bored now, though." She sighed, and her expression was mockingly wistful. "What a story this is going to make in Washington . . . me, alone on the prairie with a handsome young officer who is so moral he'd die before soiling me." She wanted to shock him, and she did, and this amused her so much that she laughed.

"You're playing a dangerous fool's game," Gary said.

"Oh, I think I've weighed the risks," Elizabeth said. "The shop girls will believe it because it has that fairy-tale quality they love. And my girl friends will envy me, whether they believe it or not. And if they don't, they won't come out and say so, because of my family background. And all the young men

187

. . . bless their one-track minds . . . will flock around me and damn the luck that put them in the Maritime Commission office instead of out here where you are."

"Only a woman would paint herself with something that might not come off," Gary said. He was mildly angry at her, for she was a woman and she aroused in him all his native suspicions of women. He didn't love her, he told himself, still he was angry at her. "Someday you'll fall in love with a man. What will you tell him, then?"

"The truth. That you're a gallant prude."

Color came to his cheeks because he knew she was right. He was a prude, a man who revered women just because they were women. "Suppose he doesn't quite believe it? Suppose a tint of suspicion remains?"

"Why, that would be wonderful," she said. "He'd watch me always and pay attention to me, and I'd never be lonely."

"You must spend all your time scheming."

"Most women do," she said, and stood up. She was ready to ride on.

They spent the night at the heliograph detachment and were on the move before dawn for their second day of travel on a four-day journey. Gary kept hoping that a patrol would be moving about this area, but he was out of luck, for the only patrol in the whole area had swung west the day before.

In the afternoon of the second day he saw some distant dust and couldn't decide whether it was a wind devil or buffaloes or Indians. Elizabeth was growing tired, and she began to complain a little. Gary couldn't blame her, for he had held to a stiff pace, trying to reach Dodge in the time Cameron had given him.

The prairie was a lonely, vast place with wind scuffing it and the sun scorching it. It was a place where a man used caution in everything he did. Gary entertained no sense of danger, for he could visualize none in particular, although many in general. He didn't want to run afoul of some stray herd of buffaloes, or a band of buffalo hunters, or some roving party of Indians off the reservations. There was an element of unpredictability about these things, and therein lay the risks.

They camped on the prairie and ate cold food, and Elizabeth was unhappy about this. She tried to keep her sharp tongue to herself, for she realized that Gary was doing what he thought best for both of them. There wasn't much talk between them, for at the end of the day they were both tired, and, as soon as it got dark, they rolled into their blankets to sleep. Gary kept waking periodically for a look around.

This time, when he woke, the night was dark, almost as dark as ink, but he could make out the vague shapes of men around him. When he started to raise up, a rifle muzzle was placed against his chest, pressing down, and an Indian voice said: "No move now!"

Elizabeth Rishel stirred and sat up, and an Indian standing near her jerked her to her feet. She smelled the rank gaminess and screamed, and the Indian slapped her hard across the face. She stood there, a hand to her bruised cheek, gasping and choking the sobs back.

Jim Gary said: "Turn her loose, or you'll hang for this."

"No hang!" The Indian called to others, and they came up with horses.

Gary was disarmed, and his dispatch case was inspected and thrown away. He was relieved to see them do that, for there was an outside chance that it would be found by a patrol — a slim chance, but still worth thinking about.

Pigging strings of rawhide were produced, and the hands of both were bound tightly behind them, and lead ropes were placed around their necks. Elizabeth Rishel was still sobbing, and Jim Gary said: "Shut up! You're going to need all the strength you've got, so don't waste it on tears." He knew very little about the life of a prisoner, but it wasn't going to be easy — that much he was sure of.

As soon as they started marching, he thought of escape. During all the next day this continued to occupy much of his thinking. They had taken his shirt and hat, and the sun burned him badly, and blisters formed on both feet. His boots were for riding, not walking.

He no longer looked at Elizabeth Rishel for, when he did, he felt so sorry for her that he could hardly stand it. There wasn't any way he could help her. When she fell down, the Indians didn't stop at once. They simply dragged her along by the neck for a hundred feet, and just before she was choked unconscious they dismounted, slapped her until she could stand, and went on. She did not fall again that day, or the next.

Distant dust forced the Indians to mount the prisoners on ponies, and they rode to the east, then south again. In the middle of the afternoon they met a band of Kiowas led by White Bird.

The moment he saw Gary his eyes brightened, and the trading began. Apparently the raiding Cheyennes did not know the value of either prisoner, but White Bird knew, and he wasn't about to tell them and have the price hoisted on him.

Gary speculated on whether it would be wise to speak or to remain silent. He chose silence. If he spoke out, White Bird would have to pay more, and he would be angry about it, and the treatment they received wouldn't be kindly. Gary told himself he was thinking more of Elizabeth Rishel than of himself, but he knew this wasn't exactly true.

She stood by him, too exhausted to care what was going

on. Gary said: "Can you hear me? Elizabeth, can you hear me? Nod if you can." He had to speak softly, in no more than a whisper, and he was afraid she had not heard him at all.

Then she nodded her head.

White Bird and the Cheyenne leader were arguing still. The Cheyenne wanted five rifles, and White Bird wanted to give only three.

Gary said: "I must tell him you're my wife. Elizabeth, did you hear me? It's either that, or some brave will take you for his wife. For God's sake, nod if you heard me! If they believe you're my wife, you'll have less value to them. The Kiowas think more of marriage than the Comanches. Elizabeth, do you hear me?"

He had spoken too loudly, and a brave whirled on him, rifle butt raised to smash him in the face. "No talk!"

Gary fell silent, but a moment later he risked a glance at Elizabeth Rishel. She made an almost imperceptible nod of her head, and he felt a little better about the whole thing. He wondered why. He didn't have any reason to feel that way.

Chapter Thirteen

White Bird's camp was in a cottonwood grove on the east bank of the Elk River, and Gary didn't think any patrol had much of a chance of finding it. Behind them were four days of marching and ahead lay death or, at best, a long period of slavery. There had been no move on the Indians' part to separate him from Elizabeth Rishel, but Gary knew it was only because they had been on the move.

He was beginning to see where the money was coming from to buy rifles and ammunition, but the knowledge wouldn't help him any. The small bands of Cheyennes and Kiowas would raid and take prisoners, and what cash they could find. The fact that they hadn't killed him right away alerted him to a bigger plan, for they never were ones to be bothered with prisoners. Kill the men and take the women. That had been their way. But their ways were changed now, and he could see why. The Comanches kept slaves. They paid a good price for them, if they couldn't take them themselves. And the Kiowas were traders at heart. They'd take horses or goods or buffalo robes for the prisoners and then convert those into cash at the agency headquarters. With money in hand they could buy the guns and ammunition from Kline, trade them again to the Comanches, get more robes and horses, make a double profit, and do it all over again.

So Gary felt that he was safe enough for the present. It was just a matter of waiting now until someone else showed up with whom to trade. He was kept under guard away from Elizabeth Rishel, and for days on end he did not see her. He worried about her, for all the good it did him.

Then Stone Calf appeared with a small band of braves, and the trading began again. The price was much higher this time, but Stone Calf paid it, and Gary was again bound at the wrists, tied to Elizabeth, and he believed they were to be marched south to the Comanche stronghold. Again he was mistaken. They kept him in a temporary camp on Horse Creek, and they waited there a week. Gary couldn't figure this out, but, when he and the girl were hustled off and placed under a wild-eyed guard, he knew that important visitors were due to arrive. White visitors — they wouldn't go to this trouble for other Indians. That night he heard the wagon and knew that Kline had arrived with another shipment of rifles and ammunition.

He lay close to Elizabeth Rishel. The guard permitted it, because he was alone and his job was made easier this way. The Indian squatted a few yards away, his attention turned toward the camp.

Gary put his lips next to Elizabeth's ear and said: "They've tied me with ropes, not rawhide. Can you hear me?"

"Yes," she said.

"I'll turn my back to you. See if you can work the knot loose."

He turned and felt her fingers on his wrist. He lay there, trying not to hope, trying not to lose his nerve, if she succeeded in freeing him. Her fingers could only do so much, but she worked steadily on the stubborn knot, and he listened to the growing gaiety from the Indian camp. Kline had obviously brought along several jugs of whiskey, for there was a lot of laughter and singing going on. *Sing on,* Gary thought. *Drink on. Get real drunk.*

Later he felt the rope give a little and drew his wrists tightly together to give her slack, and in a little while she had the knot free. He moved his arms gingerly and began to work on her knots. He had better luck and freed her wrists in a short while. Then he doubled his legs back and worked on the ankle ropes.

The night hid his activity, and he made no sound at all. Presently he felt Elizabeth move her legs independently of one another and knew she was free, also. He put his hand out and touched her hip, and she lay still.

It was his move now. The guard was still sitting there, watching the camp and probably wishing he didn't have this miserable duty. Gary gathered up the longest piece of rope and tied a string of large knots in it, spacing them about three inches apart. Then he wrapped both ends around his hands, so his grip wouldn't slip, and began to inch toward the Indian.

This was slow, heart-pounding business, but he drew within striking distance, raised up suddenly, and whipped the loop of rope over the Indian's head. Savagely he crossed his hands and pulled, and the cry welling up in the throat was shut off by a crushed Adam's apple. There was only a moment of vicious thrashing, and the Indian lay dead. Gary felt quickly at his belt, hoping to find a pistol, but there was only the Evans rifle and a knife. He took both.

Elizabeth was waiting, and he said to her: "We'll never make it, if we strike out . . . tracks . . . and we'd be afoot. They'll find us."

"What then?" She wasn't crying now, and she wasn't afraid. All that was behind her, and she had found herself and her courage, and her will was as strong as any man's.

"I think we'd stand a better chance of getting out in Kline's wagon," Gary said. "He won't stay the night, not with the Indians drunk." He took her hand, and they skirted the camp, squatting down some distance away on the other side.

Kline had his wagon parked away from the fire, the horses still in harness.

"Wait here," Gary said, and went forward. He knew the night would hide him, and the Indians were whooping it up and paying attention to no one except Ray Kline, who kept passing around the last jug.

Gary peered into the wagon and cursed. It was completely empty, with not even a tarp to hide under. Without waiting further, he went back to where Elizabeth crouched down.

"We can't hide in the wagon," he said. "It's empty, and he'd see us."

"He's a white man," she said. "Wouldn't he help us?"

Gary shook his head. "He'd kill us the minute he laid eyes on us. We know too much about his business." He took her arm. "Come on."

They moved toward the wagon, crawled beneath it, and became invisible in the darkness. He began to whisper to her. "Getting out of here just isn't a matter of walking. The Indians can't afford to let us get away, knowing what we know. Neither can Kline. But I don't think he knows we're here, which is a bit of luck for us. We've got to get at least two miles from here without leaving a mark for the Indians to find."

"In the wagon . . . it's the only way," she said.

"Or under the wagon," Gary said. He reached up and felt of the bolster, then tied the Evans rifle to it, using a knot that he could yank free with one tug. He then experimented by hooking his legs over the axle and raising himself clear of the ground by clutching handy cross-pieces. He felt that he could hang on, since his life depended on it. But he knew that Elizabeth couldn't hang on for long. Her strength just wasn't up to it. He'd have to work out something else for her.

"Why can't we steal the wagon?" she asked.

"How far do you think we'd get? No, this is the way. Let

me help you, and we'll see if you can't be wedged between the tongue and the wagon box."

"I can't ride there."

"You can't hang on for two miles, either," Gary said.

That was the truth, and she knew it, so she allowed herself to be pushed and pried into the space between the wagon box and the tongue that separated the front and back wheels. She bumped her head and bruised herself and swore a little, then she disengaged herself. They crouched under the wagon and waited, watching the camp, wishing Kline would hurry up and leave.

Finally, when the whiskey jug was nearly empty, he picked up his rifle and turned to the wagon. "Now," Gary said, and hurriedly pushed Elizabeth Rishel into place. Kline boarded the wagon, and Gary lifted himself clear of the ground as he drove away.

Instantly he knew he was in for the greatest torture imaginable. The empty wagon bounced and vibrated over every irregularity in the ground, and he thought that his fingers were being torn loose. Elizabeth groaned and clung desperately with both hands as Kline picked up speed. He was in a hurry to put distance between himself and the drunken Indians.

Gary knew that he couldn't last a mile this way, but he forced himself to hang on by taking it one minute at a time, then adding another onto it. The pain in his legs and hands was beyond belief, so strong a pain that it soon numbed him, and he clung there like some half-dragged piece of brush and nearly as lifeless. He tried to gauge the passage of time and found it impossible. He could continue to hang on because his fingers were locked into the cloth of his sleeves, and they had gone dead. He had a death grip on himself and was powerless to break it.

Elizabeth Rishel broke him loose, when she slowly slid off

196

her perch and fell to the ground. Gary, torn free, grabbed for the rifle and missed it, and the wagon passed on in the night.

He lay there for a minute, not moving, then he started to push himself erect and fell back because his hands still seemed dead. He could see Elizabeth, a dozen yards back. She was stirring, and then she crawled over to him.

"Jim, are you all right?"

"I don't know," he said. Pain was now a flame in his right hand, an agony he could hardly bear, and he couldn't understand it. He felt of his right hand, and was surprised to find that it felt pulpy, sticky. "My God," he said softly.

Elizabeth showed him what kind of woman she was. She put her arm around his shoulders. "Jim, what is it?"

"When I fell off, the wagon wheel must have rolled over my hand. I think it's smashed." She drew a breath in sharply, and he patted her cheek. "Now, now . . . it's going to be all right, if we keep our heads. The rifle's gone, but I've still got the knife. We'll make out, if we keep our heads."

It was good for him to talk. He could forget the cramps in his legs, the pain of stretched muscles. He knew she was hurting, too, but she held it back. They would have to get to their feet, get moving. He looked at the sky and the stars and set his direction, hoping to reach a heliograph detachment that he knew was some forty miles west. When he listened carefully, he could barely make out the racket of Kline's wagon in the distance. Then it faded completely, and they were alone in a black, silent land.

"Can you walk?" he asked.

"I have to, don't I? But which way?"

"That way," he said, pointing, and they started off together.

Walking brought relief from his leg cramps, and they kept it up for an hour, while a constantly spreading agony built in

197

his right hand. He knew it was coming, and in a way he prepared for it, conditioning his mind to bear it. He wanted to be
brave, to show her the extent of a man's courage, but in time
the pain broke him down, and he walked along, sobbing
softly, tears running down his cheeks.

At dawn they fell into a buffalo wallow and rested there
with the dung and flies, and he could look at his hand then.
When he did, he nearly vomited. All the fingers were crushed
and broken. He could see that at a glance. He could see Elizabeth, too, the cuts on her face and welts on her bare arms.

She tore up her petticoat to make a bandage for him and a
sling, then pushed him back and made him rest. He supposed
they slept some, but it was a fitful sleep, prodded by thirst and
hunger and the constant sun. It was a blessed relief, when the
sun finally went down, and they could go on.

He knew where there was a creek, a narrow, muddy stream
full of skimmers and slime. When they got there, they both sat
down in it and let the cool water soak into them. Then they
drank and went on and felt somewhat better.

Gary said: "Another fifteen miles . . . that's all I'll need."

"We haven't come forty miles," she said.

"I don't need forty miles," he said. "Just fifteen, and a
good sun tomorrow."

That was the extent of their talk. Shortly after dawn they
found another wallow to sprawl in. Gary sat there, the knife in
his hand, rubbing the blade back and forth on his trouser leg.
When he had it polished to suit him, he had to wait for the sun
to swing around, and in mid-afternoon it suited him. He
crawled to the rim of the wallow and lay there, the knife in
hand, catching the sun's brightness and flinging it off in a
signal to a point on the prairie miles beyond.

Elizabeth crawled over. "What are you doing?"

"Trying to attract the attention of a heliograph attachment out there," Gary said. He looked at her. "I've got a fever. Tomorrow I'll be out of my head. So I want you to take the knife, when I'm through, and keep it."

"Jim, don't talk that way."

"I've got to, and you've got to understand," he said. "I'm apt to go crazy and try to kill you. You take the knife, when the sun goes down. And in the morning, don't think about me. I'm as liable to run off as not. Don't chase me, Elizabeth. You keep going the way we have been. I'll point out the stars to you tonight. If you follow those, you won't be far off."

"Jim, don't. You're frightening me."

He patted her hand and smiled. She was as dirty as a person could get, yet he thought her exceedingly lovely. "You've got the courage for both of us. Now you'll do as I say and no argument. Is that a promise?"

"Jim, I don't want to promise that."

"You've got to. All right?"

"All right," she said, and leaned back. "Jim, why do we always have to pick these inopportune times to say the things we want to say the most? If I could have one wish, it would be to start over again with you. I'll never be the way I was. I don't want to be any more." She bent forward then and kissed him. "You've always felt that a good lick across the britches would have done wonders for me. And, of course, you were right."

"Give it a few years, and you might like this country," he said.

She shook her head. "No, I'd never like it. But I've found I'm strong enough to beat it, and that's a good thing to know." Then she pushed him back. "Go to sleep. I'll watch over you. Please . . . I want to."

Chapter Fourteen

General Cameron got up from his desk and went to the orderly room. "No signal from General Sherman, Corporal?"

"No, sir. Nothing."

Cameron nodded and went back inside and closed the door. He'd been in the field for a solid week, and it had netted him nothing but a sore back and two companies of cavalry so worn out they wouldn't be fit for decent service for ten days. The renegade Indians had scattered or had been drawn away by some force Cameron didn't understand.

He lit a cigar and sat there with his hands folded, mildly worried about the silence from Sherman. Had Gary sold the general on the delay, or was the issue still in debate? There was no word from Gary. Nothing. The not knowing could give a commander fits.

He glanced at his watch, then got up and left the office, crossing the parade ground to his quarters. Wilson Chaffee was already in the parlor, waiting, and Cameron was pouring drinks when Eastland and Bennett came down the stairs.

They sat down, accepted a whiskey, and waited for Cameron to speak. He could see by their expressions that they were more against him than for him. The whole show was being bobbled. They wanted everything to go smoothly, and it was not doing so. As the time was running out, they would have to go back soon with their impressions and opinions.

"My niece promised to wire me, when she reached Dodge," Bennett said. "My wife's concerned about it, General."

"Well, I'll send a signal in the morning." He let none of his own worry show. "Gentlemen, I see no need for worry. I'm satisfied with the general execution of my plans."

Wilson Chaffee frowned slightly. "I can't say that I am, Tracy. There are too many ifs, ands, and buts in your plans. It's a program of faith, and on the strength of it I can't see how I can recommend a ten-year expenditure toward educating the Indians, who are reluctant to surrender to your generous terms."

"That's quite a switch in policy," Cameron said. "I didn't expect that of you, Senator Chaffee."

The man shrugged. "Tracy, I've got to do right for the voters. Show me something tangible."

"How can I, when we're dealing in intangibles? Gentlemen, peace is a state of mind. It's not a birdhouse a child builds and then takes to show to his mother." He looked from one to the other. "I have Parker's word that he will be here in a few weeks to discuss peace. Isn't that enough?"

"It may be as far as Parker is concerned," Bennett said. "But you can't control the bands of renegades who're roaming around the plains."

"They can be controlled," Cameron insisted. "We've cut off their supply of ammunition. If Parker goes the way of the white man, they'll have to follow suit or starve."

"That may be true," Chaffee said mildly. "But we can't take that chance. Tracy, I'm sorry, but I'm afraid I'll have to vote against any budget allocation in this matter. It would be throwing good money after bad."

Cameron looked at Albert Bennett. "And you, sir?"

"I've never been overly impressed from the beginning. I must agree with Chaffee."

"Mister Eastland?"

"I'm a majority man. I'll vote the way the wind blows."

Cameron took the time to pour himself another drink. He

201

felt that he needed it now. "All right, gentlemen. Then how would you plan to handle this? Or do you deny that it should be handled?"

They glanced at each other, and Wilson Chaffee said: "I think we'd better recommend that Sherman send south a punitive expedition and subdue the Indians by force. Frankly, it's the only sure, complete solution. It must be settled once and for all, Tracy. Why, we get mail all the time from people who've lost relatives in Indian raids. Some that were moving West twenty years ago were hit hard and turned back. They want to know about their kin, and I don't blame them."

"It would be a hopeless business, such a search," Cameron said.

"That may be so, but it'll have to be done," Eastland said. "But that's not the point now. General, I admire your dream, and I admire your effort. I'm genuinely sorry that it hasn't worked out."

"It will work," Cameron said softly, "if I can gather about me men with faith." He paused to consider his next words. "The soldiers in my command believe in me. They're simple men, taken off the streets and sometimes even from the jails, but they have faith. Unfortunately, that doesn't increase with a man's importance. Now, if you'll excuse me, I think I'll spend the rest of the afternoon with my wife."

They said nothing, and Cameron left the parlor. Edith was in the kitchen, baking cookies, and Cameron said to her: "That's all right for a lieutenant's wife, but a general's wife . . . ?"

"I like my own cookies," she said, kissing him quickly. Her eyes darted over his face, then she patted his arm.

She knows, he thought, and sat down. *She knows Gary's missing. Gone.*

"Tracy, why don't you swear?"

He smiled. "It wouldn't do any good, Edith. I sent Gary out there alone with that girl, and, if they're dead, I'll deserve all Bennett will give me." He rubbed his hands over his face. "I guess we'll be leaving Fort Elliot soon . . . they'll order me to a change of command, probably on the West Coast, or back East where an eye can be kept on me." Then the anger he was holding back let go a little, and he slapped the table. "Damn it, I hate to turn Miles and the others loose on the Indians. It'll be a damned slaughter."

A trooper's boots resounded on the side porch, and a knock sounded. "Pardon me, General," the trooper said. "Signal for you, sir."

"From Dodge?"

"No, sir, from Elk Creek heliograph." He handed Cameron the message, saluted, and went back to his duty.

Cameron opened it and read:

Commanding Officer,
Ft. Elliot
   Mr. Gary and the Bennett girl found on prairie . . . both badly worn. Gary hurt in escape from Indians. Girl being returned to the post with escort. Gary determined to go to Tascosa.

                                        Signed:
                                        Hendricks, Sgt.

Edith Cameron stood there and watched her husband's face. "What is it, Tracy?"

He stood up so suddenly that he upset his chair, and he dashed out without bothering to right it.

Edith called after him: "The cookies will be ready soon." But he was hurrying across the parade ground, and she knew he had not heard her.

Cameron entered the orderly room so quickly that the clerks popped erect. He snapped orders. "Find Lieutenant Baldwin and send him to me on the double!" Then he slammed his door and sat down behind the desk to see what he could salvage from this.

Sherman would be sending wires to Miles and Mackenzie. Already they would be looking over their equipment and picking horses for the march. There wasn't any chance to stop Sherman now. No one ever had, once he'd started to move. And there was less chance where Miles and Mackenzie were concerned, for they both wanted badly one more chance to lock horns and get another successful battle behind them. They wouldn't pass this up, because battles were getting scarce.

Cameron wondered if he could talk Chaffee into intervening, but he threw out the idea almost as soon as it was born. He didn't want to owe Wilson Chaffee a damned thing. And such favors would have to be paid back, one way or another, one time or another.

Baldwin reported and was motioned into a chair. He was a frail-bodied man with dark, intense eyes and a restless way of moving about.

Cameron said: "Frank, I've got a job for you that is strictly volunteer, Army style."

"That's fine with me, sir. What do you want done?"

"I want you to ride into Parker's camp, unarmed, and tell him that I want the peace talk held in six days, right here at the post. Tell him that there will be food for all his people, blankets and tobacco, and that he and all his people will be my guests. Remind him that my medicine is strong, and that I want to share it with him to make him as strong." He leaned forward and looked steadily at Frank Baldwin. "You've got to sell this for me. You've got to get him here and all of his

204

people. If he comes alone, I'm lost, and so is he."

"If you say so, General."

"I do say so," Cameron said. "Sherman is going to conduct a campaign, and, as far as I know, it may have already started. You've got to get to Parker before Sherman's force does, and you've got to get Parker out of there. I've preached peace, and I think Parker believes me. But if he found out that war was being made behind his back, we'd never get him to sit down and talk. I want Sherman to find a barren prairie, Frank. I want him to waste his strength on the march, while I'm sitting here with Parker negotiating peace."

"I'll get them here, sir, if I have to kidnap their medicine man." Baldwin stood up. "I'll leave within the hour, General."

"Leave in fifteen minutes and don't worry about killing your horse."

Elizabeth Rishel had kissed him, when they parted at the heliograph station, and Gary could still feel the pressure of her lips on his ten minutes later. He wanted to look back as he rode away, but he didn't. His resolve might be weakened, and it was not too strong to begin with. He needed rest, more than he'd taken, for his fever was still strong but not so much so that it worried him. His hand was a bandaged package of pain, and, although the sling helped ease the jolt of riding, every movement the horse made transmitted itself to the splintered nerves of his crushed fingers. Still, he had one thought clear, and he knew it was enough to keep him going. He was going to kill Ray Kline. Trooper Randall had loaned him his pistol and belt. He had the tools and the determination. Now he only needed the time to make the long ride.

He spent the night on the prairie, slept fitfully, mounted early, and went on. During the day he ate cold rations, drank from the canteen loaned to him, and bedded down that evening by a small creek. The fever left him, and he slept fairly well, but before dawn he was riding again, pressing the horse as hard as he dared. In the early afternoon he reached Tascosa.

Guthrie McCabe was sitting on the hotel porch, and he got up as Gary swung down. He took one look at the bandaged hand, then said: "Come on up to my room. I'll send someone for the doctor."

Once he had Gary stretched out on the bed and a whiskey burning away inside him, McCabe said: "How did it happen?"

"A wagon ran over it," Gary said.

McCabe frowned. "How come the surgeon at the post didn't . . . ?"

"It didn't happen on the post," was Gary's only reply.

The doctor came upstairs, and McCabe let him in. He stood by while the doctor unwrapped the hand and cleaned it. The doctor clucked and chirped away to himself like a small, contented bird.

"Well?" Gary said.

"Broken. All the fingers and the small bones."

"I knew that," Gary said impatiently. "Will it be all right?"

"Too early to tell. Weather changes may bother you some, though."

Then the doctor gave him ether, and Gary lay blissfully unconscious while he straightened the fractures. The doctor talked while he worked. "Hard to splint, fingers. Small, you know. In my bag you'll find some old corset staves . . . yes, thanks." He used these for splints, bandaging each finger straight out. "There's a sack of plaster and some horsehair there." He took the ingredients and told McCabe to get a pan and a pitcher of water. Then he mixed the plaster and added the horsehair. "Any Army surgeon knows this trick," he said. "Learned it myself in the war. Eastern doctors don't think much of it, but that's to be expected. They fought the use of ether for sixteen years."

When the cast was on, the doctor washed his hands and accepted a drink from McCabe. He gave McCabe a small bottle of pills. "That's for the pain. One every four hours, if it gets bad. Tell him not to take them unless he has to. Habit-forming, you know."

He went out, and McCabe waited until Gary came around. The ether made Gary sick, but this passed. McCabe said: "What did you do . . . get horse-dragged? You ought to know how to sit a wagon."

"I was a guest of the Indians," Gary said, and explained how his hand was broken.

McCabe listened, then said: "You're in no shape to brace Kline. I'll flush him out for you."

"No! I get the first crack."

"No sense in being stubborn about it."

"How would you be?"

"Stubborn," McCabe said. "All right, Jim. Go to it."

"I'm not in shape to do much running after him, if he breaks away."

"I'll see that he doesn't do that," McCabe said grimly. He helped Gary to his feet. "Feeling a little shaky?"

"Just point me in the right direction. I'll make it."

They went downstairs and through the lobby and walked across the street together. Just before they reached Kline's store, McCabe stopped. "I'll stay here and keep him from going out the front. He's got a back door, leading to the alley, and a lot across that. He keeps his wagon there and some horses."

He reached out and unbuttoned Gary's holster flap and

tucked it behind his belt to keep it out of the way. "You'll have to pull that cross-draw, and there's no sense in being too slow. I hope you can draw and shoot with your left hand."

"You think of everything," Gary said, and went into the store.

Kline was waiting on a woman at the drygoods counter, and Gary waited until she made her purchases and went out. Then Kline looked at him and smiled.

"How can I help you, sir?" He peered closer. "Why, it's Gary, isn't it?" He looked at the cast and sling. "My, that looks like quite a hurt there. A horse step on it?"

"No, your wagon rolled over it," Gary said. "The other night when you passed out the jugs of whiskey and got the Indians drunk."

"That's a lie!"

"Kline, there was someone else with me. Now you're under arrest."

For a moment, Kline simply stared at Jim Gary, then he picked up a box of shingle nails off the counter and threw it. Gary tried to draw his gun and threw up his arm as protection against the rain of nails, but he didn't succeed in doing either. Kline started to run, and Gary made a bound for the counter, but Kline grabbed the edge of it and spun it partially into Gary's path. Gary stumbled and fell and lost the pistol, and Kline charged out the back door.

There was no time to hunt for the gun. Gary raced after him and saw Kline crossing the alley to the barn. Kline ran inside and came out with a rifle. Gary saw him shoulder it in time to hit the ground, and the bullet *spanged* off a wagon wheel. He rolled underneath the wagon as Kline reloaded, and then saw the piece of rope hanging there, just as he'd left it. Gary yanked the bow knot free, and the Evans repeater fell against him.

He worked the lever with his left hand, tucked the butt against his shoulder, and squeezed it off just as the front sight crossed Kline's chest. There was no solid kick to the .44, not like a government issue .45-70, but Kline was sent spinning, and he collapsed.

As Gary got out from under the wagon, McCabe came running out the back door of the store. They went over to Kline. He lay there, twitching and choking.

McCabe said: "You got his spine, boy. He's done for."

"I'm not sorry."

McCabe looked at him steadily. "Hell, who is?"

"I took that Evans repeater off an Indian and tied it under the wagon," Gary said. "But I never thought it would be the gun that killed him."

"He sure didn't, either," McCabe said, and he put his arm around Gary. "Come on and let me get you to bed, boy. You look like a man who's about to fall down."

"I can't do that," Gary said. "McCabe, if I laid flat, I wouldn't get up for a week." He turned and crossed the alley and went back inside Kline's store. "Lock the front door, will you? I want this place cleared out."

"It's your party," McCabe said, and ran the curious out.

Then he bolted the back door and went into Ray Kline's cramped office, where Gary was rummaging through the desk. "I'm looking for his ledgers," Gary said before the sheriff could ask. "You can't operate a business without some kind of books, even when the activity is illegal. No man can keep it all in his mind."

McCabe scratched his head. "I don't see why you're wasting your time. You got the guilty man."

"Kline couldn't do this alone," Gary said. He leaned against the desk and reached across his stomach to support his crippled hand. "Kline must have charged double for every rifle and box of ammunition he sold. Indians don't have that kind of money, not even from selling prisoners to the Comanches for slaves. You figure how many buffalo robes it would take at agency prices to buy a case of guns, and you'd see that Kline wasn't alone."

McCabe seemed puzzled. "Hell, Jim, the Indians haven't sold robes to the agency for nearly a year. Graves is the biggest hunter around these parts. Why, hardly a month passed but that he hauled in a wagonload of hides and sold 'em to Kline."

"Are you sure of this?"

"Hell, yes, I'm sure. Don't you think I know what's going on in my own town?"

"Then that's it!" Gary said excitedly. "Oh, that's got to be it, because it's so simple. The Indians hunted the few buffalo that were left and took the hides to Graves's camp. Graves would pay a third what they were worth, sell them to Kline, and make his profit. Then Kline would ship them to Dodge and make a profit. He made a fat profit all the way around. That's why it's necessary to comb his records and find out just how much he did make."

"It's too bad you don't have the hunters handy," McCabe said.

"Handy?" Gary laughed. "Hell, they're in the Fort Elliot stockade right now." He moved away from Kline's desk. "I've got to get a message off to General Cameron, warning him not to release the hunters."

"Write it out for me," McCabe said. "I'll see that it's sent."

"All right, but I'll have to get a buckboard and return to the fort. The general will want my detailed report in person."

"He'll get it, because I'll give it to him," McCabe volunteered. Then he laughed. "I must be sick, doing you a favor like this. But you're too stove-up to make the trip."

McCabe's arrival at Fort Elliot was badly timed. He entered the post and was detained by the sergeant of the guard until the officer of the day could be summoned.

Lieutenant Butler had the duty, and he knew McCabe. "What the devil are you doing, riding in at three in the morning?"

"I want to see the general," McCabe said. "Joe, you'd better wake him."

"He hasn't been feeling well. All this damned going, day and night, is catching up with him."

"Let me put it this way," McCabe said gently. "If you don't roust him out and if what I have to say waits until morning, he'll put you back to second lieutenant."

"You paint a dismal picture," Butler said. "Come along, then. Sergeant, secure the gate." As they walked across the parade, Butler said: "The whole place has been in a boil for nearly a week now. The word's out that General Sherman is marching again to clean out the whole Comanche nation in one fell swoop."

"That's what this country needs," McCabe said, "another Indian war. It would scare the damned settlers away for another ten years at least."

Butler left McCabe at the porch. "Have you heard about Mister Gary? He and the girl were prisoners, you know."

"I didn't know about her," McCabe said. "But Gary's all right. I left him in town." He reached out, snapped the brim down on Joe Butler's hat, then knocked on General Cameron's door.

An orderly answered it, and he was in a sour frame of mind. But McCabe didn't give him a chance to say anything. "Fella, I want to see the general, and I want to see him now.

So you wake him up, or I will, and, if I do it, I'll stand here on the porch and howl to do it."

"He'll have my stripes for this," the man said.

"And I'll have your ass if you don't, so take your choice."

The orderly looked past McCabe and saw Butler still standing there. Butler said: "I think it's important, Rodgers. Better wake the general."

"All right. Come on in the parlor." He went ahead to turn up the lamps, then went upstairs. McCabe sat down and rubbed his thighs; the steady riding had left him aching and sore in the joints. He looked around until he found the liquor cabinet and Cameron's cigars, and, by the time Cameron appeared, McCabe was getting comfortable.

The general was tying the belt on his robe. "I see you found everything." He poured a drink and tossed it off, then shook his head. "That stuff either wakes a man up or puts him to sleep. In the area between it does nothing for me at all." He sat down and crossed his long legs. "Now, what's worth a midnight ride, Sheriff?"

"Jim Gary blew a hole in Ray Kline with one of the man's own trade rifles."

Cameron snapped bolt upright. "He killed him?"

"As dead as a man can get. General, have you turned the hunters loose yet?"

"No, but I'm going to have to," Cameron said. "I really have nothing to charge them with. And the pity of it is that they can come back on Captain Einsman."

"You'd better hang onto those jaspers a little while longer, General. They've been getting their hides off the Indians and selling them to Kline. The way Jim Gary figures it, the Indians brought the hides to Graves, and he gave cash for them. Then the Indians spent the money with Kline for rifles and shells. Graves, in turn, sold the hides to Kline, and that way

212

the Indian agent never got suspicious. And you've got to admit, General, that you never caught on. You may have seen hides in Graves's camp and just figured that they had a few days' shooting."

Tracy Cameron sat there for a moment, gnawing on his lip. Then he slapped the arms of his chair. "By God, that's right! Can Gary substantiate this?"

McCabe grinned. "General, I'd bet that he will. But it may take a week or ten days. He's got a badly mangled hand and. . . ."

"Elizabeth Rishel told me about it," Cameron said.

McCabe puffed on his cigar. "Could you put me to roost tonight? I've been in the saddle considerable, and I've got to have my sleep."

"Tell the O.D. to give you quarters," Cameron said. "Sheriff, I never considered you a man who'd put himself out for someone else. But you did Gary a good turn. Why?"

McCabe thought about it a moment, then said: "He trusted me, when he really didn't have to. I guess I owe him something, and I always pay off my debts."

"Now the Army is in your debt," Cameron said.

"Thanks, no," McCabe said, standing up. "General, I'm just living for the day when all you people will be gone and I can run this country the way I want to." He grinned. "How the devil do you expect a man to make a little extra money, if you keep looking over his shoulder all the time? Get the Army out and we'll have a few horse thieves and cattle rustlers back. A man's got to have some business to tend."

"I'd never vote for you," Cameron said. He reached into his cigar box and handed McCabe several. "For the ride back, Sheriff."

"I get thirsty, too," McCabe said.

Cameron smiled and gave him a bottle of whiskey, then

walked to the door with him. "If it's all right with you, I'll send a detail and ambulance in for Mister Gary. The congressman's niece wants to catch the train out of Tascosa on Friday."

McCabe stepped off the porch and walked toward the stockade, and Cameron turned back inside. Elizabeth Rishel had come quietly down the stairs. She stood there, a hand on the railing.

"You have word about Jim Gary?"

"Yes. He's all right. He's in Tascosa."

"He killed that man, didn't he?" she said. Then she sat down on the steps. "I knew he would. I saw his face, and nothing would have stopped him."

"Jim Gary didn't do it because he likes to kill."

"Oh, I know that," she said, a trace of irritation in her voice. "You know, I'm a little bit in love with him now."

"Does he know that?"

She shook her head. "No, and I don't want him to know. It would embarrass him. General, you know how to put up a good fight, don't you? All of you know how. And Jim Gary taught me how, too." She patted the stairs beside her. "Come and sit down. I don't want to go back to sleep just yet."

"When my wife and I were courting," Cameron said, "we used to sit on the stairs. It was close to the kitchen in case I got hungry, and close to the front door in case her father got up to see what was going on." He chuckled. "You'd make a good wife for Jim Gary, Elizabeth."

"Sometimes I think so, too."

"Then won't you say something?" Cameron asked. "I would like to see something happy come out of all this."

She remained thoughtfully silent, then said: "What would I do if he rejected me? How would I bear that?"

"You said he taught you how to put up a good fight." He

reached over and patted her hand. "You'd better make one now, or you won't ever forgive yourself for passing up the chance."

"I think you're right there," she said, getting up. "Good night, General." She dashed up the stairs, and he waited until her door closed before going back to the parlor.

Chapter Fifteen

Wilson Chaffee and his party left Fort Elliot accompanied by a full escort of cavalry, and, after they cleared the post, General Tracy Cameron went to his office to do some thinking. The parting had been friendly enough. There was no reason for it not to be. After all, they hadn't been enemies, just men with opposing points of view.

Cameron didn't like to think of this whole affair as a game, but in a way that was just what it was. For some years now he'd been playing his game with the Indians, toying with their superstitions, running his bluffs, and getting away with it. He'd even played a game with Albert Bennett and Chaffee, painting a rosy picture and trying to keep them from evaluating the long odds. And, of course, they knew he'd do that. It was part of their game to ferret out these things, a sort of political blind man's bluff.

The fault of this lay within himself, Cameron decided. He was not a strong enough man to sway others to his thinking, and he was presenting his ideas much too early for them to grasp. He did not want to think that his concepts of peace were too radical for the times. Well, he couldn't sit and brood about it. A man had to go on until he couldn't go any further, and Cameron still felt that the cards remaining in his hand were worth playing out.

That afternoon a two-squad detail escorted the civilian prisoners to Fort Dodge for trial, and a dispatch case full of depositions accompanied the officer in charge. By moving the prisoners to Dodge, Cameron was putting off that messy business for a while. He felt that he needed unrestricted room now. He had only a few days left, a week at the outside, and he didn't want to be bothered by side details.

Shortly after sundown Jim Gary rode onto the post. As soon as Cameron heard about it, he sent a runner to Gary's quarters and had him brought to Quarters A. Cameron's wife had retired, and, when Gary came into the parlor, Cameron rose from his chair and, without a word, embraced Jim Gary. Then he cleared his throat and poured two drinks.

"I suppose," Cameron said, "that you met the company escorting Bennett and friends to Tascosa?"

"No, sir," Gary said. "I was making my best time, and I didn't see them at all." He took a sip of whiskey, then asked: "I suppose Elizabeth went along. Naturally she would. Stupid question." He slumped glumly in his chair. "I've been a fool with her, sir. Said a lot of things I shouldn't have. I wasted it all, General."

"Nothing's ever really wasted," Cameron said softly. "We're getting near the end, Jim. In a few weeks I expect I'll be transferred to some other post, something quiet. And I suppose I'm expected to gather about me all my faithful retainers and pack them along. That's the usual procedure . . . in that way they get rid of the problem and the sympathizers. But I'm not going to do that to you, Jim. I'm going to leave you behind. The work will still have to be done, and a post needs all the good heads it can get."

"I thought it would be that way, sir." Gary finished his whiskey and put the glass aside. "But if you'll pardon me for saying so, sir, I hate like hell to see you give up before taps are blown."

Cameron smiled. "I'm still playing out this hand, Jim. Lieutenant Baldwin is trying to persuade Parker to bring his people here. I know Sherman's given the order for Mackenzie

217

and Miles to march. I couldn't hope to stop that. But I want them to find empty prairie, not Comanches ready to fight."

Gary's expression turned grim. "I messed that up for you, sir, by getting captured. If I'd got through. . . ."

"You probably would have failed, anyway," Cameron put in. "Jim, I don't think Sherman's mind could have been changed. I believe he had already promised the others they could have a crack at the Comanches." He shook his head. "I'm not going to complain about not having had a fair chance, because I did. Any chance is a fair one, Jim."

"It boils me, sir, to see something good come to nothing."

"That happens every day. What we don't get now, we may get tomorrow. One thing you must learn to survive is not to take defeat personally."

He stood up and walked about for a moment. "I can't understand why Baldwin isn't back." He wiped a hand across his mouth and smiled. "Well, he'll get here, when he can. And if it's too late, I'll know without asking that he tried. You'd done a damned good job yourself, Jim. That business in Tascosa was a little unorthodox, but the results justify the methods."

Cameron walked over to the bell cord and gave it a tug, and, when he heard the orderly coming down the hall, he excused himself and went out to speak with him. When he came back to the parlor, he said: "Waiting is pure hell, and I've done it for years."

Gary stretched his long legs out and crossed them. He let his plaster-covered forearm rest on his stomach; the protruding fingertips were swollen and discolored. He said: "I feel a lot older all of a sudden. Something in the climate, I think, that ages a man fast."

A slight sound overhead caught his attention. "I think I woke your wife, General. I'm sorry. Talking too loud and too long is getting to be my habit."

A woman's step came down the stairs. Cameron said nothing. Jim Gary remained in his chair, his back to the hall archway. Elizabeth Rishel stopped there and said: "Jim, aren't you going to say you're glad to see me?"

He moved in a bound and hurried to her. He stood before her for a moment, then brought her to him with a rush. Cameron saw them kiss, and turned away to pour another drink for himself. When he looked at them again, they had both stepped into the room and stood with their arms around each other.

Cameron said: "I guess it's settled then."

"That was a dirty trick to play on a man, General."

"Dirty tricks are my stock and trade." He glanced at his watch. "I see no reason for me to remain up. Doubtless you have things to say to each other."

"There are a few things," Elizabeth said. "And General, will you send my uncle a wire? He heartily disapproves, you know."

"Yes, in the morning," Cameron said. "Good night."

Gary said nothing until Cameron went up the stairs. He made Elizabeth sit down, and he sat beside her, holding her hand. "You can make a man feel ten feet tall, Elizabeth."

"Do I really?"

"Yes. I'm in love with you. I found it out too late. Or I thought it was too late."

"I was going to leave," she said. "But at the last minute I couldn't. I just had to stay and tell you that I'd fallen in love with you. Even if you rejected me, it was something you had to know. Something that had to be said."

"The general said I'll be staying here," Gary said. "A second lieutenant's quarters is far from grand."

"We'll manage," she said. Then she laughed. "I always

thought long engagements were proper and church weddings a must. Now I wonder where that notion went." She put her arm behind his head and pulled him to her. Then she let her head rest on his chest. There must be some way, since he did love her, to persuade him to request a transfer away from the frontier.

Gary went to the mess early, and on the way he saw Lieutenant Beamish herding a detail of prisoners with the "honey" wagon. He thought: *Some things just haven't changed at all.* He waved at Beamish, but Beamish ignored him, and Gary went on to the mess.

Breakfast took longer than usual, for the officers demanded that he recount his recent exploits, particularly the shooting affair in Tascosa. All this embarrassed Gary, and he left as soon as an opportunity presented itself.

He expected to find Cameron in his office. The man seemed to be the first awake and the last asleep. The orderly room was full of activity, when Gary passed through, and, as he stepped into the general's office, Cameron was concluding a conversation with the signal officer.

"You're ten minutes late," Cameron said. He paused to pour a glass of water and take some pills; he kept a bottle in his desk and dipped into it frequently. Then he spun several messages across his desk. "There's a group of journalists heading this way . . . they should arrive this afternoon. And a dispatch from Ash Creek. General Sherman is on his way here to give me the sad news in person." He coughed and drank some more water. "Gary, I haven't the time or energy to babble to reporters. Take care of it for me. I haven't heard a word from Baldwin, and I've had a damned upset stomach for three days. I want you to give Captain Evans an exact description and the number of the Indians that held you and

Elizabeth prisoner. When we catch them, we'll build one big scaffold and hang them on the parade ground."

"General, I don't think you ought to do that."

Cameron's glance came up, hard and irritated. "Mister Gary, I like you, but I'll run this command. I've been too easy all along."

"No, sir. I'm sorry to disagree, sir, but you've said it before . . . someone has to be the first to quit. Someone has to take his bloody nose and not hit back. Well, sir, *I* was captured, and, if I had to, I could forget where I was and who took me prisoner." He hesitated. He had gone too far and knew it, but he had to go on now — all the way. "What would you gain now by a reprisal? The Indians wouldn't understand it, and I wouldn't appreciate it. General, it's your command, and I can't say that you've made many mistakes in it. But a vendetta now would be a mistake."

Cameron remained silent for a moment, then he nodded. "You're right, Jim. I have to let this go, don't I?"

"Yes, sir."

"I don't want to let it go, but in a way I'm dealing with children. I can't overdo the punishment." He sat down and put his hands over his face. "I'm tired, Mister Gary. Tired of the fight. Tired of the working hard and losing out."

"General, you ought to get some rest."

Cameron laughed. "I'd like to say that I don't need it, but I'm down to the last shot in the carbine." He stabbed at Gary with his finger. "And I want you to go see the contract surgeon about that hand."

"Yes, sir. Will that be all, General?"

"What else is there?"

Gary went out, thinking that one more pound of weight on Cameron and he would collapse. The man needed a real rest, more than a few nights' sleep.

He found the contract surgeon unoccupied. "The general thinks you ought to have a look at this," he said.

The surgeon patiently sawed through the cast, and examined the fractures carefully. He made some wry comments about the cast, mentioning Army horse doctors and a rather backward medical profession. Gary was a little irritated. He didn't give a damn for any opinion except for how his hand was healing.

"Your fingers will be a little stiff," the surgeon said. "But I think you'll have full use of the hand . . . within limits."

"What limits?"

"You'll lack dexterity."

"No clever poker tricks?"

The doctor smiled. "Well, if you have some notion of practicing the fast draw, I'd forget it. Your hand will always be slightly stiff." He brought out bandages and plaster. "The swelling has gone down. You were due for another cast anyway." He wrapped and applied plaster, talking all the while he worked. "If you've got any influence with General Cameron, try and get him to bed earlier. And convince him that he ought to get at least nine hours of sleep every night."

Gary asked: "What's the trouble with the general, Doctor?"

"Overwork."

"Is that a cause or a symptom?"

"Good question," the doctor said. "Mister Gary, Cameron's not a kid. Sometimes he drinks too much, and he has a liver complaint to begin with. Our organs grow weaker as we get older, Mister Gary. Try and get him to slow down."

"I'll do my best, but I don't think it can be done."

"Neither do I . . . still I must try."

Gary left the infirmary with a new cast on his arm. He checked his watch, and then spent three hours arranging a party for the reporters. The officers' mess was reserved, the cooks alerted, and enlisted men picked to serve.

When he went back to headquarters, he found Cameron pacing up and down his office. "All this time and not a dispatch from Baldwin. Gary, can he be dead? By God, if they've killed him, I say wipe them all out!"

"General, you don't mean that," Gary said.

Cameron stared at him for a moment, then said: "No, I didn't mean that at all." He slapped his desk. "It's just that I'm dog-tired, and my nerves are raw, and my head's splitting."

"General, why don't you go to your quarters and get some sleep?"

"You're out of your mind," Cameron said. "Sherman will be here in the morning."

"Yes, sir, and you'll want to be feeling well, sir."

Cameron frowned heavily. "That damned doctor has been talking to you, hasn't he?"

"Yes, sir, and I must say that I think he's right. General, from the first time I met you, I thought you were driving yourself too hard. I realize that it's impertinent of me to say this, but it has to be said. You've got to slow down, sir. A man can't stay up all hours of the night and go all day, too. Not week after week. I strongly suspect that you've been doing this for years."

"Mister Gary, you're poking your nose into something that's none of your blasted business!" He glared for a moment, then sat down. "Get out of here. I feel so rotten this morning that I'm liable to say anything, and I hate like hell to apologize."

Gary saluted, and left headquarters. He stood on the porch for a moment, undecided, then walked to Quarters A. By chance he came around to the side entrance, and he saw

Elizabeth Rishel on the back porch, sleeves rolled up, a cloth about her hair, bending over a washtub.

"What are you doing?" Gary asked, slightly horrified.

"Washing clothes," she said. "Next week I'm going to have to wash yours, Jim, so there's no time like the present to start."

"We'll send out our laundry," he said flatly.

"And squander thirty-five cents a week?" she laughed.

"But they'll talk about you."

"Jim, they'll talk about me as soon as we're married." She saw the question in his eyes, and it seemed to amuse her. "My, you're innocent, Jim. Can't you imagine what they'll be saying?"

"No, I can't."

"Why, they'll start looking for me to get fat. After all, it will be a rather sudden wedding, and they'll feel sure that it was caused by some misbehavior on our part. We were alone together for some time, Jim, and who would we be to resist temptation?"

"I'll flog the man I hear speaking such a thing!"

"You will not," Elizabeth said. She patted his cheek with a wet hand. "People have to talk about something. It doesn't matter."

He studied her for a moment, then laughed and kissed her, and she grew red-faced and pushed him away.

"Jim! Not here where anyone can see us."

"So it's all right to be talked about, but not to be seen."

"Now you're teasing me," she said. "And that's not fair."

"Nothing's fair in love and war, or something like that."

"I rather hate slogans," Elizabeth said. "And I hate politics, too. I feel sorry for General Cameron, all of that work for nothing."

"He'd tell you that it wasn't for nothing. It has a value.

224

Not now perhaps, but one day it will make another man's job a little easier." He laughed without humor. "I never used to think philosophy had much value, but I can see how it can cover some sharp disappointments. I ought to say honestly that I wasn't too happy to get this assignment in the first place, because Tracy Cameron has a reputation as a no-fighting commander. Of course, I hoped for Ranald Mackenzie, or some thirsty blood-letter . . . to make a big name for myself, you know. But the talent Cameron has is pretty rare. He can draw a man to a cause without seeming to try. That's why I'm glad I'm going to stay at Fort Elliot, Elizabeth. I want to be here the next time. And there's going to be a next time."

"I hope he gets a post where he can rest," she said. "His wife worries, you know. And that's something you should think about, too." She gave him a gentle shove with her hand. "Now go on and let me wash my clothes."

He kissed her again, and she pretended to be indignant, but he knew that she liked to have him kiss her in public. He went back to headquarters, because his place was there. Tracy Cameron was sitting at his desk, head in hands. He motioned for Gary to sit down.

"I think I will go to my quarters, Mister Gary." He slowly shoved himself erect. "Of course, you'll notify me the moment General Sherman arrives?"

"Yes, sir."

Cameron gave Gary a pat on the shoulder, in passing, and went out, his step slow and deliberate, as though he were counting each one. As he crossed the parade, Gary went to the window to watch him. There was a man running down, he thought, and it worried him, for Cameron would always drive himself far harder than he'd drive anyone else.

The remainder of the afternoon was spent in taking care of

225

final details and pestering the signal officer for word from Lieutenant Baldwin. There was no word, and Gary inherited Cameron's worry. Baldwin was either dead or was still trying to convince Quanah Parker that he ought to bring his people to the post.

The newspapermen arrived in a mud wagon, and Gary had the officer of the day escort them to headquarters. They were held in the outer office and their cards were presented, then Gary invited them in. There were five of them, and they looked at him inquiringly. Obviously they expected the general to meet them.

Gary queried: "Mister Osgood, from *Frank Leslie's?*"

"Osgood here," a man said, and nodded. He was a slender, handsome man in his early forties. "I assume, sir, that you are not the commanding officer."

"I'm General Cameron's aide, Lieutenant Gary." He glanced at another card. "Mister Simonson from San Francisco?"

"I'm Simonson." He shook hands with Gary.

They were all made known to Gary, and he invited them to sit down. An orderly brought in extra chairs for them and closed the door.

"General Cameron has instructed me to extend every courtesy," Gary said. "I've taken the liberty to arrange a party tonight at the officers' mess. Strictly stag, with the best liquor on the post being served in endless bottles."

"That sounds good," Simonson said. "Mister Gary, may we ask questions?"

"Of course."

"Well, I have one that I'd like an answer to. In Dodge City the word was going around that General Sherman was planning a full-scale campaign against the Comanches."

"Since I'm not on General Sherman's staff, and since he rarely consults me, I can hardly verify that. However, the general is scheduled to arrive late this evening. Perhaps in the morning he'd answer that himself."

"I can wait," Simonson said.

Osgood had a question. "We had the pleasure of being in Tascosa when Congressman Bennett's party arrived. He spoke unfavorably of General Cameron's peace efforts. Would you care to comment on that?"

"I might say that, while General Cameron has had his finger on the pulse here for three years, Congressman Bennett has been exposed to it for less than a month. In a military matter such as this, I am inclined to accept the judgment of a military man."

"Is it true that the congressman's niece is remaining here?" This was from Mr. Daniels, a Chicago man. He had a dry, humorless expression and a hard, Midwestern twang in his voice.

"Yes, she's consented to be my wife," Gary said matter-of-factly.

They smiled, and Osgood said: "Well, it wasn't a total loss, then, was it?"

"The final judgment is not yet in on General Cameron's program," Gary said. "If there is any acknowledgment of defeat, he'll make it. For my own opinion, I would say our position is still strong."

"Explain that," Simonson invited.

"I'm not at liberty to explain it."

The man smiled. "Secrets, Lieutenant?"

"We all have them. I dare say, there's a matter or two you'd not care to discuss with your wife."

They all laughed, and the New York man said: "He's got you there, Walter." He glanced at Gary. "Have you met Parker?"

"No, I never have."

"I interviewed his mother. She lives back East, you know. She was a prisoner for many years, then one day she just walked off, and they made no move to stop her. That's peculiar, isn't it?"

"No, not from their point of view," Gary said. "I understand that she was taken as a very young woman and was the wife of a Comanche leader. Quanah Parker took her maiden name out of pride. They keep slaves, but after eight or nine years they no longer guard them. If they want to leave, they can, and in some instances they are given a horse and weapons and food. I don't know if Quanah Parker ever thinks of his mother, but I assume that he does, because he took her name."

"A blood-thirsty devil, there," Osgood said.

"Don't believe everything you read," Gary cautioned him. "In the last eight or nine years, the Comanches have kept to themselves. I believe the records will bear me out in stating that they have not been engaged in active fighting with the white man. You see, while the Sioux and Cheyennes and Kiowas spent their strength, the Comanches hoarded theirs. Now, when the Kiowas can barely fill a hundred saddles, Quanah Parker can put a thousand braves on ponies. Quite a force, when you consider they're the finest light cavalry in the world."

"And that's what Sherman wants to fight?" Simonson asked.

Gary smiled. "I told you once that I'm not in a position to say what Sherman wants."

From the look on Simonson's face Gary knew that he was playing the game and staying ahead. These men would pull an answer out of him, or trick him, or misquote him, if he gave him a chance, while he stood there and talked a lot and said nothing much at all. They wanted to know everything, and they didn't care whether it was good or bad, as long as they could write it down and stretch it a little and make people read it.

He fenced with them for an hour, and then had an enlisted man show them quarters and a bath. After that, he went to the mess hall to check the last few stray ends of detail, had a bath and shaved himself, and felt like tackling a long night of gaiety. As long as the liquor was being poured, he could stave them off. General Sherman ought to arrive sometime between ten and midnight. Then Cameron would take over, and Gary could chuck the whole affair.

He had to make an excuse to Elizabeth Rishel, and he wasn't quite certain how she took it. She was a woman and looked a little askance at anything men told her. It was a natural suspicion, and he didn't mind her having it. Probably in future years it would keep him in line.

The party was a bore to Jim Gary, and at eleven o'clock he was grateful when an orderly interrupted him and asked if he would come to Quarters A. He excused himself and stepped out into the cold night air, and, as he walked across the parade, he was disturbed to see so many lights on in Cameron's house. Damn the man, anyway. He just wouldn't go to bed and sleep.

Gary entered through the front door and found Elizabeth there. He was surprised, and let her see it. "What are you doing up?" he asked.

"Jim, the general's sick. The doctor's with him now."

"Well, it's no wonder, with all the ramming around he's been doing, getting only four hours of sleep a night."

She turned suddenly cross. "Oh, for heaven's sake, don't be analytical! Go on up to him . . . he's been asking for you."

"Damn, but you're bossy," he said, and hurried on up the stairs.

Chapter Sixteen

Gary found Edith Cameron on the upper landing by the general's door. Her face was slightly puffed, and her eyes were red from crying. Jim Gary simply put his arms around her.

"Tell me what's the matter," he said.

"Oh, Mister Gary, I'm so glad you're here. The pain began to get him shortly after he came home. He thought it was gas and finally went to bed after taking some soda."

The door opened, and Doctor Talbot looked out. "Oh, there you are, Gary. I thought I heard voices." He motioned for Gary to step into the room, then he spoke to Edith Cameron. "Madam, why don't you lie down a bit? Go on now. I'll call you soon." He waited until she walked down the hall, then he closed the door.

Cameron was in bed, his complexion wan. He breathed rather heavily and through his open mouth. Talbot came close to Gary and said: "I believe this attack of gas he thought he had is a mild stroke. I'm afraid the general's out of the harness for a while." He stepped over to the bed and took Cameron's wrist and timed the pulse.

Gary asked: "This is sudden, isn't it?"

"A stroke usually is," Talbot said. "I think he'll recover from it, but he'll have to change all of his habits . . . and retire, of course." He paused to finger his mustache. "The ranking officer of the post is Major Riley . . . in supply. He ought to be notified."

Gary said: "I hardly know the man. As a matter of fact, I don't believe I've spoken to him. He never leaves his office, and I have had no reason to go there. Doctor, what of the general's plans? Are they going to go to hell now that he's not around to execute them?"

"I don't think so," Talbot said. "Gary, we all knew what the general wanted. Even the orderlies in the infirmary knew. We'll pick up the pieces somehow and carry on. I think you'd better tell Riley of his new duties."

"Yes, of course." Gary looked at Cameron. "Is he conscious?"

"Not now. It's best this way. Go on . . . I'll stay with him. And I'll do all I can." He took Gary by the arm. "As far as Missus Cameron knows, it's still gas. Let it stay that way for a time . . . all right?"

"Anything you say."

He went out and down the stairs. Elizabeth was waiting, her worry plainly written in her eyes. "Jim, it's serious, isn't it?"

Gary nodded. "The doctor doesn't want to tell the general's wife just yet."

"All right. How serious?"

"A stroke." She gasped, and he put his arms around her. "He'll be all right. Things will simply have to slow down, that's all. It'll mean retirement, but he's earned it." He patted her and drew away. "I have a lot to do now. I may not see you until tomorrow."

"It's all right, Jim."

He left the house and walked across the row to Major Riley's quarters. As he paused before the door, he could hear Riley's young daughter, Grace, playing the spinet. It was a pleasant, bright sound, and at the end of the piece the family applauded.

Gary knocked, and Major Riley came to the door, an elderly, balding man who had devoted his career to the supervision of records. He had a reputation for being a detail man.

"I'm sorry to intrude at this late hour," Gary said. "But I'm afraid the general's ill, and you'll have to assume command of the post."

"Come on in," Riley said. "We'll go in the kitchen. Grace, time for bed now." He smiled at his wife. "Excuse us, Martha." He took a lamp and led the way into the kitchen and closed the door. "This must be serious, Mister Gary."

"Yes, sir, I'm afraid it is. This is in confidence, sir."

"Of course. Sit down, Gary." He pulled a chair around for himself. "I don't know where to begin really. Will you continue on as my aide?"

"Yes, sir."

"Good. You had the old man's ear. I know he relied on you as much as he relied on any captain on the post." He blew out a long breath. "Suppose we closet ourselves at headquarters in the morning, Gary? You can bring me up to date."

"I'm sorry, sir, but that will have to be done now . . . tonight. General Sherman will arrive before morning, and I'm sure the major will want to receive him properly."

"Good Lord!" Riley said, and leaned back in his chair. "All right, what do you suggest? Full honors at two in the morning? It will wake the whole post."

"Damn the honors," Gary said sharply. "We'll explain that General Cameron is ill, and he can get pecked about it or not." He shrugged. "Anyway, I don't think Sherman expects the old man to be up and about at such a late hour. I'll return to headquarters, sir, and remain there until reveille. The general will have arrived and most likely will sleep until ten o'clock. It will give us some time to work up a review company and other nonsense."

232

"All right," Riley said. "And thank you, Mister Gary. I appreciate this."

Gary went to Cameron's office and sat down in his chair and hoped no one would come in and catch him there. The chair didn't feel right to him, and he knew he would never be comfortable sitting in it. The presence of Tracy Cameron was strong in the room. Gary had to stifle the impulse to look around to see if the man were standing there.

He's put his touch on every man on this post, Gary thought. And it would remain long after he was gone. Mostly a change in command meant a lot of new orders, a new way of doing things, the promise of many changes, and perhaps the officer who was sent to replace Cameron would start out that way, but he wouldn't get far. This was Tracy Cameron's post, regardless of where he was. Gary knew that it would go on that way, for the man was more than a man with rank. He was a leader who inspired by his ideals rather than by his deeds. *They even may put him in the history books,* Gary thought, and the idea pleased him.

Gary slept right there, his head on the desk, and the O.D. woke him by shaking his shoulder. Gary sat up with a start. "What is it now?"

"The sentry reports the approach of a large force, sir."

Gary spoke, while he splashed water on his face. "It can't be the general. Hasn't he arrived yet?"

"No, sir."

Gary didn't know what time it was, but the sky was beginning to tint to a lighter shade. *Probably a little after four,* he thought.

He dried his face hurriedly and went with the O.D. to have a look. In the distance he could make out an incredibly large group, and, as the light grew stronger, he could recognize them as Comanches. They were approaching the fort —

women, lodges, and all — a mass movement led by Quanah Parker and Lieutenant Baldwin.

"I'll be damned," Gary said. "He did it!" He took the O.D. by the arm. "I want the regimental band rousted out right away, full dress, and playing the 'Gary Owen' in ten minutes. Roust A and F Companies out in full parade dress for a double row inspection. Tell the sergeant of the guard to open the gates as the Indians approach. Now get on with it, and, if it isn't done properly, I'll have Cameron roast your fat, if it's the last thing I ever do."

"Hell, I'll do it," the O.D. said, and hurried away.

Gary wondered where he would quarter Quanah Parker. The man was a chief and proud, and he wouldn't accept a slight of any kind. He thought of the officers' mess, but that was in a shambles from last night's party. He couldn't billet him in the bachelor officers' quarters — that just wouldn't do at all.

It was insane to think of Quarters A, but he *did* think of it, and it was his answer. He ran across the parade ground and knocked on the door. One of the servants was up. He opened the door and scowled, then erased it quickly when he saw Gary.

"I've got to see Missus Cameron immediately," Gary said.

"She's resting now, sir."

"Yes, and I'm terribly sorry, but this is of the greatest importance."

"Come in, sir. I'll tell her you're here."

Gary paced up and down the hallway until Edith Cameron came down the stairs, a robe tightly bundled about her. "What is it, Mister Gary?"

He snatched off his kepi. "Madam, I don't want to bother the general when he's ill, but I'm afraid I've run into a sticky problem. Quanah Parker, the Comanche leader, is approaching the post with his people. It's what the general dreamed of, and wanted . . . a chance to talk peace."

"He won't be able to receive him, of course," she said. "The doctor's been with him all night. He seems to be resting now, but. . . ."

"I had no notion to trouble the general," Gary said quickly. "Madam, time is of the essence here. Parker is no more than fifteen minutes away. He's an important man, and the general would want me to woo him, if I could." He cleared his throat before going on. "Madam, I want to quarter him and entertain him in your home."

This staggered her. She raised a hand to her throat, then said: "Of course, Mister Gary. You do what you feel is best."

"Thank you. And I'm sorry the general's condition hasn't improved."

"We'll have to hope for the best," she said. She turned to the stairs, and paused. "I've prepared two messages. Will you see that they're sent to our sons?"

"Yes, immediately."

"I'll send one of the servants over with them a little later," she said.

He went out, wishing he could stay. She seemed so alone now, bewildered. But he had his duty, the damned duty that kept him from doing what he wanted to do.

The sergeant of the guard was wheeling out two small saluting cannons. He said: "I thought you might want to use these, sir."

"Bless you, Wiggins, they're just the ticket."

There was much ceremony to put in order and very little time to do it in, but it got done — not, perhaps, in a manner that would have satisfied a visiting general, but Quanah Parker would be suitably impressed.

When he came onto the post with a host of his best warriors and a bearded Lieutenant Baldwin, the band struck up the rousing march and the cannons went off, frightening the horses. Two companies presented arms smartly, and Quanah Parker dismounted with great dignity and pumped Lieutenant Gary's hand.

"You are welcome to Fort Elliot," Gary said. "Well done, Baldwin."

"Where's the old man?" Baldwin asked.

"Stroke."

"Good God!" Baldwin exclaimed, and said no more.

"I come to talk peace," Parker said solemnly. "My people come in peace."

"We offer you peace," Gary said. "Baldwin, will you make up a detail and see that Parker's people are camped and comfortable. Take a couple of wagons of food to them. See that they have bacon and coffee and sugar."

Then he took Parker's arm. "General Cameron wishes for you to share his house. You will live with him during your stay and eat at his table."

"That is good," Parker said.

He was impressed with the post and the men and the band music. Gary kept shooting him sidelong glances as they crossed the parade to Cameron's quarters. The commotion had aroused the whole post, and Gary knew that within half an hour every man would have the full details.

As they approached Cameron's quarters, the door opened and a servant appeared, bowed to Parker, and ushered him in with a great deal of ceremony. Mrs. Cameron came from the parlor, dressed in her best gown, and with the pleasantest smile Gary had ever seen said: "We're so happy you could stay with us."

Gary saw that Parker had a comfortable chair and one of Cameron's cigars. Parker sat there, puffing on it and grunting

236

softly to himself. There was a strong, musky odor about him, and his war-like trappings were out of place amid the sedate furniture.

"We will eat soon," Gary said.

"Good," Parker said. "Much hunger." He slapped his bare stomach.

"Oh, dear," Edith Cameron said faintly.

"Where is general soldier?" Parker asked.

"The general is not feeling well," Gary said. "I am speaking for him."

"You are not big soldier," Parker said. "How can you speak?"

"It is our way," Gary said. "Any man can speak for another when he has permission."

Parker grunted and didn't seem to care to debate the point. He said: "Winter come soon now. Cheyenne friends go back to reservation. Kiowa go back, too. No buffalo. No meat. Peace is better than war."

"And there will be peace," Gary said. "We will talk many days and write the words on paper as they are spoken. Then we will all sign, and there will be no more war."

"How do I know this is true peace? Many years ago soldier Mackenzie make us put down weapons. No more war, he say. But there was no true peace. Kiowas, Comanches meet and talk. They have guns and fine ponies. We grow poor."

"All men are tired of war now, Parker," Gary said. "The day for war is past. The buffalo hunters are gone. Men of peace live in this land now. It is so, and you know it."

Parker thought about it, nodded, and puffed on his cigar. A man's step sounded on the stairway, and Gary looked around, but Quanah Parker did not. Doctor Talbot paused in the parlor archway, looked at Gary, then shook his head almost imperceptibly. Edith Cameron drew her breath in sharply and caught it, a hand half raised to her mouth.

Gary said: "Madam, I'll entertain our guest, if there's a matter you wish to attend to." He got up and took her hand. "You're a great lady. The general was immensely proud of you."

He escorted her to the door, as Elizabeth hurried down the stairs. She was crying silently. The two women put their arms about each other and went up together.

Gary turned to Parker. "I believe I smell coffee from the kitchen. Would you like some?"

"Coffee good," Parker said, and went on puffing his cigar.

Gary excused himself and walked to the kitchen. The house was quiet now, and, strangely, he could not feel sad. Somehow, by his magnificent strength, Cameron had lived to the end of his dream. Parker was in his house, a guest, on a mission of peace. It was all ended. There was no more fighting. The period had been placed, concluding the sentence of his life, and another line had been written.

A good line, Gary thought. He even thought General Sherman would see it, once he got over the pique of being out-maneuvered.

He brought the coffee back to the parlor, and they drank it black. Gary sat there and listened to Parker talk about his plans to go East and see his mother and learn more of the white man's ways. And it was an enjoyable thing, this talk between friends.

WILL COOK

THE DEVIL'S
ROUNDUP

Will Cook has long been regarded as one of the finest writers of the Western's Golden Age. These five short novels, among Cook's best, are all set in Hondo, Texas, and the surrounding ranching community, and take place over a period of twenty years. Many of the same characters appear throughout as they age, marry, have children and fight to survive in a wild and violent land. This thrilling saga reveals an entire frontier community's growth through moments filled with excitement, drama and highly memorable characters.